## "We dance well together," Garth murmured.

"I couldn't have had a better teacher." Kitt studied the shadows on his face, pleased that a gentle smile played about his lips.

"When I first saw you last night, I had the idea that we might call a truce in the hostilities."

Kitt tried to cover the shiver that ran down her spine. His breath was hot and smelled of lemons, and his voice was a raspy growl that curled around in her ear and then began sliding down through her bones like hot syrup.

"That's what I thought last night. And then today I thought I'd just like to settle the past. Heal the old wounds."

"That sounds all right." She suddenly wished she were wearing a parka, the way his fingers kept slipping up and down her back.

"But right now, I'm thinking something different."

"What . . . what are you thinking?"

He whispered close to her ear, "I'm just thinking how good this feels. . . ."

Dear Reader,

Happy New Year and welcome to another exciting month of romance from Silhouette Intimate Moments. We've got another irresistible lineup of books for you, as well as a future treat that I'll be mentioning in a moment. First, though, how about a new book from one of your favorite authors, Nora Roberts? *Night Shift* will enthrall you—and leave you eager to read *Night Shadow*, coming in March. Readers of historical romance may recognize the name Catherine Palmer. Whether you know her name or not, you will undoubtedly enjoy her debut for Silhouette Intimate Moments, *Land of Enchantment*. Round out the month with new books from Sibylle Garrett and Joyce McGill, two more of the authors who make this line so special.

Now for that future treat I mentioned. Next month we're presenting "February Frolics," an entire month made up of nothing but first novels written by authors whose futures look very bright indeed. Here at Silhouette Intimate Moments we're always trying to find fresh new voices in the romance field, and we think we've come up with four of the best. Next month you'll get a chance to see whether you agree with us—and I hope you do!

In coming months, look for new books from more of your favorites: Dallas Schulze, Heather Graham Pozzessere and Marilyn Pappano, to name just a few. And every month, enjoy some of the best books in romance today: Silhouette Intimate Moments.

Leslie J. Wainger
Senior Editor and Editorial Coordinator

# CATHERINE PALMER

# Land of Enchantment

## SILHOUETTE·INTIMATE·MOMENTS®

Published by Silhouette Books New York

**America's Publisher of Contemporary Romance**

SILHOUETTE BOOKS
300 East 42nd St., New York, N.Y. 10017

LAND OF ENCHANTMENT

ISBN: 0-373-07367-4

First Silhouette Books printing January 1991

Printed in the U.S.A.

## CATHERINE PALMER

loves creating stories with locales and backgrounds that are as exotic and diverse as the ones she grew up in herself—and as the daughter of missionaries, she's been to quite a few places! One of the most exotic—Kenya, Africa—brings back fond memories of living on a nineteen-thousand-acre cattle ranch and thrilling to the sight of wonderful animals such as gazelles, lions and giraffes.

She now resides in Artesia, New Mexico, with her husband and their young son, and between writing, her membership in the Romance Writers of America and the local art guild, she is kept very busy. Though her first joys are her family and her writing, she also enjoys crafts, tennis and swimming.

For those who heal broken lives.

Especially:

J.C., Libby Bennett, Andy Jamison, Bill Harrison, Chris Manzanares, Burma Kernal, Mike Hickey.

My thanks for research assistance to:
Bobbie Ferguson, Terry Koenig,
Dr. R. Lally, Dr. J. Moreno, Dr. G. Agogino.

# Chapter 1

Kitt Tucker brushed away the powdery brown dust and stared down at the gleaming skull. Two gold front teeth, still in place, glittered in the brilliant New Mexico sunshine. She rocked back on her heels and ran her gaze over the unmarked grave. Two gold front teeth . . . a memory long hidden slipped from the recesses of her mind and struggled forward. She flipped her long brown braid over her shoulder and leaned over the skull again.

"Dr. Tucker." The voice startled Kitt from her concentration, and she shaded her eyes as she looked up from the six-foot-deep pit to find the portly Dr. Dean standing over her. "Dr. Tucker, he's back."

Frowning, Kitt rose and placed one foot in the step she had carved in the side of the pit, which let her stand high enough to survey the old cemetery site. The summer archaeology students were hard at work in the afternoon light, excavating the graves and taking out the remains that soon were to be reinterred in another cemetery—one safely distant from the dam that would flood this area.

"I had to run him out of my tent. He was fiddling with the skeletal material. He's over there by number fifteen now." Dr.

Dean, who had become self-appointed watchdog for the crew, nodded in the direction of the numbered grave of a small child.

"I'll ask him to leave," Kitt murmured.

The grizzled old man standing in the cemetery had proven to be harmless—though something of an annoyance—since his first appearance at the project site nearly three weeks previously. Kitt climbed out of the grave and walked up to the old man. Gently, she touched his arm.

"Eh?" The old man glanced at her, his watery blue eyes distant. "What's the matter, young 'un?"

"Sir, I'm afraid you'll have to leave the site. I've told you before, we cannot allow unauthorized people at the project."

The blue eyes surveyed her calmly. "Why not?"

"Because..." How many times had she been over this with him? she wondered. She watched a young summer student listening as he worked quietly in the grave beside them. Somehow, she had to make the old man understand.

"Because this is very sensitive work...even dangerous. There may be living viruses in this soil. We're all vaccinated, you see." Kitt paused. "The smallpox virus can live for three hundred years in skeletal remains. Have you been vaccinated?"

The old man gave her a long look.

"Even more important," she went on, "the cemetery dates back only to the late 1800s—people in this county have relatives buried here. We're trying to conduct our work in a respectful manner."

"Respect for the dead."

"That's right, sir. We're not allowing the press or anyone else on the site until the project is complete."

The old man took off his brown felt hat and looked away. The afternoon sun had sent a rivulet of perspiration down his cheek. Kitt watched it meander into a crease, then fall beneath his worn white collar.

"The twilight is coming," he said at last. His gnarled fingers twisted the brim of his hat. "The twilight is coming and I'll be here to see it."

She opened her mouth to protest, then noticed that a tear had escaped the old man's eye. He brushed it away with the side of his finger and put his hat on his head. Kitt cleared her throat.

"It's not long until dusk." She shifted from one foot to the other, unsure the man had been talking about the time of day. "I'm sorry, you'll just have to leave. The rules are set by the Bureau of Reclamation and I—"

"I'll stay." He looked at her so matter-of-factly that she decided it was useless to argue. He'd always gone away before, but he seemed too harmless to be a threat to the project.

"Listen, sir—what's your name?"

"They call me Hod." The old man grinned, knowing he had won. "I'll just sit under that cottonwood. You'll never know I'm here."

Kitt nodded in resignation. "You can sit there today, Hod. But I can't permit you to come back again. If you do, I'll have to—"

"Oh, I'll be back. I'm here to watch the twilight."

Kitt looked at the student, who had continued laboring, silent but curious. He winked and tapped his temple. "Guess he's coming back."

Without answering, Kitt turned on her heel and headed to her own work site. She could see Dr. Dean watching her, and she knew she should come up with a good reason for letting the outsider remain. She had directed a number of similar projects for the bureau—and she always felt it important to present a professional operation to the visiting professors and government assistants. After all, she had worked her way into the bureau's top archaeologist position with her no-nonsense attitude and levelheaded dedication.

"Looks like he's here to stay," the anthropologist said with a smile as she approached. "You've always got a few hangers-on to deal with, haven't you? Curious children, wandering bums, pesky reporters."

She sighed in relief. Dr. Dean had been at the site from the start, but unlike many of his stuffy predecessors, he had proven to be a warm and enjoyable addition to her crew. "His name is Hod and he seems to ramble a little. He's awfully old."

"Maybe he's got a friend buried here."

"A friend? He couldn't be *that* old."

The professor chuckled. "Nineties, I'd say. Maybe a hundred. Remember—I'm the physical anthropologist. I'm trained to figure out things like that."

"On skeletons."

Kitt grinned and knelt at the lip of the grave pit again. She could see a few rib bones protruding from the dirt. The skull stared vacantly at her. Two gold front teeth. How odd, she thought. Most of the people buried in the cemetery had been impoverished pioneers. The dig had uncovered nothing of value—a few unmatched buttons, a scrap of denim, a bone wedding band.

"You have a message in the tent."

She looked up in surprise. She had forgotten the professor's presence in her growing curiosity about the skeleton. "A message?"

"In the tent."

Sighing in frustration, Kitt stood and brushed off the knees of her jeans. What now, she thought as she followed Dr. Dean. If it weren't some doddering old codger who wouldn't leave, it had to be a broken camera lens or a hailstorm or a new government form to fill out.

The professor led her to the large yellow nylon tent where he examined the skeletal remains in order to determine age, cause of death, sex and various other information. Kitt walked into the tent and swept the folded phone message from the card table. Flipping open the note she scanned it as he began digging through a crate of yellowed bones.

"Damn." Kit stuffed the note into her back pocket.

"Problems?" Dr. Dean looked up. He held a skull in one hand and a set of calipers in the other.

"Oh, I'd forgotten a meeting I agreed to." Kitt brushed a wisp of brown hair from her cheek. "A man named Burton—an Affiliated Press reporter from Albuquerque—is passing through and wants an interview. I agreed, as long as he stays off the site. He's waiting at my motel."

"So go. These skeletons aren't going anywhere, you know . . . at least we hope not."

Kitt grinned in spite of her annoyance. She wouldn't have time to change clothes or prepare what she wanted to say. But more frustrating, she would have to leave the grave she had started on. The strange skull flashed through her mind again and she lifted her chin in determination.

"Well, Mr. Burton is just going to have to wait a few minutes for his interview," she announced. "I have a more important date—and he's been waiting nearly a hundred years for me."

She could hear Dr. Dean chuckling behind her as she hurried into the relentless sunlight. Glancing at her watch, she gave herself twenty minutes to complete a cursory examination. She would have to leave the detail work for a student. Project rules prohibited leaving any graves open overnight.

Climbing into the grave again, she picked up her small brush and began expertly dusting the skeleton. Soon she had finished cleaning the skull and started on the shoulders. She brushed a filmy layer of dust from the skeleton's scapula and noticed a small protrusion buried in the bone. Taking an old toothbrush and a chopstick—her favorite tools—from her back pocket, she cleaned away all the debris until she could clearly see the knife tip. From the look of the bone, which had calcified around the metal, the man had lived for several years with the blade embedded in his shoulder.

Her curiosity mounting at the discovery of the man's violent past, Kitt carefully worked her way down the remainder of the skeleton. Nothing unusual turned up, and she was just about to climb out of the grave when her eye fell on a folded corner of newspaper. It was always strange to discover what time had chosen to preserve. The buried man's pants had rotted long ago, but in the spot where the pocket would have been, the scrap of newspaper lay in the dust.

Perhaps this held a clue to his identity. Shivering slightly at the prospect, she gingerly picked up the paper, heaved herself out of the grave and hurried across the cemetery to the yellow tent.

"What do you have there?" Dr. Dean looked up from his examination of a set of bones. "Looks interesting."

Kitt nodded and sat on a high wooden stool beside the table. With tweezers, she carefully pried open the section of yellowed newspaper. The side folded in revealed nothing more than a listing of books and maps for sale—an atlas of the United States, a geography of the Mississippi area and a map of the New Mexico Territory. In one corner, the owner had scribbled what looked like an address. Probably the source for the maps.

She flipped the paper, hoping for something more revealing.

"Cattle market results," Dr. Dean announced, leaning over her shoulder. "The poor fellow must have had a few head of cattle. Did you finish the grave?"

She shook her head. "No time—and I took longer than I'd planned anyway. I'll have to let one of the students do the sifting work." She hurried to the camera table and photographed both sides of the newspaper clipping. Then she refolded it and set it into the box she would use to store the skeleton.

"It's the strangest thing," she murmured, half to herself. "The skull has two gold front teeth."

"Two gold teeth? Didn't I read about a fellow...that Indian who ran with James Kirker, the old scalp hunter. What was his name? A real terror, as I recall. Black Dove—that's it." Dr. Dean said the name that had been playing at the edge of her mind. "Of course, he was buried down in Mexico. You ought to know that as well as anybody."

"Guadalupe Y Calvo. It's down in southern Chihuahua." Kitt brushed her forehead with the back of her hand. "Dr. Frank Oldham found the records of his burial while we were working together at Northern New Mexico University."

Dr. Dean smiled. "I read that paper, you know. Fine work. Dr. Oldham is the authority on Black Dove and the Indians of the Southwest, in my opinion. You must have learned a lot working with him."

"I wish he were still teaching at the university. The students loved him." Kitt smiled in memory. "I'm expanding the paper into a book for the NNMU press. Should get some attention—the white scalp hunters have been getting a lot of play in the journals since our account came out."

"You're the person to do the book, if anyone."

"Well, I guess I'll head into town—I've kept that reporter waiting long enough. If I'm lucky he'll have gone home. Shut things down for me, will you? And let me know what you find out about our mystery man."

Dr. Dean nodded, already absorbed in his examination. Kitt slung her leather bag over her shoulder and picked up the worn bush jacket. A skull with two gold teeth, she thought...how odd.

Hurrying out of the tent toward the Bureau's pickup, she glanced at the site. The students moved around in the waning sunlight. She watched them for a moment as they worked in the cemetery, silently digging, photographing, conferring. The scene warmed her heart, let her know she belonged, gave her purpose.

As she started the engine, she glanced down at herself—faded jeans, dusty boots, khaki work shirt. This was who she was...Kitt Tucker, head anthropologist-archaeologist for the Bureau of Reclamation in New Mexico, Oklahoma and West Texas. Thirty-two years old. Single.

Throwing the truck into gear, Kitt looked up. Her gaze fell on a lone figure beneath a stately cottonwood tree. Old Hod tipped his hat to her and nodded. "The twilight is coming," she heard his voice whisper to her through the recesses of her memory. "The twilight is coming."

Kitt focused on the dry landscape as she drove down the highway toward town. The clay soil and arid climate had worked unusually well to preserve the remains at the cemetery, she thought, keeping her eyes trained on the pavement. Too bad she hadn't had more time to examine that skeleton. By tomorrow the skull with the two gold teeth would be sealed in a new coffin, and soon it would be set in the ground to rest in silence forever.

Black Dove... the legendary Shawnee war chief... Kitt's thoughts retraced time to the two years she had spent working with Dr. Frank Oldham. Her primary focus in the paper had been the white scalp hunters of the early 1800s—men who had slaughtered Apaches for the Mexican and United States governments at up to two hundred dollars a scalp.

Kitt remembered a few details from Black Dove's life. He had been one of James Kirker's right-hand men for many years; he had ruthlessly massacred men, women and children for bounty; he had been tall, powerfully built and handsome; he had had two gold front teeth.

And he was buried in Guadalupe Y Calvo, Mexico.

A tumbleweed rolled across the highway, and Kitt swerved to miss it. Those had been good years at the university. She had entered as hardly more than a child, aching to fill the void in her heart left by the sudden end of her brief, tempestuous marriage. She had worked hard to put away her past, to grow beyond it. And nine years later she had completed her doctorate, a mature woman, certain of her intelligence and skills.

Kitt rounded a bend in the road. The small oil town of Catclaw Draw came into sight, pink-glazed by the setting sun. The thought of her marriage opened a new floodgate of memories. How far she had pushed that year of reckless love, mad and whirling passion...that year as the wife of Garth Culhane.

Even his name had an unfamiliar ring. She had severed it from her own name not long after he walked out the door—just as she had tried to sever all the memories...the hot nights of flaming love in their little trailer, picnics and laughing down by the creek, their parents arguing ceaselessly over the hasty wedding and the child...most of all their child.

Blinking back tears she never allowed herself to cry, Kitt sped into town and spun the pickup into the motel parking lot. No—she wouldn't cry now. She was too knowledgeable for sentiment. All the statistics showed the marriage had been doomed. It couldn't have lasted—they had been too young, far too filled with fun and irresponsibility. Their parents had fought it from start to finish. Babies born to teenagers were often small, often premature, the figures showed. The odds had been stacked against them from the start.

There was no point in going over barren ground. She had closed off that part of herself.

Kitt climbed out of the pickup and hurried to her turquoise-blue motel door. Fortified against her past, she inserted the key, stepped into the darkened room and shut the door behind her. She had just lifted her hand to the light switch when a hard pounding sounded on the door.

For a moment she stood in silence, staring into the blackness. Then—with a melting wash of relief—she realized it must be the reporter. Sliding her leather bag onto a chair, Kitt turned and pulled open the door.

"Hello, I'm—" She stopped, her words frozen at the sight of the man leaning against her door frame. His dark blond hair blew gently away from his forehead and at first she couldn't be sure...the shoulders were different somehow, and the jaw... and then she looked into his eyes. Gray-blue with a golden halo around the dark center.

"Garth."

"Kitt." His voice was deeper than she remembered. He stood up to his full height—and he was taller than she remembered. "What... are you doing here?" he asked.

"This is my room. What are *you* doing here?"

He looked away for a moment, his jaw rigid. Then he turned back. "I came to get a story on some archaeological site... I came to interview the project director in room 112."

"But Mr. Burton—"

"Burton's down with the flu in Las Cruces. I was heading back from an assignment at Carlsbad Caverns when I got the call to fill in for him."

"You're a reporter? You're supposed to be a farmer."

"And you're supposed to be a farmer's wife." Garth looked at Kitt again, uncertain whether this tall, willowy woman standing before him really could be that wispy girl he once had known... "I've been with the Affiliated Press for eight years. I went to college, you know... So—do you work for the project director or something?"

"I *am* the project director." Kitt stared into the blue-gray eyes. "I went to college, too. I've been the anthropologist-archaeologist with the Bureau of Reclamation for six years. The cemetery relocation is my project."

"Kitt Culhane—"

"Kitt *Tucker*."

She watched him shove his hands into his pockets and lean against the door frame again. He had larger hands now, sun-baked to a golden brown. And his shoulders were broad and massive...but of course Garth was a man now. He was what— thirty-three? He had been just a boy when he had last leaned against her door frame and looked into her eyes. *I'll always love you,* he had whispered. *And if you ever need me*...then he'd stopped speaking.

Kitt had nodded and shut the door on him. But she *had* needed him! She'd clung to his words, believing that somehow he'd know to come for her. He hadn't come. He'd never come back—until one day she knew she didn't need him anymore. She had made it on her own, and she didn't need anyone, least of all Garth Culhane.

"Can I come in and do my interview?" His voice startled her again. When had it lost that youthful lilt? "Just give me the basics and I'll get out of your way."

Just walk in and then back out. Like he'd done before. "No," she said suddenly. "No, I agreed to an interview with a Mr. Burton. Not with you. I had a lot of work to do—"

"Look, I've been waiting for you for three hours." Garth again rose to his full height. "And digging up a bunch of old graves isn't my idea of hot news anyway. So let's just—"

"Excuse me." Kitt turned into the room and shut the door firmly behind her. And it felt good...so good. Years ago, Garth had walked away from her, and she had always feared that if he came back she would weaken and open wide the doors to her heart. But he hadn't come until now. And she'd been able to shut the door.

Trembling, still aware of his physical presence imprinted on her consciousness, she flipped on the light and hurried across the room to the closet. She would shower and change and then take herself out to dinner. A fine dinner...

The knocking began again. Harder this time.

"Kitt Culhane, open this damn door." Garth's voice was deeper, almost a growl.

Kitt stared at the turquoise door shuddering on its hinges. Who was he, this stranger pounding outside? The Garth she knew would never have stayed and slammed his fist on her door. He would have gone away...quietly, gently...as he did everything. He had even left her tenderly, sadly.

"Open this door," Garth called louder. "I'm talking to you, Kitt Culhane—"

"Kitt *Tucker*!" she yelled. "Tucker, Tucker, Tucker! Now go away. Leave me alone."

She ran into the bathroom and slammed the door. No, she wouldn't cry. She buried her face in a towel and pressed her eyes tightly closed. She hadn't cried over him yet, and she wouldn't start now. Just because he was out there, so close...just because they'd loved each other once. No, he was not the same man!

Kitt whirled and turned on the shower full force so she couldn't hear him. She peeled off her dusty boots, jeans and work shirt. Then she stepped into the stall and scrubbed the day's dust away with a thick white washcloth. Letting the water cascade over her sunburned face, she unbraided the long coil that fell down her back and thoroughly shampooed her hair.

She expected her tension to melt as it always did under a good, hot shower. But this time she couldn't pull her thoughts from Garth. They had showered together often...in the early days when all was well. She could almost feel his fingers caressing her shoulders, his lips on her wet neck, his strong young body hungry against hers...she could almost smell that undefinable scent of his skin, so male...could almost sense the way his flat brown nipples pressed to hers, sliding, circling, teasing her to tightened arousal. And then when she had begun to swell with the baby, he had run the bathtub full with bubbles. He had gently washed her back and then they had marveled at the moving hills on her stomach as the child turned inside...

Whisking open the shower curtain, Kitt fumbled blindly for a towel. She quickly dried herself, wrapped her hair into one towel and tucked another around her body. She had business to think about. She needed to check in with Dave at the Bureau and file the stack of notes heaped on her table. She stood for a moment with her hand on the doorknob listening. The shower dripped. Cars sped by outside the tiny frosted window. A truck honked. But there was no sound at the bedroom door.

Pulling open the bathroom door, she stepped out onto the carpet and reached for the telephone on the dresser, then dialed the number from memory.

"Is Dave in? Thanks, Sue." She stroked her fingers along the plastic wood-grain veneer. "Hi, Dave. Kitt. Just wanted to let you know we're almost through... Oh, five or six unmarked graves since we last talked. Nothing of any interest really... Looks like some syphilis and smallpox deaths. A lot of children... Babies."

Kitt swallowed as she listened to Dave. She nodded. "Poor folks, mostly. Tin and bone wedding bands. Hardly any boots. Oh, one fellow was a little strange—he had two gold teeth. Gold, yes! I know, I didn't expect that...Black Dove is the one you're thinking of. But he was buried in Mexico, remember? Guadalupe Y Calvo. Yeah, I guess so... I'd say no more than four days should do it—I've ordered the monuments. No, not really. There's this old fellow who keeps hanging around the site, but I've told him—" A gentle breeze lifted the corner of the towel around Kitt's thighs, and she turned in surprise to the open window.

"You've changed in twelve years." Garth's voice seemed to fill the room. He was sitting in an orange armchair, his boots propped on the bed.

"How did you get in here—" She caught her breath. "No, Dave. It's okay, it's just this reporter who... Yeah, I'll get rid of him. Call me when you get that final survey."

She set the receiver down, her eyes narrowed.

"You left the window open." Garth unfolded himself from the chair and stood up. "I climbed in. That's one thing I've learned as a reporter—never let a story get away."

"What story? Just some boring old cemetery relocation." She planted her hands on her hips. "Get out of my room, Garth—"

"A cemetery relocation—and a skull with two gold teeth. But you say it couldn't be Black Dove. I just did a feature story on New Mexico's Apaches. Did you see it? Most of the papers picked it up—the *Journal*, the *Tribune*... Old Black Dove was quite a character. Massacred the Apaches left and right. So, where were the gold teeth on that skull? In the front?"

"That was privileged information, I'll have you know. The results of the dig will be formally released to the press when I feel it's appropriate."

"Appropriate? Black Dove will be back in the ground by then, along with all his secrets."

"Black Dove is buried in *Mexico*. If you'd done any research for your feature story, you'd know that. Go read your history books." She glared at him. She was a little surprised he'd even heard of Black Dove. The only extensive mention of him was from his years with Kirker. And what was this hulk of a man she hardly recognized doing in her bedroom, anyway? "Garth, I'm telling you to get out of my room or I'm going to call the desk."

"Were the teeth in the front? The two top ones?" Garth whipped a narrow spiral notebook and a ballpoint pen from his back pocket. He forced his thoughts from the swell of her breasts against the damp white towel, from the droplets that beaded her clear bare skin. The floral scent of her damp hair filled his nostrils. He focused on his notepad. He'd stroked her bare skin once, tasted the sweetness of her breasts, turned their rosy tips into honeyed pebbles against his tongue.... "Black Dove disappeared in New Mexico, didn't he?" he asked, scribbling with determination across the thin blue lines on the notebook page. "Right after his stint with Kirker—"

"Black Dove is buried in *Mexico*. I helped Frank Oldham write the paper that proved it, for heaven's sake." She couldn't believe she was standing here in her towel watching Garth Culhane write furiously in his little notebook. Was he totally unaware of her—all his senses trained on his story? And why did she give a damn where Garth Culhane chose to place his attentions? "The full paper is in the NNMU library. It's all written down, Garth. There's no story *here* about Black Dove. The only story is that the Bureau is moving a historical cemetery to make way for a dam that's going to flood the area—"

"Were the teeth in the front? Just tell me that." Garth looked up from his pad, his eyes filled with an intense light Kitt had never seen there before.

"You're just the typical obnoxious reporter, aren't you?" She took a step toward him. The steam drifting from the bathroom had lent a misty moistness to the air. "Sticking your nose into places it doesn't belong. Trying to make something of nothing so readers will buy more papers. You'll insinuate that Black Dove is buried here, and then history buffs and treasure seekers will come pouring out of the woodwork—disturbing historical sites, moving grave markers, trespassing on government property—"

"So the teeth were in front?"

"Get out—"

Garth's hand shot out and grabbed Kitt's wrist. "When did you get to be such a—"

"Professional? After you walked out of my life." She stared into his eyes, willing herself to see only the hardness in them. Willing herself not to feel his fingers burning into her skin, his hot breath on her damp cheek. He was so close now, the warmth of his body almost filling the empty space around them. The muscle in his jaw flickered, and his strong lips held a magnetism that beckoned her. She lifted her chin. "I worked hard to get where I am today. And I'm not going to let you desecrate the things I believe in."

"And what do you believe in, Kitt Culhane?" He dropped his voice. He could feel her wrist trembling in his grip. That was the Kitt he remembered . . . soft, giving, a little scared of life. But when had she flown away and left this rigid, angry shell of a woman? He ran his eyes over her face, searching for traces of the girl he'd loved so deeply—so much he thought he'd never be able to put his shattered life together again.

There had been no choice but to leave her . . . he had nearly ruined her life. He had convinced himself it was all his fault. If she hadn't been so young when he'd loved her, their baby might have had a better chance. The birth—he couldn't even call it that . . . the removal of that lifeless body inside hers had nearly killed her, too. And afterward, the cold emptiness in her eyes had haunted him. She had been so young to suffer such a loss.

He stared at her now. Her eyes were the same—deep golden brown, with long black lashes that fluttered when she talked. And yet the gold in them, which once had been like molten lava, now was as hard and cold and empty as an ingot. "What do you believe in?"

"I believe that you should get out of my room. Get in your car and go back to Albuquerque." She fought back the tears that his gaze had melted inside her. She tightened her lips. "I don't want you here, Garth. I don't want you in my life anymore."

"Get dressed and I'll take you to dinner." He dropped her wrist and walked toward the orange vinyl armchair. "I'm hungry."

Kitt knotted her fists. Anger boiled inside her. Without thinking, she stormed to the telephone. But as she reached for the receiver, Garth's warm hand closed over hers. She turned, her lips forming the hot words that would unleash the years of pain, disappointment, loneliness. But he lifted her hand in his and kissed it gently.

"Just get dressed, Kitt," he said softly, and his voice sounded almost as young and loving as she remembered. "I'll take you out to eat for old times' sake. We won't even talk about your project or Black Dove—"

"Black Dove is *not* in that grave." She stopped, reeling from the chaos he had evoked in her. Part of her wanted to shout at him, to beat her fists against his chest for hurting her so much, to prove to him that she didn't need him ... And part of her longed to fall into his arms, to lay her head against that very chest, to feel his fingers stroke her hair... "I'm going into the bathroom to dress and you'd better be gone by the time I come out."

Kitt pulled her hand away from Garth's and hurried to the closet. Grabbing the first dress she found, she jerked it from the hanger and went into the bathroom. She quickly toweled her hair and ran a comb through the long, damp tresses. She should wear it up, tight and in a chignon. He would hate that— he had always loved her hair hanging long and loose down her back. But then, she'd told him to leave. He probably would go this time.

Leaving her hair, she slipped into the loose-fitting white cotton shift she had bought on a trip to Mexico with Dr. Oldham. The last she had heard the professor was retired in Albuquerque. That could mean trouble—no doubt Garth would think he had to contact Dr. Oldham about the skull. How ridiculous the whole notion was. She had seen Dr. Oldham's full report—interviews, photographs, tapes.

Kitt leaned over the sink, brushing a little mascara over the tips of her dark lashes. She had no need for cosmetics with the ruddy sun glow on her cheeks. In fact, she would have to be more careful to wear her hat in the severe summer heat. As she rubbed a little lotion on her skin, she stopped and held her hand to her nose. A scent clung to her fingers—a scent so evocative that she closed her eyes and leaned against the wall. Garth's scent ... spicy, a hint of musk ... but mingled within it the sense of *him*—his skin and his breath and ...

Jerking upright, Kitt shook herself slightly to free the hold of the memories. She turned on the water and lathered her hands with the tiny bar of motel soap. Then she dried them carefully, lifted her chin and walked out of the bathroom.

Her room was empty. She stared for a moment at the imprint of Garth's boots on her bed. The Indian-print coverlet was slightly rumpled, dented. So he had gone. Good. She hurried to the bed and smoothed out the spread. Erase him, Kitt. Erase him again.

She slipped into her sandals and threw a jacket over her shoulders. For a moment she stood alone in the room. His scent was here, too. No one would have known but she...she had lived with it once. She looked at the garish orange chair. He'd sat in that chair. He'd walked on this carpet.

For one brief moment, he'd come back...mistakenly—but he'd entered her life again. And now he was gone. This time she would hold up her head in defiance against the pain. She would know that he'd grown hard and brutish and stubborn. He wasn't the man she had once loved. It was over.

Picking up her leather bag, she flicked off the light and stepped out into the night. She took a deep breath of cool air and hurried to her pickup. Climbing in, she set her bag on the seat beside her and rummaged for her keys amid the pens and scraps of paper, loose bills and bottled soil specimens. At last her fingers closed around the keys. As she lifted them to the ignition, the door on the other side of the pickup swung open and a tall, lean figure climbed onto the seat.

Catching her breath, Kitt stared at the face lit by the dome light. Garth smiled at her. His hair had fallen over his forehead.

"Sent a message to the bureau chief to get in touch with Dr. Oldham. And I had to get my jacket," he said lightly, pulling the door shut. "At night, it's cooler than you think here in the desert."

"Garth—"

"Let's go." He gestured to the keys lying idly in her palm. As she numbly fitted the key into the ignition and started the engine, he pulled out his notebook and pen. "So—were the two gold teeth in the front of the skull?"

"Garth, you promised..."

"At dinner. Nothing about work at dinner." He flipped open his notebook and began scribbling. "But right now I want to know about that skull. Remember—you owe the Affiliated Press an interview, Mrs. Culhane."

*"Tucker!"*

# Chapter 2

Kitt cut her enchiladas into seven neat rectangles. Then she cut the rectangles into squares. She could feel Garth's eyes on her, watching every move. They had hardly spoken on the way to the restaurant. She had refused to let out one tidbit of information. He had clamped his jaw in frustration.

"You planning to eat any of that?"

Glancing up, she saw the hardness had gone out of his face. His eyes had darkened to teal in the soft candlelight. His hair looked thick and clean. Touchable. Once, he had been all ears and crewcut and sunburned neck beneath his Cummins Diesel cap. His arms had been long, gangly with sinew. Now, white shirt sleeves rolled halfway to his elbows, he displayed the solid, rock-hard muscle and ropy veins of a man. Thick silver-gold hair swept over his forearms. His hands were large and square, their blunt-tipped nails white against his deeply tanned fingers.

He dipped a tortilla chip into a bowl of salsa. As he sat back, his knee brushed her leg under the table. A high-voltage tingle zipped down her spine. She sat up straight. Instinctively, she clamped her knees together so tightly it would have taken a crowbar to pry them apart.

She took a bite and chewed with intense concentration. At this moment, she felt about fifteen years old—skittish, twisted into a hundred knots, her heart pounding like thunder. She felt out of control, and she didn't like it one bit.

"Decent place to eat for a small town." He watched and waited for a response.

Kitt gave an indifferent shrug. Though the restaurant claimed great fame for its Mexican food, the stuff was bland and nearly tasteless compared with the hot, spicy dishes of northern New Mexico. The decor appeared to have originated in some border town flea market—faded piñatas, ceramic parrots, sombreros.

Perhaps she was being a little harsh. With Garth Culhane sitting across from her, she could taste confusion and hurt more strongly than red chilis.

"Where do you live, Kitt?" he asked. So far he'd gotten either anger or stony silence out of her. She was no longer the skinny chatterbox who lay in his arms and told him everything she was thinking and feeling. This woman had an exterior of ice.

"Santa Fe."

"Pretty expensive up there, isn't it?"

Kitt gave another little shrug. She didn't want him to know anything about the world she had built for herself. It was her world. Private. Closed. If he knew anything about it, he would become a part of it in some small way. And she had worked too damned hard to forget.

"So, how many more days until you finish up the project?"

"You heard what I told Dave Logan on the phone. Don't play games with me, Garth."

*Can't you see I don't want you?* The message couldn't have been more plain if she had spoken the words. Garth watched her face for any break in the facade. But there was none. Maybe it wasn't a facade, this rigidness. Maybe she was a block of stone right to the core. If so, it was his fault. He swirled his tea, watching the ice cubes go around and feeling uncomfortable. His fault. He had to take part of the blame for killing her spirit. A big part of it. But maybe somewhere inside she was still soft and warm . . .

He looked up. She was pouring honey down the steaming throat of a sopaipilla. Her fingers, tanned by the sun, were still as long and beautiful as he had remembered them. Her hair was draped across her shoulders to her waist in shades of deep brown that lightened almost to ribbons of gold. It was tempting to find out what lay beneath those harsh words and the frigid silences.

"I guess I should have expected you to do something in history or anthropology," he began. She was poking at her frijoles. "Remember how we used to meet in the Southwest history section of the library at lunch? It was the quietest place—"

"Don't, Garth. I don't want to talk about the past." Of course she remembered it. She remembered everything. The chairs were hard brown wood. The floor was off-white tile. The books smelled musty. The librarian wore bright pink lipstick and sat with her back to the room, eating her lunch of peanut butter sandwiches and bananas.

Kitt sat on Garth's lap and they would make the pretense of reading about New Mexico—about Geronimo and Cochise and Victorio. They studied Billy the Kid and the Lincoln County War. And Kitt would feel Garth's arms slide around her waist, his fingers heating the skin just beneath her breasts. His lips would move down her neck, and his breath would send coils of fire into the pit of her stomach. She would wiggle her hips a little against him, settling into his hard young body— and relishing the way his breath shortened over the words he was trying to read.

"So, you don't want to talk about the past. And you won't tell me about the present." Garth watched her struggle to focus. She had been remembering it. He could see the way her lips had softened and her face had gentled. "What about the future, Kitt? What do you plan to do when this dig is over? You going to stay with the Bureau?"

"It's my job," she said, fighting to stabilize the wall of coldness that had started to topple. "I'll be rehabilitating some irrigation ditches that date back to the Spanish settlement."

"Where are they?"

"Near Taos."

"Why do they need an anthropologist for that?"

"I'll be trying to document the antiquity of the ditches. I think they're pretty unique, but the locals want to line the ditches with glaring white concrete."

"So what can you do about that?"

"The old ditches are really as organic as the things around them. I'm hoping to come up with a creative idea to preserve some of their totality with the environment."

"You find a lot of conflict between progress and history."

"Yes." She felt like he was interviewing her again. But it was a lot more comfortable than reminiscing about making out in the Clovis High School library.

"So what do you think you can do to preserve the integrity of the old ditches? Do you have any ideas?"

"It's my job to take problems that are given to me—the parameters are set—and solve them. The locals won't give up the ditches, and I'm not willing to let them become twentieth-century horror stories. I imagine we'll compromise. I'm thinking of earth-colored concrete."

"Colored concrete." He had to smile. Maybe the fun and zest had gone out of her—maybe she was prickly and analytical—but this new Kitt was also intelligent and resourceful and dedicated. He liked that.

"It would work," she said.

"I'm sure it would. So, when did you decide to go into archaeology and anthropology?"

She folded her napkin and set it beside her plate. The past, the past. Why couldn't he stick to easy subjects?

"I took a course in college."

"Where did you go to school? NNMU?"

"I need to be getting back to my room, Garth. I've got a lot of things to go over."

"I got my degree after the war. Finished up in '78."

The war? Kitt tensed. She hadn't known Garth had fought in Vietnam. "Were you in the army?"

"I volunteered right after the . . . right after I left Clovis. I was a communications specialist at a Comcenter. It kind of gave me a taste of the field. When I got back I studied journalism at Texas University in El Paso. I got hooked on the stuff. Worked for the local newspaper for a while. Finally the Affiliated Press took me on."

"Have you been in Albuquerque's Affiliated Press bureau all those years?"

"Digging into the past, are we, Mrs. Culhane? I thought that was forbidden territory."

"Digging into the past is my *job*."

"It's my job, too."

"You have an uncooperative subject tonight."

"I'm well aware of that." He could see that she was trying to maintain her expressionless facade. But she wasn't succeeding. One corner of her mouth had turned up. "I was in El Paso for a couple of years. I really liked covering the border. Drugs, racial tension, illegal aliens. Good stuff. But they got shorthanded in Albuquerque and sent me up there."

"And what's in your future? Are you trying to move onward and upward?"

"I've applied for an overseas post." He looked away, studying the print on the curtains. "The hotter the spot they plant me in, the better. Kabul, Jerusalem, Moscow, Bogotá, Beirut—I'll go anywhere."

Why? She wanted to ask. Why had he gone off to a horrible war where he could have been killed? Why would he purposely request to be sent to Beirut or Bogotá? She had seen pictures of reporters stepping over mutilated bodies, photographers dragging wounded comrades from the line of fire.

"You were going to be a farmer." The words slipped from her mouth, barely audible in the busy restaurant.

His eyes darted to hers and locked there. "Things change."

"You used to take me out on that big green tractor of your dad's. And we'd ride all over the place, remember? You'd show me the fields and you'd talk about milo and cotton. You had big plans for that farm. You were going to try all the new methods, remember? And you'd tell me how much you had to pay for seed and fertilizers and insecticide. And you'd show me the barn owls up in the hay barn—"

"Yeah, I remember those barn owls." He leaned across his plate, his elbows resting on the table. He felt almost malicious, forcing memories on her that she'd chosen to destroy. But he had held onto those moments—they'd gotten him through some tough times. "We'd walk into the barn, acting like we were going to watch the barn owls. You'd be trying to

look like you belonged on a farm. You wore that checkered
shirt and those overalls. Smallest pair of overalls I ever saw."

Kitt bit her lower lip to keep from falling under the spell of
his words.

"Designer overalls. But you looked so damned cute, Kitt.
We'd be standing in the barn looking up at the owls, and I'd
start rubbing your shoulder, and you'd stick your hand in my
jeans back pocket."

"Garth." Kitt glanced at a waitress wheeling past a cart
loaded with salsa and chips.

He leaned over and lowered his voice. "And then I'd un-
button those top buttons on your little overalls. You'd close
your eyes and take my hand. We'd start climbing up the bales
of hay to the very top where we were almost level with the owls.
And they'd watch us with their big yellow eyes. You'd start
kissing the back of my neck, right there."

He touched the place just below his ear. He could see that
her brown eyes had gone almost black. She wasn't hearing the
clink of silverware of smelling the green chilis. She was far
away in that barn, lying on top of that hay with him.

He liked the way she looked just now, her lips damp and
parted, her breasts rising and falling beneath the thin fabric of
her white dress. And he liked the way he felt, a little like that
strong young buck who could hold a girl and make her sigh in
his arms.

"Remember, Kitt?" he said, across the forgotten enchiladas and frijoles. "Remember how we made that agreement
that we'd keep it safe—but we'd do everything we could to
make it good? I'd hold you and you'd hold me and we'd roll
around on top of the hay—"

"You sure are wordy, Garth Culhane." Bristling, Kitt slid
out of the booth.

"Words are my business."

"I prefer silence." She grabbed her purse and fumbled
around for her keys. "I'm going back to the motel now. I have
to make sure I ordered the right monuments. And there's a
stack of papers waiting to be filed. Maybe you can find a
way—"

"I'll go with you." He rose and took the check from her
hand.

"Give me that," she snapped, ripping the paper from his fingers. "I'm paying for my own dinner."

"I figured you would. I just wanted to see how much I owed for a tip."

Wanting to crawl inside herself, she stalked to the cashier's desk. She had not felt embarrassed in years. Everything she did was orderly and calm. Now she felt all at a loss—off kilter. How could she have been lulled into listening to that story about the barn? How could she have sat there almost in a trance as he rambled on and on about things she had long ago chosen to forget?

Not one of the men she had known in the past fifteen years had been able to embarrass—or even tease—her successfully. Not one had been able to encroach upon her methodical approach to life. They respected her intelligence and skill. They admired her. She was an equal, a colleague. She was Dr. Tucker, fellow historian—not some hot-blooded girl rolling on the hay in a barn.

Kitt sucked in a breath of chill night air as she started the pickup. Her knees still felt a little weak. Garth sat beside her, his big body filling the cab. He smelled like he always had—warm and masculine.

She rolled down the window.

"That oil refinery puts out quite a perfume," he said after a minute. Looking like a tangle of white Christmas tree lights, the refinery stood out against the darkness. It made Kitt think of some weird science fiction city, all angles of pipes and jets of white steam and ever-burning flares. The unreality of it as she sped past seemed to match the skewed sense of proportion in her brain.

She was riding in a pickup with Garth Culhane. The flat darkness of the highway engulfed them, and she stared out at her headlight beams. Garth and Kitt in a pickup. At sixteen, she was snuggled up against him as they spun down dusty farm roads. He'd have one hand on the steering wheel, his elbow cocked on the open window. The other hand was dangling over her shoulder, perilously close to her breast. She'd lay her head on his shoulder and settle her thigh along his. He'd be chewing a long piece of straw. He'd take out the straw and lean over and kiss her. She'd laugh. And pretty soon he'd pull over under a big old cottonwood tree.

Without turning her head, Kitt glanced at Garth in the darkness. He was all spread out across the pickup's seat, his knees jammed against the dashboard, his arm stretched along the back, his fingers tapping the red vinyl. Perilously close to her shoulder.

"Remember that old Chevy pickup I used to have?" His voice came out of the blackness.

"No," she said quickly.

"Yeah, you do. It was white. Gray seats. A gun rack on the back window. I used to take it around the farm after school and check on the cattle. Remember the time we got that flat tire and I couldn't figure out how to work the jack? And then you—"

"No. No, I don't remember that. I don't really remember much of anything from those days, Garth. To tell you the truth, I keep my focus squarely on the here and now."

"You never were a very good liar, Kitt."

They rode without speaking. She kept her eyes fastened on the road. Maybe she had been lying. But she was *not* going to think about the past. It was over and done with. She didn't know why he had to bring it all up—what he thought he could possibly accomplish. He was only making her angry. And when she got mad, she withdrew. So if he hoped to get her to feel all those old feelings again, he was dreaming. She felt nothing, she told herself. Nothing.

"Okay, we'll talk about the here and now." He pulled a miniature tape recorder from his coat pocket and clicked it on. "Tell me about the dig. What have you found? Anything interesting?"

She spun the pickup into the motel parking lot. "Nothing much. A lot of violent deaths. A lot of…babies." She snapped off the ignition and threw her keys into her purse. "I've decided to call a press conference tomorrow afternoon at two. You can come to that."

She threw open the door. He clamped his hand down on hers, pressing it into the cool vinyl seat. "Where will the conference be?"

"At the new cemetery where we'll be reinterring the cas-
kets. Chisum Memorial Cemetery. It's just the other side of
Catclaw Draw."

"I'd like go out to the project site and take some pictures in
the morning."

"It's against Bureau regulations."

"Why?"

He hadn't taken his hand away. It felt warm and strong en-
compassing hers. "You haven't been vaccinated."

"I'm up to date with everything. Covering the border, you
know."

Kitt stared into his eyes. The orange and blue neon sign over
the motel office sent flickers of color across his face. He wasn't
smiling.

"Regulations," she said softly.

"I'd be quiet as a mouse."

"Is causing conflict part of your job description, too?"

Garth looked at their hands. Her fingers were icy. He closed
over them with his palm, lifted them onto his thigh. She tried
to pull back but not hard enough. He turned her hand over in
his and uncurled her fingers. She kept her nails short. Un-
painted. He ran the tip of his finger over her palm in a circle
and felt a small callus across the heel. From digging, he imagined. He took her little finger between his thumb and index
finger and pulled down gently, over the knuckle, over each
joint to the tip. Then he started on the next.

"I suppose stirring things up a little is part of my job." His
voice sounded low, raspy.

She closed her eyes. "You used to be quiet all the time. I
never could get you to say what you were thinking."

"I learned how to talk. Some people think I'm very wordy
now."

He finished with her thumb and started up her wrist. She
held her breath, aware of the little ache that had started between her hips. She hadn't felt that ache for years. She wanted
to savor it, savor the warmth of it and the growing pulse. But
it was Garth Culhane who had caused that ache. She drew her
hand away and clamped it onto the steering wheel.

"I have to go call the local papers about the conference."

"Good night, Kitt."

She shut the metal door, leaving him in her truck. She opened the turquoise door, knowing he was watching her. Inside her dark room, she sat on the bed and squeezed her hand between her knees.

"I'd like room 118."

The motel owner held out his hand for a credit card. They conducted the transaction in silence. Credit card, license number, key. Garth studied a poster on the paneled wall. Visit New Mexico: Land of Enchantment.

He walked down the sidewalk to his room. Their doors were side by side. Her curtains were drawn, her lights off. She was making all those phone calls in the dark?

Garth smiled a little tiredly. He felt more wrung out now than he'd felt trailing a couple of DEA officers around for three weeks in Juarez while they followed up on an aborted drug bust. Of course, it wasn't every day you ran into your ex-wife.

In his room, he pulled off his boots, reached over and turned on the TV. He tossed his coat onto a chair. The tape recorder clunked against the arm. He took it out and stretched across the bed with the tape deck sitting on his belly.

Against the background jabber and sporadic laughter of a talk show, his thoughts turned. No, he hadn't expected to run into Kitt—ever. He had stayed as far away from Clovis as possible for fifteen years. Now he had to smile, imagining the Kitt he'd pictured still living there.

She had stayed in that fine brick house of her daddy's for a couple of years, soaking up the comfort of home and forgetting all about him and their baby. Then she'd probably met some fellow—some junior vice president in her daddy's bank or something. They'd gotten married. He'd moved her into another fine brick home. She'd had a couple of kids . . .

No, Kitt hadn't had any more babies. Kitt wasn't a housewife or a Junior Leaguer or a country clubber. And she wasn't Mrs. Kitt Culhane, either. He had to admit that.

She was Dr. Tucker. She had more education than he did. Damn . . . how about that? He grinned, and shook his head. She worked out in the sun, supervising big projects. She figured out charts and compiled reports. She probably dated professors.

As much as he knew about her, he realized there was a hell of a lot more he didn't know. And he wanted to find out everything. Had she ever married again? Were her parents still alive? Did she still like pecan pie better than anything else in the whole world? Did she still sleep with her sheet over her head in case bugs fell on her face? Did she still put food on her pantry shelves in alphabetical order? Was she still ticklish behind her knees...

Garth sat up. He thought he heard a sound through the wall. He flicked off the television. Her voice was muffled as she spoke on the phone. She was making those calls after all.

Why had he antagonized her? Why had he insisted on bringing up their past when she clearly wanted to forget everything?

He had told her the truth—conflict was part of his life now. He hardly ever had a conversation without digging into somebody's secret pain. He probed everyone from senators to little Mexican boys selling roses on the Avenue of the Americas bridge. He never let simple answers be enough. That was why he was so good at what he did—that was why he'd won awards at every Affiliated Press conference—that was why he expected his overseas post to come through by the end of the year.

But did he have to touch Kitt's pain? The facts were pretty clear. She didn't want him. She didn't want the memories of their life together. She'd built her own world. She was her own person now, separate and strong.

He closed his eyes and lay back on the dingy pillow. Tomorrow, he'd keep his distance. He'd cover the press conference. He'd let the skeleton with the gold teeth rest in peace. He'd write up a story, send it in and head for Albuquerque.

But for now, he thought... for right now, he was going to think about Kitt Culhane. Kitt Culhane, that skinny girl who ran through the milo with him and fell down laughing, and pulled him onto her...and kissed him. Kitt Culhane who lay on her bed in the room next door. A beautiful, intelligent woman who shivered when he touched her fingers in the pickup truck.

He flicked off the light and pushed the button on the little tape deck. It whirred softly, rewinding. He pushed play.

*"Tell me about the dig. What have you found? Anything interesting?"* His voice sounded professional. A little cocky. There was a pause. He could hear her breathing.

*"Nothing much. A lot of violent deaths. A lot of . . . of babies."*

Kitt lay curled in her bed with the sheet over her head. She felt hot, a little sick. Maybe it was the Mexican food. Maybe it was the fact that she'd peeked out her curtain and watched Garth move into the room next to hers.

Everyone she had phoned was coming to the press conference. The *Catclaw Draw Daily Call* would be there. So would the Carlsbad paper and a couple of others. With Affiliated Press covering the story, most of the dailies in New Mexico could pick it up and run it.

She thought about getting up and compiling a few more notes. But she already knew what information she would give out and what she wouldn't. Garth was going to be disappointed. She wouldn't have Dr. Dean's final compilations on the last few skeletons for several days. The skull with the two gold front teeth would be classified information for now.

Kitt stiffened. The comforting murmur of the television next door suddenly stopped. She could hear a bedspring squeak. A loud thud sounded on the wall near her head. She imagined Garth's headboard swaying as he settled into bed.

She pulled the sheet more tightly over her head. Garth used to sleep naked. His long body would be sprawled all over their lumpy double bed in the little trailer. Sprawled all over her. Covers crumpled on the floor. Sheets smelling of their passion.

The sound of his voice filtered through the wall. He was talking to himself. No, her voice suddenly followed his. The tape. He was playing the tape. He was listening to her as he lay on his bed. Naked.

Kitt pulled the pillow from under her head and shoved it over her ears. She carefully tucked the sheet all around. A little cocoon. Dr. Kitt Tucker was wrapped in a cocoon of sheets and pillows all because her ex-husband was staying at her motel.

Grow up, Kitt. Other women saw their former husbands and lovers all the time. They chatted amicably and worked out details of their lives—trading children back and forth, calmly discussing their work and their interests and their other loves.

But Kitt had no other loves. It was hard to admit that after fifteen years the best she'd been able to do was a man who had run off and left her all alone in a tiny, freezing trailer. Left her with empty arms and an empty womb.

Now she lay like some half-dead mummy. She was thirty-two, for heaven's sake. Wasn't this supposed to be her most sensual time of life? Wasn't she supposed to be enjoying wild nights of incredible passion? Wasn't her body supposed to be throbbing from dawn to dusk with a sexual drive that equaled or even surpassed that of a seventeen-year-old boy?

She felt more like a withered-up old prune that had fallen behind somebody's refrigerator shelf and molded there for fifteen years. She felt barren inside. Her breasts might have been a couple of prairie dog hills for all the joy they ever gave her. The secret places Garth had once fondled and kissed were...

She closed her eyes, thinking of the ache that had started inside her when he had held her hand in the pickup. Even now, just thinking about him, she felt it again. A warm, tingling, glowing ache. It coiled between her hips, curled up to her breasts and warmed and tightened their tips. Then it settled down inside her, down deep inside her, and made her heart thud against her chest.

In a sudden swift movement, she shoved the pillow between her knees and squeezed it tightly. She clenched her fists and held her breath, willing away the thought of him. Then she crushed the pillow tightly to her chest and listened in silence.

*"Tell me about the dig. What have you found? Anything interesting?"* His voice said the words for the twelfth time. She had counted.

*"Nothing much. A lot of violent deaths. A lot of... of babies."*

## Chapter 3

Kitt leaned over the sink and peered into the mirror. A couple of sandbags were sitting beneath her eyes. Any genteel woman would hurry to the refrigerator for cucumber slices, she thought. But there was no time for that sort of luxury. The sun was up, the day was still cool, and work was waiting.

She grabbed a hank of long brown hair and began brushing at the bottom, working her way up. Garth had left his room a half hour earlier—she'd heard his door shut as she lay staring at the purple light of dawn on her ceiling.

The tape of their voices had run on for hours in the night, stopping at the end, rewinding, starting again. Somewhere in the early morning his room had gone silent. She had waited, tense and listening, imagining him asleep. But within a minute his television had come on. So, Garth had wrestled with his own private demons last night. She was glad. He deserved every toss, every turn, every painful memory.

She began braiding her hair, starting at the top of her head, her elbows crooked up high behind her. She felt tired, emotionally drained. One more day, she thought, and Garth would be gone again. She'd just have to get through this day—through the press conference—and she could get back to living her normal life. She lowered her arms, swung the braid around and started working on the bottom half.

Minus the sandbags, she looked like she always did. Tall, a little thin, not exceptionally pretty but good enough. She had on a white sleeveless T-shirt beneath her old plaid work shirt. The same faded jeans she'd had on the day before were buttoned to her waist and cinched with her worn leather belt. She had on steel-toed black work boots and thick cotton socks. All in all, she decided as she came to the end of the braid, she was definitely not a genteel lady. But she was herself.

She clamped the end of the braid between her teeth like a lariat and started rummaging through her cosmetics bag for an elastic band. She remembered the day-old powdered-sugar doughnuts in a bag beneath the seat of her pickup. She'd grab a cup of coffee in the motel lobby on her way out, and that would take care of the morning meal.

"Kitt!" A hammering began on the turquoise door.

She swung around, her teeth sinking into her braid.

"Kitt, I've got breakfast."

She dropped the braid and stared at the door for a moment. "I'm in a hurry to get to work."

"It's fast food."

"Very funny, Garth. Listen, I'm trying to get dressed."

"Let me in, Kitt."

"I've got my own breakfast in the pickup."

"Let me in, Kitt."

"I told you I'd see you at the press conference."

"Kitt."

She walked to the door, aware that her braid was slipping apart.

"Morning." He shouldered past her, his arms heavy with a huge white sack. At the table, he began unloading a breakfast of steaming scrambled eggs in little disposable containers, English muffins, jelly, hot black coffee. She watched his big shoulders moving beneath his blue oxford shirt. He looked every bit the journalist. Khaki pants, loafers, argyle socks. Notebook jammed into his back pocket. She wondered if he'd left the tape deck in his room.

"I usually eat doughnuts for breakfast," she said.

"Unhealthy, you know."

"Eggs have cholesterol."

"Protein, too." He studied her as she stood by the open door. *Now,* she might really fit in on a farm. Her scuffed black boots were turned up at the toes; the knees of her jeans were worn and dusty. Her long hair hung over her shoulder, half braided. But she looked beautiful—so beautiful. She looked more real than she used to in her fancy boutique dresses and shiny high heels.

Kitt slowly shut the door and walked across the room. It gave her a perverse pleasure to see that he was wearing his own set of sandbags. His face looked pale, too. Despite the city-slick appearance of his clothes, his hair was newly washed, springy and falling over his forehead and ears. It gave him a disheveled, rakish air.

"I have to be at the dig at seven." She sat on the edge of the chair and picked up a plastic fork.

"You'll be there."

He was glad she had decided to eat with him. It made what he was going to talk about a little easier. His decision to stay at a distance from her had faded pretty quickly once he began to look at the situation more clearly. He'd realized it some-time in the night after listening to her voice over and over. She was here and he was here. It was time to take care of unfin-ished business.

"So, what are you planning to do today?" she asked in a conversational, reserved tone.

"I thought I'd check out the town. Talk to the local edi-tor—see if there are any other stories that might be worth-while." He was planning to spend a good part of the morning at the town library researching Black Dove and his two gold teeth—but this wasn't the time to tell Kitt that.

"There'll be three or four papers represented at the news conference." She wanted him to know he wouldn't be getting a scoop.

He nodded, trying to think up something mundane to break the tension. "So, Kitt, tell me how one goes about digging up an old cemetery."

He was stirring his eggs around, hardly eating. She watched his fork move aimlessly across his plate and stab his English muffins a couple of times. His eyes were locked on her face.

"I do a lot of contract work. I put together a design of the project I'm working on. Then I contract out various aspects of the job to other people. Mostly I plan and oversee the work. But with something as small as this cemetery relocation, I can get involved personally... Aren't you going to get out your little notebook, or turn on your tape recorder or something?"

He shook his head. "This is just for me."

Kitt took a swallow of coffee. It felt strange to sit with him like this, eating breakfast as they always had. Talking over their plans, sharing thoughts. Keep it light, Kitt, she thought. Just get through the day.

"So, tell me how you make a project design," he said.

"I take a serious look at the area to be flooded. I search for missing pieces in the historical picture—the archaeology and anthropology of the site. I issue my findings to the public. Private companies or universities submit proposals to suggest how they'd work the project. I pick the best one and award a contract. Then I administer it."

"You have to make a follow-up report?"

"I really write up three kinds of summaries. One is an interpretation of the project. Another is for archaeologists. A third is just for the general reader. There are a lot of history buffs around here."

Garth leaned back in his chair. She might look like a farm girl—but she was every bit the archaeologist-anthropologist that went along with her doctoral title. She knew her stuff, and he imagined she did her job extremely well.

There had been a time, early in his career, when professionals like Kitt had intimidated him. He would be trying to get a story out of them, well aware that they were experts in their subject and he knew next to zip. But it hadn't taken long to figure out that his skill was in getting people to convey to him what they wanted to get across—along with a lot of other things they might have wanted to keep under wraps.

The time had arrived to put his professionalism to work. First, the direct approach.

"Kitt, remember how we used to just sit around and talk to each other?" He watched her face. If he'd had a notebook, he would have recorded the way her eyes darted to the window. She remembered.

"We used to be able to talk about everything," he said gently. "You'd get me to open up to you about stuff I couldn't share with anyone else."

Kitt surveyed the mulberry trees as she tried to make herself think about the project. Everyone would be driving to the site. Dr. Dean would be asking where she was. The summer students would start climbing into the pits. The bulldozers would roar to life.

But in her mind's eye, she saw a gangly young man leaning across the table, his hands twisting a Cummins cap around and around. His mouth moved as he talked about his father—about the pressure to succeed, about the pressure to stay quiet and to be obedient at all times. He talked about his mother and the old hickory switch she used when he got out of hand. He talked about the farm and his dreams.

"I remember," she answered.

"Remember the time you told me how much your father hated me, because I was beneath you—I was nothing but a farm boy who'd never amount to anything?"

She nodded, fingering a crease in her jeans. "Garth, what do you want—"

"I want to talk about what happened between us, Kitt. I want to talk about the baby."

She pinched the crease. "No, Garth. It was a long time ago. It's over now."

"I want to talk about it."

"Well, I don't!" She heard her voice lose its professional detachment.

"I want to know what happened."

"What happened? You know what happened. You were right there! The baby died. It just died. That was it. They took it out. We went home to the trailer and three weeks later you walked out the door and didn't come back."

"Kitt, I want to tell you—"

"I don't want to hear it, Garth. It doesn't matter anymore, can't you see that?"

She got to her feet and he leaped up. He grabbed her wrist. "It does matter. You mattered to me!"

"If I mattered to you, then why did you run off and leave me?" Snatching her hand away, she stalked to the bed. "Don't try to make it all better now, Garth. It's been fifteen years. We've gone on. We're okay people in spite of it. I want to stay okay. And talking about what happened and bringing it all up and going over everything is not my idea of okay."

"You want to heal it, Kitt. I can see that in you. You want to heal it as badly as I do."

"Tearing the scab off an old wound is not healing. It's...it's reinjuring." She settled her hat on her head and sighed. "Look, this was a weird thing, us running into each other. It's just made us both start thinking of things we haven't thought about in years. I'm sorry, Garth. If you'll excuse me, I'm late for work."

He nodded, watching her face as she tried to compose it. She was right, of course. They should drop it. But there were a few things Kitt didn't understand. She thought she knew him. She thought he was still her old Garth—the boy who found it so hard to talk, the boy who took suggestions as orders. The good boy. She didn't know what the years had done to him.

He was blunt now. Head on. Like a bulldog, he'd latch on to a problem and not let it go until he'd solved it. He put puzzles together just like she did. And the way their lives and their marriage and their love had fallen apart was the biggest puzzle he knew. He had his teeth in it now, and like the mature bulldog he'd become, he was going to get to the middle of it.

Time for the back-off tactic.

"Okay, Kitt," he said. "You're right. Skip it. Sorry I brought it up." He shrugged and walked to the table. "See you at two, if I can make it."

She pushed her hands into her pockets. "If you can make it?"

"To tell you the truth, things are starting to pile up on my desk. I really didn't have time to take Burton's place on this story anyway. I'm thinking about heading to Albuquerque this afternoon. You can send me the report when you get finished and I'll write the piece on the relocation from that."

"Okay." She felt suddenly deflated. It had been strangely good to get angry, to shout at him. But she'd gotten her way, just like that. The subject of their past was closed. Now he would walk away from her again.

It seemed too soon. There was more anger inside her. And other things she hadn't even known were there. Tears...she could feel them trying to well up. Fear...fear of letting go, fear of taking hold. And hunger...she had discovered that in the night. She knew it now, watching him in the early morning light. He was big and handsome. He smelled good. His eyes kept calling to her. His lips, when he spoke, seemed to beckon.

She smiled an empty smile and slung her bag over her shoulder. "Well, thanks for the breakfast."

"You're welcome."

"Well...bye."

"I'll clean this stuff up and shut your room for you."

"Thanks."

"Bye, Kitt."

She hurried out into the sunshine. The pickup started with a cough. The steering wheel felt hot under her frozen fingers and she gripped it tightly as she drove.

Hod stood beside one of the graves, peering intently into its depths. "I told you not to come back," Kitt snapped.

The old man glanced up in surprise. His face in the morning light looked even more ancient than she remembered. Unshaven chin, hooked Roman nose, stringy white hair that needed a thorough washing. He smelled a little of perspiration and liquor and wood smoke.

"I had to come," he said simply. He had lost most of his teeth, and his words were hard to make out.

"I told you before, it's against regulations... Look, is there some specific reason you're here?"

"I'm here to see the twilight."

"Oh, don't start in on that twilight business." She felt grouchy, impatient. Her hair was unbraided. Her stomach was half empty. And she had a headache. "If you have some reason for being here—"

"The gold."

"There's no gold here, Hod. None. This is a cemetery. You're looking for... what? Some kind of an old mine?"

He nodded. Gnarled hands straightened the patched black wool suit he wore. "My father's gold mine. He took me there when I was nine years old."

"I see. And I do understand your interest. But I can assure you, there's no mine here."

"Oh, I know that. The mine is on a mountain. Rocks all around. A pine tree bent by the wind into the shape of an L."

"This is a cemetery, you see. Flat ground. Graves. There are people buried here."

"Yes. Mothers and fathers."

Kitt took off her hat and began coiling her loose hair into a knot. "Mothers and fathers?"

"What's your name, young lady?"

"Kitt Cul—" She jammed her hat onto her head. "Kitt Tucker. Dr. Kitt Tucker."

"Dr. Tucker, I *have* to stay. Let me stay."

"I'm sorry, Hod. I'm responsible for the site." She felt like the wicked witch.

His shoulders hunched, the old man turned toward his battered truck.

"You all right this morning, Dr. Tucker?" Dr. Dean laid a hand on Kitt's arm. "You're looking a little worn."

They walked toward the nylon tent. The dew on the long grass was drying swiftly as the sun rose higher in the pale blue sky. The Pecos River, winding between cottonwoods, scrub oak and salt cedar, whispered between the silences of the morning. Locusts sang. Hundreds of little white butterflies drifted up from cow patties, then settled again. Bees darted among the purple-tipped alfalfa blossoms. A mockingbird wheeled overhead. its black and white wings flashing in the light.

"Thanks for getting things started up out here," Kitt said as she stepped through the tent door. "I had a late night. I've called a news conference this afternoon over at Chisum Memorial."

"You finish up with that reporter from Albuquerque?"

"I guess so." Finished up was right. "Find out anything new on that skeleton with the gold teeth?"

"Nothing else was in the grave. He had a knife tip in his scapula. Two inches long."

Kitt nodded, fiddling with a set of calipers. "I saw that."

"Just the gold teeth and the knife tip and the newspaper clipping. He didn't have a casket so we won't have any wood to date the age of the grave."

"Anything on the skeleton itself?"

"I haven't started the measurements. Just looking, I'd say he was a pretty old fellow, which is strange considering most of the men in here died violently when they were fairly young."

She glanced up. "You don't think he died violently?"

"Hard to say. The knife tip in his shoulder didn't kill him. and there were no bullets in the fill dirt. 'Course someone could have slit his throat or knifed him in a vital organ and we'd never know it . . . The skull looks a little odd to me."

"In what way?"

"I haven't had time to do a thorough examination of the remains, but his teeth look different to me. He's definitely not Negroid or Oriental. His features appear to be Caucasian—but the front incisors are shovel-toothed . . . well, I'll let you know after I complete my study."

"Thanks." Kitt set the calipers on the table. As an archaeologist, she had the job of piecing together the puzzles of history. She had always enjoyed compiling hypotheses based on the information that came out of dig sites. The old Muddy Flats cemetery interested her in that way. She had imagined putting together the final reports she had described to Garth— the charts and diagrams, the factual information and her own conclusions.

But faced with this strange gold-toothed skull, she felt uncharacteristically reticent. She wished she hadn't dug it up. She wished it didn't have those gold teeth. She wished Dr. Dean had said it was obvious the man had been just another of the poverty-stricken pioneers of early New Mexico.

It was Garth's doing, she thought as she stepped into the glaring sunshine. If he hadn't latched onto the ridiculous notion that the skull resembled the description of Black Dove...if he hadn't pestered her for an interview…if he just hadn't come at all…

Kitt spent the morning as she had for two months—sitting at the edge of grave pits drawing outlines for the summer students. She watched them trowel away the dirt and remove the collapsed coffin lids. She helped one young man pick the soil away from a skeleton then sift all the remaining dirt with a screen. They found three tin buttons and a bullet in the chest area. Another violent death.

But instead of engaging in the usual banter that kept the whole group informed and feeling like a team, she lapsed into deep silence as she worked.

Garth had been right, she realized. She did want to find a healing. Somewhere inside herself she wanted to understand what had happened. Why had everything fallen apart so quickly? Why had they been chattering best friends one minute—and mute adversaries the next? Why had their passion suddenly died? Why had Garth left her all alone in that battered, windblown trailer?

She wasn't going to get the answers now. It was ironic to think that her career was built around digging up the past and finding answers to unsolved riddles. But she would never understand what had happened in her own past. She would never know why she and Garth had come apart at the seams.

Holding up the sole of a boot she'd just uncovered, she turned it back and forth. The leather had worn partly away to form a hole in the center. The sun shone through tiny holes where thread once had laced the sole to the upper. On the left side, the heel had eroded, leaving a sort of triangular wedge.

"Looking at that heel, I expect the poor fellow had bandy legs," the summer student said. "Probably a horseman. A cowboy. He must have done some walking, though, to have worn out the sole that way. Or maybe he inherited the boots from somebody else. Isn't it pretty unusual that they left this guy's boots on when they buried him, Dr. Tucker?… Dr. Tucker?"

Kitt's eyes darted to the young man. "That's right, Sam. Very unusual. The people in the Muddy Flats area were so poor they passed their shoes from person to person."

"How about that fellow with the gold teeth you uncovered yesterday, Dr. Tucker? He wasn't like the others we've found here. Two gold front teeth . . . he must have been pretty rich."

"I expect so, Sam."

"He was rich enough to have gold teeth—but not rich enough to have a coffin or a stone marker. How about that?"

"Maybe nobody liked him. Or maybe he was a stranger passing through Muddy Flats when he died. He might have had a disease. Or maybe he was some kind of an outcast."

"Like an Indian or something. What do you think, Dr. Tucker?"

She shook her head. "We'll see, Sam."


Kitt shaded her eyes as she looked out over the group of gathered reporters. An attractive young woman had come from the Catclaw Draw newspaper. A thin blond fellow represented the Carlsbad press. Old Hod sat beneath a distant cottonwood, his hat in his hand. Garth was not present.

She hadn't expected him to be. After lunch, she had gone to the motel to change clothes. She'd spent some time going over what she wanted to release, and she talked with her supervisor at the Bureau. They set the closing date of the site for the following week. She hadn't seen the gray car that had been parked outside Garth's door the previous night. His room had been silent.

The two o'clock sun was blistering at the Chisum Memorial Cemetery. Recent graves lay scattered across the irrigated green grass, their stone markers topped with wreaths and bouquets of brilliant artificial flowers. A pair of big oak trees cast a paltry shade over one section. A canopy had been stretched over a new grave. Beneath it stood a woman and a little girl, holding hands, staring down at the spaded dirt.

Kitt shifted her attention to the untouched site where the Muddy Flats cemetery would be relocated. It had been her idea to recreate a similar setting and atmosphere to the historical cemetery—shaggy kochia grass sprouting from bare brown dust, sandstone rocks, prickly pear cactus, stands of yucca, even an occasional rattlesnake. The Muddy Flats residents would rest much as they always had, with nature as their gardener and caretaker.

"On behalf of the Bureau of Reclamation, I'd like to thank you all for attending this press opportunity." She began speaking and everyone quieted. "Within four to six weeks the old Muddy Flats cemetery will be relocated directly behind me in this open field. The headstones are being restored. New markers will be placed on every previously undesignated grave."

The reporters had begun taking down her words in their notebooks. Some had tape recorders. Hod kept turning his hat in his hands. Kitt brushed her palm across the back of her damp neck.

"I'll go over what we're doing out at the Muddy Flats site, and then you may ask questions. A contractor from Catclaw Draw is working with us. His men dig down until the first signs of remains are discovered. We've found that the skeletal material at the site is in remarkably good condition due to the clay soil. Photographs of the remains are taken while they're still in place. Our physical anthropologist, Dr. John Dean of Northern New Mexico University, will use these photographs in his study. The bones are then put on a board and taken into Dr. Dean's tent. There he performs fifty-eight examinations on each skeleton. He tests for signs of disease, as well. We've done six to eight skeletons a day..."

A gray compact car sped through the cemetery and pulled to a halt just beyond the ring of reporters. Garth Culhane got out.

Kitt pulled her focus back to her listeners. Her heart thudded heavily. "The remains are put into metal boxes, along with the coffin material and other archaeological artifacts found in the grave. We've finished excavating all the marked graves and we've placed a numbered lath at each one. We then moved the soil fill from the surrounding area and started trenching to see if there were any unmarked graves."

Garth took out his tape recorder and switched it on. He stood head and shoulders above the other reporters. The sunlight caught the blond streaks in his hair; it carved shadows beneath his cheekbones. He looked as he had that morning—blue oxford shirt, khaki slacks. His sleeves were rolled to his elbows. An air of assurance, of bold belief in himself, was evident in the compact way he walked and moved. He gave the impression of solidity, confidence and reliability—the sort of man's man whom employers loved, co-workers envied and women pursued.

As she continued to speak, Kitt found herself thinking about Garth's jaw. She had grown used to the squareness of it now. She didn't find it so startling to see him as a man, no longer her rangy, loose-limbed lover. In less than a day, she had become accustomed to seeing his shoulders broad, his chest hard and solid beneath the oxford shirt. He had grown tall, and it felt almost normal to look up into his face. How strange to lose the boy and accept so swiftly the man he had become.

Only one thing about Garth Culhane remained the same. His blue-gray eyes. They followed her movements as they always had. They studied her mouth as it formed words. That deep-set gaze raked through her hair and down her body, just as she remembered. Though Garth's outer self projected confidence and professionalism, he also wore—not far beneath the surface—the natural sensuality of a leopard on the prowl. She felt as if his eyes were devouring her.

"We've found thirty-seven graves to this point," she heard herself say as she looked at her notes. She was right where she should be. "Of the fourteen males from ages eighteen to forty-five, ten died violent deaths. There are lots of infants buried at Muddy Flats—some no more than four weeks old. Childhood diseases such as diphtheria and whooping cough are probable causes. Married women normally had a baby every two years, and the children were hard to nourish..."

Garth studied Kitt as she talked about the little babies. Her voice sounded tight and professional. She spoke in a clipped sort of way, as if she were analyzing the data as she relayed it. But he knew just by watching her what was going on beneath that cool, unemotional facade. He'd heard her voice on the tape recorder all night long.

It hadn't taken much time that morning to make the decision that had been playing in the back of his mind since he'd reentered her life. He was going to find the real Kitt again.

Sitting in the quiet of the local library, he had outlined a rough plan. Even put it down on paper in his reporter's notebook. The plan had had a good beginning already. And with the help of a few history books, his plan now had a modus operandi—a method of procedure that involved a certain gold-toothed Shawnee war chief. The only weakness in his plan was the ending.

He had no clear idea of what he hoped to accomplish by bringing Kitt out of her silence. He supposed that just the healing they had talked about that morning would be enough.

But Kitt appeared to need no healing, he thought as he listened to her voice. She was stunning in the afternoon sunlight, her long hair drifting loose at her waist. She had on an outfit that would have turned heads even in Santa Fe—a white cutwork blouse, an Indian broom-pleated skirt of purple cotton that hung almost to her ankles, huge silver earrings, a heavy concho belt and leather sandals. Five silver bracelets marched up one arm. She looked like a gypsy and sounded like a professor. The mixture was intriguing.

"Yes, there have been a few surprises," she was saying. The reporters had begun to ask questions. She had relaxed a little and was enjoying herself. This was her domain. "The myth of the tall, rugged John Wayne type cowboy certainly has been dispelled at Muddy Flats. Most of the men were barely over five feet tall. The women, of course, were very small as well."

"What sort of artifacts did you find in the graves, Dr. Tucker?" a short blond man asked. "Can you give us some details?"

"We found very little, actually. These people were terribly poor. Only two men were buried with their boots on, and only six of the graves contained shoes. We found copper or brass buttons, like you might see on a pair of jeans today. There were some scraps of denim. We also found buttons of shell, bone and glass. The buttons rarely matched. There were lots of nails, all square. Some of the coffins had handles. One infant had a pin that been engraved with the word Baby. We did find . . . we did find safety pins in the infants' graves. It was a difficult thing to see . . ."

Garth watched her face as it seemed to sag momentarily. Her eyes drifted to the ground and studied a clump of dry grass beside her foot. He thought he would go to her—but then she was speaking again, her shoulders straight and her chin high.

"There was hardly any jewelry. Three males had on cuff links. One pair was made of onyx. There was a matching collar stud. One woman wore a necklace of bone and glass tubular beads."

"What about wedding rings?" Garth asked.

Kitt's hand tightened on her notebook. "A few. Some were made of iron, others of a kind of hard rubber. Some had rings of gold alloy."

"Did you find any valuable items in the graves, Mrs. Culhane?"

Kitt's face darkened. "I think you've mistaken me for someone else, sir. My name is Dr. Tucker. And no, we found nothing of any value in the graves—small brooches, the head and arms of a ceramic doll, scraps of black broadcloth, a piece of folded newspaper."

"What about the skeletons themselves? Did you find anything unusual or interesting about any of them?"

The other reporters had turned to stare at Garth. Their looks were a little hostile. After all, this was a historical cemetery relocation, not a major crime scene. Did he have to hound the charming professor, they seemed to be asking.

"As a matter of fact," Kitt said briskly, "we were able to substantiate some of the local legends that have been circulating around the Catclaw Draw and Muddy Flats areas for nearly a century. The grave of William Jackson, who was said to have been shot at close range by his father-in-law, contained many pieces of buckshot. Another man by the name of Johnny Southern was rumored to have been shot. We found a slug in his grave near the heart area."

"Anything else?"

Kitt looked steadily at Garth. "One elderly man whose grave was unmarked had two gold teeth and a knife tip embedded in his scapula."

"Where?"

"The scapula . . . it's the shoulder blade."

"I mean the teeth. Where were they—in the front?"

Kitt clenched her jaw. Of course she knew he'd meant the teeth. And what could she say? If she were evasive in front of the media it would arouse suspicion. "Yes. In the front. The two top incisors were made of gold."

"Would you say, then, that what you found in the Muddy Flats cemetery confirmed or dispelled the written and oral history of the area?"

"Without a doubt, it confirmed it. I had believed, actually, that the local stories were rather exaggerated. I thought the tales of the old Wild West were just a myth. But based on the number of violent deaths in the cemetery, I would have to say that the legends are probably quite accurate."

"You've changed your mind, then?"

Kitt stared at Garth. What was he getting at? "Yes, I would say I've changed my mind."

"So you would agree that you—as a historian—have a responsibility to change your opinion about something if it can be proven different than you had thought? Let's say, for example, you turned up evidence that made you question some historical information you had always believed. Would you then feel obligated to pursue that evidence until you were satisfied about its authenticity—even if it disproved what you had assumed was true?"

Garth was studying her, his gray-blue eyes locked on her face. She felt angry, cornered. He wanted her to admit that the gold-toothed skull was unusual—that she should probably question it more thoroughly. Under normal circumstances, she would. But she *knew* Black Dove was buried in Guadalupe Y Calvo just as certainly as she knew that Garth Culhane was trying to raise her hackles.

Maybe she could turn the tables on him. He wouldn't want to reveal his suspicions about Black Dove. Reporters were notoriously protective of their scoops.

"What are you driving at, sir?" she asked bluntly. "Are you referring to something specific?"

Garth grinned, acknowledging her move. "Just a simple question about archaeological technique. Does a historian have a responsibility to try to solve an archaeological puzzle—even if the solution proves the historian wrong?"

"Yes," she said. "Generally speaking, that would be true."

"Thank you, Doctor."

"Are there any more questions?" Kitt glanced around. "Then if you'll excuse me, I need to close down the site for the day."

Flipping her notebook shut, she started toward the Bureau pickup. Garth was at her side before she had taken five steps, his long-legged stride eating up the distance between them.

"Black Dove's out there, you know," he said, placing his palm flat against the door so she couldn't open it.

"Black Dove is in Mexico. Guadalupe Y Calvo. Just go look at a map—it's there."

"I looked at a map this morning in the library. Guadalupe Y Calvo is there. But Black Dove isn't. I studied some history books, Kitt. I'm sure he was buried at Muddy Flats."

"You go take a look at Dr. Oldham's research notes if you're so sure about that. He substantiated everything. There are interviews, records, the whole bit."

"I'm throwing down the gauntlet, Kitt. Pick up that puzzle piece like a good archaeologist should—try to prove that old Black Dove isn't in the grave at Muddy Flats."

"I don't have time, Garth. I have to finish this project. There's no time for chasing down some insignificant historical figure whose death has already been substantiated."

"Come on, Kitt. Take the challenge."

He was smiling at her. His eyes had softened at the edges. Their blue-gray was not so much the color of steel now—more the shade of a winter lake. A ladybug sat on his shoulder and she could tell he didn't know it was there.

"You know, you're obnoxious, Garth," she said. But her voice was soft. "It's really no wonder they haven't given you an overseas bureau post. You'd probably start a war."

She took the door handle and pulled it. Garth bent his elbow. Dipping her knees, she stepped beneath the bridge of his arm and got into the truck. He leaned through the open window, his arms crossed.

"You don't work on Saturdays, do you? I'll pick you up at nine. We'll take a drive. I have a load of things on Black Dove to go over with you. Those librarians are thorough."

"I'll be busy tomorrow, Garth." She started the engine. If he just weren't leaning through the window like that, smiling so comfortably and smelling like the boy who once had turned her heart. If his hair didn't look all soft and shiny. If his arms weren't brown and thick with muscle. It was that jaw, most of all. That square, hard man's jaw.

"Nine o'clock," he said.

Kitt rolled her eyes, let out a sigh and stepped on the gas. As she drove past the cottonwood, old Hod tipped his hat.

# Chapter 4

Kitt slammed the dryer door a little harder than necessary. A young woman with pink plastic rollers in her hair looked over the top of her gossip magazine. Heaving the plastic basket into her arms, Kitt walked across the laundromat. The sickly sweet perfumes of fabric softener and detergent mingled with the scent of overdried clothes. She dumped her clean laundry onto a linoleum-topped table. Someone had left a pile of religious tracts next to a wadded gum wrapper. Kitt shoved her hand into the hot pile of clothes and pulled out a T-shirt.

It was still light outside. A few stores were open—a card shop, a boot repair store, a newsstand. The laundry was next to the movie theater. Both fronted the main street, as did most of the other businesses and restaurants in town. There was only one show at the theater, and it cost a dollar to get in. Shoppers walked by, glancing surreptitiously at their reflections in the laundromat window. Cars carrying teenagers cruised past, "draggin' Main."

Memories of her own high school years brought a soft smile to Kitt's lips as she folded her laundry. The same scene had existed in the small New Mexico towns of her youth—kids cruising the Sonic drive-in at one end of the street, the hamburger joint at the other.

The in crowd hung out together in one group—cheerleaders, football players. Their status symbols had been heavy gold class rings with wads of tape to make them fit girlfriends' fingers; expensive perfume; enough hair spray to keep three companies in business; low-slung sports cars with full gas tanks.

The "stomps" rodeoed and belonged to FFA or 4-H or both. They exhibited projects at the county fair and didn't mind hosing down a hog or rubbing lanolin on a cow's udder. They had their own symbols—pickup trucks, roper boots, cowboy hats, five-inch silver buckles on braided leather belts.

There were other groups, of course. Rebels with leather jackets and rock-star haircuts; intellectuals with arms full of books; shy wallflowers who didn't fit in anywhere.

The kids had inherited their parents' traditions—along with their prejudices. And by the looks of Catclaw Draw's main drag, the subcultures were still intact. Hardly anyone crossed group lines.

But Kitt Tucker had. She was supposed to be in with the rich kids. Her father was president of the bank, after all. They lived in a big brick house in Colonial Park. Her parents had given her a brand-new red Corvette when she turned sixteen. They made sure she wore the latest styles. She went to society functions and she even spent one summer at a camp back East to learn proper etiquette.

None of that had kept her from Garth Culhane. The moment she moved to town and set foot in the high school, they had been drawn to each other like magnets.

That's when the fighting had begun. Her parents fought with each other. Why had they moved to this Podunk town, her mother wanted to know. Couldn't her father have gotten a better job? Kitt's father was quick to shout back. Why couldn't her mother have raised a daughter who knew how to behave? He'd worked damned hard to become bank president and he wasn't about to see his daughter marry some poor cotton farmer.

Garth's parents argued as well. He wasn't getting any of his chores done. Was he too good for the country folk now? Who did he think he was, anyway? He'd better get his backside out into the field and onto a tractor or he'd get a licking he'd never forget. He'd be better off with the young people he'd grown up with in Sunday school. Didn't he know someone like Kitt Tucker—a girl who drove a Corvette and wore short skirts and makeup—was bound to be fast?

Kitt shook her head and pulled a pair of socks from the pile of warm laundry. It hadn't mattered a bit—all that fighting. They'd spent every spare minute together anyway. Her time with Garth Culhane formed the sort of memory a woman took from the shelf now and then, dusted off and studied for a minute.

The last thing she had expected was for that memory to come barging back into her world, big as life, twice as handsome and with more of that old magnetic pull than ever. She hurled the sock ball into the empty basket at her feet. The woman in curlers lifted her eyes over the magazine again.

*Throwing down the gauntlet,* indeed. Of all the nerve. Kitt flung a second sock ball into her laundry basket. Damn that skeleton for having two gold front teeth. And now she was faced with a new fact. Dr. Dean's words played back in her mind as clearly as if they had been captured on Garth's little tape recorder.

"I've finished the examinations on that skeleton of yours, Dr. Tucker," the physical anthropologist had said that afternoon when she returned from the press conference. "Quite a fellow. He was six feet tall, very powerful, and handsome. I'd make him about sixty-five at death, but his body had held up remarkably well. He'd lived a violent life—broken femur, two broken ribs, knife tip in his scapula. He had been very active, right up to the end. Very active."

"Thanks, Dr. Dean." She had almost hoped that was all.

"One more thing. There's no question about his race, Dr. Tucker. Other than the two gold teeth, his six remaining front incisors were shovel-toothed. He was an Indian."

Now he had two gold front teeth *and* he was an Indian. One fact was becoming clear—she was caught in a real dilemma. Garth had been right that afternoon at the press conference— remains that so closely matched the description of Black Dove should be given careful consideration. It *was* her job. More than that, these tantalizing clues might add up to something really fascinating. She felt the old tingling thrill at the thought of tracking down and fitting together the pieces to an intriguing puzzle.

If only she could send Garth packing. Head him back to Albuquerque where he belonged. Kitt hurled a third sock ball into her basket. She glanced at the woman in curlers, but though her eyes had lifted from the magazine, they were riveted to the laundromat door. Kitt turned to follow the line of her gaze.

Garth was leaning against the metal door frame and grinning like the Cheshire cat. "Hi, Kitt. I passed your truck on my way to dinner. Doing your laundry?"

When she didn't answer, he strolled across the room. She jerked up a pair of jeans and began the futile exercise of smoothing their set-in wrinkles. Twenty-four hours ago, she fumed. Just twenty-four hours ago, her life had been calm, purposeful and orderly. Now she had an ex-husband who was determined to dog her like a bloodhound, a gold-toothed skull that refused to rest in peace, and a misbehaving heart.

"There's a street dance two blocks down." Garth leaned his hip against her table and crossed his arms over his chest. "The high school rodeo association's putting it on for the state championship finalists."

"How about that."

"Want to go?"

"I know you're having trouble with this little item, Garth, but I'm not in high school any longer. And you're not a rodeo cowboy."

"The dance is open to the public."

She hadn't danced in years. But the very thought of singing fiddles and couples swirling across scattered hay made her feet itch. She could almost smell the hot apple cider.

"I'll help you do your laundry, and then we'll go to the dance. I was always good at laundry, remember?" He heaved himself up on the table and picked up a red T-shirt. "What was that place called? You used to hate it. The very idea of washing your clothes in the same machine that somebody's else's dirty clothes had been in was disgusting. 'Oh, Garth,' you'd say. 'This makes me sick.'"

"U Washem . . . that's what it was called." Kitt shook her lowered head, a grin playing at the corners of her lips.

"Ah, the old U Washem Laundromat. Those were the days."

Garth was folding a shirt on his thigh just the way he always had. Beneath her brows, Kitt watched his big hands smooth over the cotton sleeves and down the front. It was a vaguely sensual movement . . . long, tanned fingers stroking the breast of her shirt as it lay on his leg.

She pulled herself back to matters at hand. She should tell him about Dr. Dean's exam results. Though everything would be in her final report, it was only fair that he know now, when it interested him. But if he were aware that the gold-toothed skull belonged to an Indian, he'd have even more reason to hold her to his challenge.

Garth studied Kitt as she sorted through her laundry. She was clearly uncomfortable performing this remembered ritual with him. Her back was ramrod straight and her shoulders rigid beneath her soft clothing. It was almost as if by holding her breath, she could wish him away.

But he was enjoying this. It reminded him of the good times they'd had. Spotting a pair of filmy pink panties buried among the utilitarian T-shirts and jeans, he drew them out and set them on his leg. It was like her, he thought, to be feminine and delicate beneath that professional demeanor. Little pink bows were sewn in among the white lace on the panties. He touched a bow, wondering suddenly whether she wore transparent pink panties just for herself—or for someone else.

"I don't fold my underwear," Kitt said, whisking the panties off his leg and dropping them into her basket.

He picked up a skimpy little scrap of a bra. One glance at her breasts lifting and falling beneath her white cutwork blouse showed him the flimsy garment in his hands would hardly be adequate. She had been small in high school. Small enough to fit in the palms of his hands. He'd enjoyed that about her. Now, turning her bra over and examining the ample cups, he decided he'd probably enjoy the new Kitt just as much.

"Nice lingerie, Kitt," he said, handing her the bra. She took it, nested the cups one inside the other, and set it in her basket without betraying any emotion.

"If you're going to fold, fold," she said.

Their eyes met, challenging. "So you never got married again, Kitt."

She shook her head.

"Well, what about . . . I know it's your own personal business . . . what about dating? You do that a lot?"

"Some. You?"

"Some." Garth picked up a pair of blue panties. "Anything special with any of these men?"

Kitt watched him hook his index fingers through the panty waist and stretch the elastic a little. It occurred to her that he was nervous. Maybe even a little jealous.

She almost wished she could dangle some delectably handsome, wealthy professor in front of his nose. But the truth was too blatant to hide.

"I travel a lot," she said softly. "There's not much time to get deeply involved."

He nodded. "I'm on the road two or three weeks a month. I pull a lot of laundromat duty."

She laughed. "I can't believe I keep doing this. When I got the job with the Bureau, I went straight out and bought a washer and dryer. They're still practically new."

"You should see my apartment. I'm hardly ever there. Looks like some kind of bare mausoleum. I've got an orange plaid couch and a lawn chair in the living room. A frying pan and a stew-pot in the kitchen. My folks gave me the old bunk bed I had when I was a kid."

"Bunk bed! You sleep on a bunk bed?"

"Yeah. Remember how it sagged in the middle when you'd sneak over to my house and we'd lie—" He glanced at her.

Her hands lay unmoving on the pile of folded laundry. She was staring at them. "I'm sorry, Kitt. I know you don't want to talk about the past. It's just that seeing you again brings it back. We did have some good times, you know. Really good times."

"It's not easy for me to think about them. I do better when I stay in the here and now."

"I admire what you've done with yourself, Kitt."

She couldn't bring herself to look up. "Thanks. I like myself again."

"I know you don't want to go into everything—but I do want to apologize for...for what you went through when I left. What I really mean is, I'm sorry I walked out on you."

"Why *did* you leave me, Garth?" She lifted her eyes. His face was solemn.

He shook his head. "I thought you hated me. I thought you blamed me for the baby. For giving you the baby...and then for its death."

"You didn't cause the baby to die."

"I thought you were blaming me, though. You were so silent. From the time we found out the baby had died, right through to the birth—"

"Garth." Kitt heard the panic in her voice. She wasn't ready to talk about it. She couldn't go back over that time. "I'm sorry...I can't..."

"Come on, honey." He slid off the table and put his arm around her shoulders. "Let's head over to that street dance. It'll do us good."

"I really don't feel like dancing, Garth."

"Then we'll just watch."


She let herself be led out into the evening. Tucked against Garth's warm body, she felt some of the ache lessen. They set the laundry baskets in her pickup cab and wandered down the street.

The dance was in full swing. A truck bed formed the platform for two fiddlers, a guitarist and a banjo player. Beside them on a bale of hay a young man in a red-checkered shirt belted out a rollicking tune. Couples of every age whirled around the street, their boots keeping time to two-steps and waltzes. Hay bales lined the sidewalks for those choosing to sit out a dance. Against the brick wall of the local bank stretched a long table with lemonade, steaming hot apple cider, hot dogs and popcorn for sale.

Garth settled Kitt comfortably against his side as they observed the dancers. Through the white cutwork blouse he could feel her warm skin. Her hair brushed his arm. Even though she didn't quite fit in with all the tight jeans, cowboy boots and silver buckles of the other dancers, he was glad she was wearing the purple skirt. The fact of the matter was, Kitt was the best-looking woman in the place—and he felt an odd sense of boyish pride to have her on his arm.

Her foot had begun tapping the moment they rounded the corner. He considered asking her to dance. But he decided against it. If he had changed, she had changed, too. There was a new depth to her, a serious, secret side that he was learning to understand and respect. If she didn't want to talk about their baby and all the things that had happened, he'd let it rest for a while. And if she didn't feel like dancing, that was okay, too.

She turned to him, her brown eyes glowing. "Want some lemonade?"

"I'll get you some—"

"No, I'll get it." She left his side and moved toward the long table. He watched her hair brush the outer curve of her hips as she walked. She was all swaying movement—hair, skirt, body. Picking up two paper cups of lemonade, she reached in her skirt pocket and pulled out some loose change. Laundry money. Her arm looked slender as she paid for the drinks.

Seeing her from afar like this, he realized how thin she really was. Strapped sandals curved around delicate ankles; big silver bracelets seemed to weigh down her wrists. Even her waist was matchstick thin. If it weren't for the maturity in her eyes and voice, he wouldn't have put her much over twenty.

Rejoining him, she stood at his side and they sipped lemonade. Their arms barely brushed against one another, but from the lightning zipping up and down Garth's spine, he imagined he could have counted every single silky hair from her wrist to her elbow without looking. He could feel the hem of her skirt swaying against his pants leg—and it suddenly came to him that these weren't old feelings renewed.

This was not nostalgia.

Kitt was desirable for who she was at that very moment. And he knew if he had just met her for the first time, he wouldn't be feeling a bit different.

"Dr. Tucker!" A sandy-haired boy waved from the other side of the street. Kitt waved back.

"It's Sam," she said softly. "One of the student workers out at the site."

The young man began weaving through the crowd, his eyes pinned on Kitt. Garth glanced at the woman beside him, uncomfortable with the gnawing irritation he felt over her glad smile.

"Sam, I didn't know you'd be here." She spoke with genuine pleasure in her voice—a tone exactly the opposite to what she'd been using with Garth for the past twenty-four hours. "Are the other guys here?"

"Jake and Matt are. Tom's coming later."

"Great! Sam, I'd like you to meet Garth Culhane. He's with the Affiliated Press out of Albuquerque."

Sam stuck out his hand and Garth shook it.

"So—would you like to dance, Dr. Tucker?"

Kitt's eyes darted to Garth for an instant. Without waiting for any sort of response, she hurried into the street.

"See you later, Garth!" She waved blithely, as if he were a pet flea she was setting free.

In the next moment, she was spinning around and around in the arms of some kid named Sam. Some scrawny, long-legged boy in skin-tight blue jeans. And she was laughing! Her head flew back. Her hair swung low and whisked away from her waist. Worst of all, they kept perfect time—his hand settling right along the curve of her hip, and his skinny legs following the beat right next to hers.

Garth downed his lemonade in one gulp. You weren't supposed to care who your ex-wife danced with. You weren't supposed to admire the turn of her ankles and the swish of her hair. And you sure weren't supposed to wish it was you holding her tight—instead of some baby-faced yokel.

But the fact was, he did care. Damn it all. He did care.

Crushing the paper cup in his palm, he tossed it into a trash can and started through the crowd. In half a minute he had caught up with Kitt, politely freed her from Sam, and taken her in his arms.

"Garth—that's rude," she said. But a smile tugged at her lips.

"I imagine ol' Sam can find somebody else to dance with."

"She won't dance as well as I do."

"True." Garth drew her closer, reveling in the balsam scent of her hair. As they stepped and turned, her skirt wrapped around his legs, pulling them tighter. She kept her eyes on his face, and he could see in the growing darkness that her lips were damp and full.

"You told me you didn't want to dance," he said.

"I changed my mind."

"We dance well together, Kitt." His voice sounded a little ragged, the way she remembered.

"I couldn't have had a better teacher." She studied the shadows on his face, pleased that a gentle smile played about his lips. His strong fingers were woven through hers, pressing their palms together. His belt buckle clinked against the silver conchos at her waist.

The song ended, and she tried to move away. But his arm behind her back was as solid and unmoving as steel. And when the next tune—a slower waltz—started up, he eased her into the street.

"When I first saw you last night," he whispered close to her ear, "I had the idea that we might call a truce in the hostilities."

Kitt tried to cover the shiver that ran down her spine. His breath was hot and smelled of lemons. He seemed towering and huge, bending over her like that. And his voice was a raspy growl that curled around in her ear then began sliding down through her bones like hot syrup.

"That's what I thought when I saw you last night," he murmured. "And then today I thought I'd just like to settle up the past. Heal the old wounds."

"That sounds all right." She suddenly wished she were wearing an Eskimo parka, the way his fingers kept slipping up and down her back. "I mean, okay to a certain extent."

"But right now, I'm thinking something different."

"What . . . what are you thinking?"

"I'm thinking how good this feels and how much I like talking to you and seeing you smile. And I'm thinking, Kitt, that maybe we could get over the hostilities and work our way past the things that happened."

"That might be possible, I guess. But I do have the project, and I know you need to get back to Albuquerque—"

"And what I was thinking was . . . that we might work ourselves up to the point of being friends again."

"If we had time, I suppose. I think we're probably past the hostility stage for the most part. But I really don't want to go over what happened."

"I think you do."

"No."

"Fifteen minutes ago you asked me why I left you."

Kitt closed her eyes and let him take her across the haystrewn street. Yes, she did want to know. But to know, they would have to talk. And talking would mean reliving. It had hurt so much.

"I'll be staying in Catclaw Draw this weekend and into next week," he said. "The bureau chief wants me to cover the state rodeo finals and do an update on the nuclear waste storage plant that's being built near Carlsbad. It's Burton's territory, but he's still—"

"Still down with the flu," Kitt said with a wry smile. "Good old Burton."

"Hey, I'm beginning to think a lot of old Burton. We can credit his flu bug with our happy reunion."

Great, Kitt thought. She felt she really couldn't let the Black Dove puzzle get away from her—but she was certain she didn't want Garth to be a part of it. Not that his input wouldn't be useful. She had been hoping he would leave soon so she could set her teeth in the problem. Now it appeared he was going to stick around until she agreed to his challenge.

The song ended and the fiddlers relaxed. "We'll take a ten-minute break, folks," the singer announced, "and then we'll be back to wake ya'll up. Don't run off, now!"

Kitt stepped out of Garth's embrace. "That was fun. Thanks."

"My pleasure. Want a hot dog?"

"No, thanks. You wouldn't believe the stack of papers waiting for me at the motel. I'd better get going."

"Had supper, Kitt?"

"No, but—"

"I'll buy you a hot dog and we'll stroll. Come on, two old buddies, right?"

"Garth, please don't push me—"

"I'm not pushing, Kitt. I never push. I simply issue strong invitations. And I can tell you really don't want to go back to that motel room."

"Oh, is that right? How can you tell?"

"Honey, the moon is in your eyes," he said in a playful tone. "The music's in your blood. And you're with the most handsome, charming fellow you've been with in a very long time."

"A little vain, are we?"

"Just truthful."

"Go get me a hot dog, Prince Charming." She gave his bottom a little swat and he set off for the refreshment table.

They wandered down the street, eating hot dogs, drinking sodas and studying the contents of store windows. Kitt felt the knots that had started in her stomach the night before slowly begin to untie. They talked about nothing—whether hot dogs needed only mustard, or catsup, too. They meandered into a card shop and Kitt bought a couple of postcards.

"Are you enjoying the street dance?" the shop manager asked as he slipped the cards into a sack. "You with the rodeo?"

"No, we're just visiting Catclaw Draw," Kitt answered. He was a nice-looking blond fellow with a friendly face. Probably a hometown boy.

"Your first visit? Where are you staying?"

"We're over at the Thunderbird Inn."

"Honeymooners?"

"Oh, no—" Kitt began.

"Sort of—" Garth overlapped.

The young man glanced from one to the other.

"No, we're definitely not—" Kitt began again.

"More like a reunion than a honeymoon," Garth said.

"We get a fair number of honeymooners passing through," the manager explained. "Carlsbad Caverns, you know. Well, if you do make it a honeymoon some day, come on back through Catclaw Draw."

"We'll do it," Garth said.

"Enjoy the dance."

The temperature had dropped with the sunset and Kitt shivered as they retraced their path.

"Nice fellow." Garth slipped his arm around Kitt's shoulders.

"You gave him the wrong impression, Garth. That wasn't necessary."

"Just being polite."

The fiddlers were heating up the crowd with "Cotton-Eyed Joe" when they rounded the sidewalk onto the street. Sam and three other young bucks leaned against the bank wall, watching as Garth swung Kitt into step. Linked arm-in-arm with a long line of dancers, they kicked up their heels and stepped out with fancy footwork as they circled the moonlit street. The faster the fiddles hummed, the swifter the lines wove around and around. Pretty soon their hearts were thumping double time and the bank wall tilted and spun at a crazy angle.

Laughing, Kitt glanced up at Garth. He was smiling at her. His hair bounced with every move; his long legs skillfully kept the rhythm. The lines grew swiftly shorter as couples dropped out, gasping with laughter and exhaustion.

Garth outdanced every high stepper in the place. Trade in that blue oxford for a denim work shirt and those loafers for a pair of cowboy boots, Kitt thought, and he would put every rodeo cowboy on the street to shame. As it was, he appeared more like some Wall Street type gone mad—shirttails flying, pens jiggling in his shirt pocket, notebook flapping out his back pocket. She grinned, heady with secret bubbles that seemed to burst up inside her and made her want to giggle out loud.

She was having fun! Nothing like the satisfaction she felt attending museum openings or art gallery showings or the Santa Fe opera. Nothing like the solid pleasure of dinner with a colleague or shopping at the Indian market. This was something she hadn't felt in years. It was silliness and gaiety. As she swayed at Garth's elbow, she felt like a little girl again. Her hair danced around her shoulders, and her feet were light as air. Her breath came in short gasps intermingled with laughter.

The fiddles sang as if they might burst into flame. Faster, faster. Kitt whirled around and around. Garth's feet became a blur. Faster, faster. And as suddenly as it had begun, the song ended. The crowd broke into a roar of clapping and cheering. Kitt sucked in a deep breath. She glanced around. She and Garth were the only ones left in the street.

A crooked grin tugged at one corner of Garth's mouth as his eyes met hers. "I'll be damned," he said.

One of the fiddlers stepped up to a microphone. "Now ain't these two showed all you cowboys how it's done?" Laughter rippled through the crowd. "Let's hear it for the city boy and his gal!"

As the clapping began again someone called out— "Give her a kiss!"

Kitt swung around, fairly certain the voice belonged to Sam.

"Give her a kiss! Give her a kiss!" The crowd took up the chant.

"I reckon you'd better oblige the folks," the fiddler said, leaning over the mike. "Pucker up, you two!"

Garth put his hands on Kitt's shoulders. She was stiff and rigid, and all the swaying fun had gone out of her in an instant. As he turned her around to face him, he saw that her eyes had gone wide and dark. Suddenly he wished he hadn't goaded her away from her laundry and her piles of papers. She was happier in her own regimented little world. There wasn't a chance he was going to kiss her here in front of this rowdy crowd of cowboys—killing the spark that had slowly come to life between them. The best he could do now was slip her out of the crowd.

Kitt saw the wariness veil Garth's eyes as he drew her toward him. He wasn't going to kiss her. She knew him well enough to read that clearly in his eyes. Like some huge panther, he hovered near, ready to protect her from the whistling, hooting cowboys. But she didn't need protecting! At this moment, she felt as alive and eternal as a teenager. And suddenly she wanted that kiss.

"Thanks for the dance, Garth," she said, rising on tiptoe and sliding her arms around his neck. Before he could put his own plans into action, she brushed her lips lightly across his.

For an instant, Garth stood rock-still. Unbelieving. Before his brain engaged, his body took over. Her scent—spicy as an Oriental evening—flooded his nostrils. Her lips moved with a warm dampness over his. Her arms fairly singed his neck.

As she backed away, his hands closed around her waist, locking her against him. Their eyes met, brown and blue-gray, challenging, consuming.

"Kitt," he murmured.

She lifted her chin. His mouth found hers tentatively at first, then with a growing intensity. Her moist, full lips promised other, hidden delights. Splaying his hands along her back, he ran his fingers down the valley of her spine and touched each separate vertebra. Her breasts pressed into his chest and he could feel her nipples pebble-hard against him through the thin fabric of his shirt. He stroked her closed lips with his tongue, aware of the roar of the blood in his temple.

And then she was backing away. The crowd was cheering. Cries of, "Dr. Tucker! Dr. Tucker!" reverberated across the street. The fiddles struck up a new tune. Dancers wove past, feet kicking out another two-step. Somebody's elbow jostled Garth, but he didn't feel it.

They stared at each other. Kitt's mouth tasted dry. She suddenly couldn't remember why she had kissed Garth. She wasn't a teenager who could live forever. He wasn't a strapping, gawky farm boy. This man was drenched in male sensuality. His kiss had held promises of magic—not the fleeting magic of first love, but that magic reserved for adults who had loved one another long and intimately. He was every bit a man. And she was every bit a woman. And they were capable of anything.

The thought scared her half to death.

The only way out of this was to be professional, polite and distant. Otherwise, he might want to take her for another stroll, or drive her back to the motel. But his kiss had released something wild and unpredictable deep within her. Tonight, she wasn't at all sure the wild thing was going to let her behave.

"Garth," she began.

"Kitt—" His voice overlapped hers.

"No, let me talk—"

"I just wanted to say—"

They laughed a little sheepishly.

"I've got to get back to my room, Garth."

"I need to talk with the organizer of the rodeo for a few minutes."

They understood each other.

"Thanks, Garth."

"See you in the morning?"

"Fine."

"Good night, Kitt."

He stroked her cheek with the tip of his finger, then headed off in the direction of the refreshment table.

Kitt started down the sidewalk toward the laundromat. But her feet didn't want to maintain the steady pace she had set for them. Before she knew it, she was running. Skipping. Dancing the two-step.

Laughing deep in the pit of her stomach, she flung open the pickup door and slid in. She sat catching her breath, legs sprawled askew across the seat. Then she picked up a handful of folded laundry and tossed it into the air. She started the engine and drove to her motel with a pair of pink panties perched on her head.

# Chapter 5

For miles, the road west of Catclaw Draw stretched out flat as a sleeping kitten's belly. Occasional pronghorn antelope lifted their heads and studied the passing gray car. Yuccas covered in thick cream-colored blooms stood tall amid swaying kochia and gramma grass. Lack of rain had left everything a dusty brown that lightened to yellow in patches. Gray-green prickly pear cacti struggled to peek over the top of the grass. Purple thistles provided the only spots of bright color. Straight fences followed the highway, keeping herds of black cattle on the safe side. Meadowlarks, mockingbirds, quail and doves flitted overhead or perched stoically on the barbed wire.

As though someone had scratched the kitten's belly, the road slowly began to ripple and rise. The Sacramento Mountains materialized straight ahead, with the snow-capped Sierra Blanca peak shining like a crown in their midst. Salt cedar and mesquite gave way to piñon and juniper. Grass grew knee-high and green. As the car climbed into the mountains, pine and juniper trees rose higher, finally towering overhead. Sparrows and blue jays played among their branches. Chokecherry trees flourished in ravines. Indian paintbrushes danced with orange blossoms along the roadway.

Kitt kept her eyes on the window, so aware of the man beside her that she forced herself to concentrate on anything but him. When he'd met her that morning outside the motel, Garth had looked completely different than he had the two previous days. His hair was damp from his morning shower. A navy T-shirt molded to the hard planes of his chest. The short sleeves of the cotton knit shirt hugged the muscle in his arms. He wore a pair of faded jeans with a hole in one knee, and a pair of white running shoes. The gray car with its leather seats and briefcase on the floor may have said "professional." But his body—tanned, fit and catlike—was every bit the athlete.

Already, Kitt was half sorry she'd agreed to come. Not only did Garth look great, he smelled like he always had—an outdoorsy scent tinged with spice. Not overwhelming, but clean and masculine. His male presence filled the compact car with an almost palpable sensuality.

She felt ill-equipped to handle him this morning. Her sleep the night before had been interrupted with bouts of worry, mingled with confusion and giddy happiness. His television had remained on until the wee hours.

Her nerves stretched almost to the breaking point in the sleek metal and leather prison of his car, Kitt made up her mind to stay detached. She would get him to reveal the information he had compiled on Black Dove—though no doubt it was nothing new. They would spend a pleasant morning together, perhaps ease some of the pain that had built at the end of their ill-fated marriage. After that, she could see him on his way and get back to her work and her life.

"Sunflowers," Garth said. He gestured with his chin.

Kitt leaned against his shoulder to crane out his window. Yellow blossoms crowded the banks of the Rio Peñasco. The scene stretched along the road, looking like one of those quaint but sweetly artificial paintings on café place mats—winding rivers, flowers, pine trees and blue, blue sky. Black-and-white cows dipped their noses into blue-green alfalfa. A mounted man galloped a horse across a narrow wooden bridge.

Garth pulled the car into a picnic site along the river. Wild sunflowers grew in thick patches right up to the water's edge. Red hot pokers, tiger lilies, peonies and blue flag irises nudged places for themselves among the lush green grass and limestone rocks. Box elder trees towered beside walnuts. A trumpet vine with red-orange flowers climbed a cottonwood tree.

Kitt chose a spot of mingled shadow and sunlight beneath a huge old cottonwood. Garth cleared away fallen branches and spread a motel blanket. He'd ventured out early to a convenience store to round up armloads of lunch meats, apples, potato chips and sodas. They ate in silence, Garth tossing pebbles into the river and Kitt listening to the thick rustle of green leaves overhead.

"Hod—this strange old fellow who keeps appearing at the site—likes to sit under the cottonwoods out at the cemetery," Kitt said. "He'll pick up a fallen stick and whittle it awhile without even looking at what he's doing. Then he'll drop that stick and pick up another one and start all over again."

"Who is he?"

"Just some old man who mutters to himself a lot. He told me he's been looking for a lost gold mine all his life. His father showed it to him once when he was a boy, but he forgot where it was."

"Poor guy. Does he think you're going to dig up his lost gold?"

"I don't think so. Dr. Dean guessed he might have a relative buried in the cemetery. He sure is persistent about coming around. I think I finally ran him off for good yesterday."

"What a meanie."

Kitt glanced quickly at Garth, who grinned disarmingly.

"It's for his own safety. Besides, I'm strongly opposed to strangers wandering around out of curiosity. I won't have the site turned into a circus."

"One old geezer isn't much of a circus."

"I know. Maybe I should have let him stay." Kitt studied Garth as he stretched out on the gray blanket, palms cupping his head. "Actually, I kind of like Hod," she went on. "Dr. Dean thinks he may be close to a hundred years old. I bet he could tell some stories about the past."

"Speaking of the past, what about that gold-toothed fellow you dug up?"

"What about him?"

"Are you going to give me that interview?"

"You came to the press conference, Garth."

"But you promised Affiliated Press an interview. A private interview. Really, Kitt, your selective professionalism surprises me."

Garth rested with his eyes closed and a little smile that was almost a smirk on his mouth. She watched his chest rise and fall beneath the navy T-shirt. The shirt had come untucked in the front when he lay down, and she could see a thin line of dark hair running into his jeans.

"What do you mean, my 'selective professionalism'?"

"First you break Bureau rules by letting an outsider on the site. Then you refuse an interview that you had originally scheduled—never mind that the reporter drove all the way to Catclaw Draw to cover the exciting cemetery relocation story. And then—"

"The reporter drove only thirty miles from Carlsbad for the story and he was on his way to Albuquerque anyway. And if the relocation story is so dull, why doesn't the reporter go on back to Albuquerque where he belongs?"

"And worst of all, you blatantly choose to ignore an intriguing trail of clues leading to the identity of the unknown gold-toothed skull in the Muddy Flats cemetery."

"I am not ignoring the clues, Garth."

"Then why don't you pursue them?" He opened his eyes and fixed her with a blue-gray scrutiny. "Are you afraid you're going to look bad when part of your paper is proven inaccurate? Or are you trying to protect Dr. Oldham? Or are you just afraid to take my challenge because you'd be working with me?"

It was unnerving the way the boy who used to twist his Cummins cap around and around when he tried to talk had become so clever with words. More unnerving was the way he was able to see right through her.

"What are all these clues anyway, Garth?" she asked. "All I know is that a poor guy in an unmarked grave in a New Mexico cemetery had two gold teeth."

*And he was an Indian,* she added silently.

Garth rolled onto his haunches. "I'll get my files."

A moment later they were poring over copied newspaper clippings and passages from books. The pickings were fairly slim, but enough to excite the historical treasure seeker in Kitt.

"The first we hear of Black Dove is just a mention in this article on James Kirker, the white scalp hunter," Garth explained. "Black Dove, it says, was a Shawnee from Ohio who was run off his land by white settlers. He and a band of these displaced Shawnee joined up with Kirker in 1836 at Bent's Fort. Apparently Black Dove followed Kirker through a whole series of escapades. But I couldn't find anything on Kirker's activities until 1840, when he went to the town in Mexico where you think Black Dove is buried."

"Guadalupe Y Calvo?"

"That's right. So what happened in the lost years? What did Black Dove do while he was hanging around with Kirker from 1836 to 1840?"

Kitt leaned against the ragged cottonwood trunk. "That's easy. Kirker played a huge part in my report. He left Bent's Fort with Black Dove and the other Shawnees and Delawares who formed his gang. He was hired by a couple of fellows named Robert McKnight and Stephen Courcier to protect the Santa Rita copper mines over in southwestern New Mexico."

"Strip mining?"

"Santa Rita was owned by the Mexican government and they used Indian labor to dig deep pits in the ground. Apparently it was very primitive and cruel. The Mexicans sent the copper in long mule trains from Santa Rita to Chihuahua City to be minted. But along the way, Apaches usually attacked the trains, stole the copper and murdered everybody. Finally the mines had to shut down."

"So Kirker and Black Dove and the others were hired to protect the copper trains."

"That's right. Kirker and his men ambushed Apaches and scalped them. In essence, they were bounty hunters. The Mexican government paid them a certain amount of money per scalp."

"Sounds like interesting work." Garth shifted through his file until he came to a picture he had copied from a book. "This is supposed to be a daguerreotype of some of Kirker's men. Which one is Black Dove?"

Kitt glanced at the familiar portrait. "No one's ever proven this is really Kirker's gang, you know. But it does seem to fit the description. They were mostly displaced Shawnee and

Delaware Indians, but he also had a few Frenchmen, Englishmen, and maybe a Hawaiian or two.''

"Hawaiians? You're kidding?"

"No. And there was a giant black fellow named Andy who
ran with Kirker. This is supposed to be Black Dove."

She tapped the chest of a towering figure dressed in a strange
combination of beaded Indian buckskin and Mountain Man
fur and flannel. It was his face, however, that drew an ob-
server's attention from the rest of the motley crew. Black Dove
stood tall, powerful, light-skinned and incredibly handsome.
He had a high forehead, prominent cheekbones, a Roman nose
and malicious black eyes.

"How did he get the gold teeth?" Garth asked, his eyes
fixed on the photograph.

"Supposedly when he was a kid, he got in a fight with another boy and bit his ear right off. As a punishment, his two
front teeth were knocked out by order of the chief. They say
Black Dove never opened his mouth to speak again, until he
was able to get his hands on some gold and have those new
teeth fitted."

"Sounds like a pretty mean fellow." Garth glanced at the
river for a moment and narrowed his eyes. "It's possible to do
computer enhancements of photographs, you know. A group
of researchers have studied some photos of a fellow who
claimed to be Billy the Kid. Remember that? They compared
the photographs of the guy with the one true shot of Billy.
We've got a photograph of Black Dove—and we've got a
skeleton. With a computer enhancement, it shouldn't be too
hard to match them up."

"Not if you've got a research grant, government permission and a bunch of money—and can find anybody who's interested in an obscure Shawnee with two gold teeth. I hate to
say this, Garth, but you're really the only one who cares much
about poor old Black Dove."

"True, he's not exactly a major historical figure. But he is
interesting, and there may be more to him than we know. If he
was buried in the Muddy Flats cemetery, somebody in Guadalupe Y Calvo invented the death Dr. Oldham was told
about." Garth set the photograph on the pile of papers. "So
Kirker, Black Dove and the gang spent a few years scalping

Apaches for the Mexican government. Why did they leave and move to Guadalupe Y Calvo?''

"Problems. They were incredibly successful at killing Apaches. Kirker became famous. Men called him the king of New Mexico—the scourge of the Apaches. The Santa Rita mines opened again. But then the Apaches began attacking Chihuahua City itself. So the Mexican Society for War Against Hostile Indians asked Kirker to protect the city. He promised to eradicate every Apache from the face of the earth. And he might have done it. But soon he became pretty unpopular. See, Kirker kept all the cattle he took when he raided Apache villages—no matter whose brand was on them. And he was an embarrassment to the Mexican army, who really should have been fighting the Apaches. When a fellow named Conde became governor, Kirker lost his contract."

"I bet the Apaches were happy about that."

Kitt grinned. "They went right back to attacking Chihuahua City."

"So that brings us to Guadalupe Y Calvo." Garth rummaged around in his stack of papers. Kitt studied the top of his head as he bent over his portfolio. Sunlight tipped the golden shafts of his hair and made it gleam. His brow was furrowed in concentration. His strong farm-boy hands riffled through the papers with a surprising gentleness.

The fact of the matter was, Kitt realized suddenly, she was having a wonderful time at this. In some ways it reminded her of the old days in the Clovis High School library—she and Garth poring over old books and papers. They had always shared this love of lore.

But Garth had changed in many ways. The Black Dove scavenger hunt had story potential, and Garth was pursuing it with all the skills he had honed through his years as a reporter. His news nose was on full alert. It could be something really good. The tingle along Kitt's spine told her the same thing. His research skills and news sense—combined with her knowledge of history and ability to solve puzzles—might lead them to something worthwhile. Not to mention the pleasure both would feel in the chase.

A wariness filtered over her as he slid a page from his file. It was too easy, too much fun to be with him again.

"Guadalupe Y Calvo sounds like a really weird place to me," he was saying. "Sort of a Shangri-la. It's southwest of Chihuahua in the Sierra Madre mountains. I had a heck of a time finding the right town. Did you know there are six or eight cities in Mexico called Guadalupe? And then there's the Guadalupe mountain chain in New Mexico and Texas."

"Our Lady of Guadalupe is the patron saint of Mexican Indians. There's a famous shrine to her in one of those Guadalupes you looked up. Tourists flock there."

"Tourists must not go to Guadalupe Y Calvo much, because I could hardly find anything about it in the library. There's a short reference to it in this guidebook. It says, 'Guadalupe Y Calvo sits at an altitude of almost ten thousand feet. It can be reached only by air. The town was settled by Englishmen who began mining gold and silver there in 1835. Most of the houses bear a strong resemblance to thatch-roofed English cottages. No roads lead into Guadalupe Y Calvo, and no wheels have been on its streets—neither automobile, truck, wagon or cart.' That's it. That's all I could find."

"Wow. Dr. Oldham corresponded with the priest there. But we never knew the place was remarkable in any way. No roads. No wheels. English cottages. That's strange."

"So Black Dove lived in Guadalupe Y Calvo with Kirker and his men. Why were they there?"

"Apaches again. They raided the gold trains that left town for Chihuahua City. Robert McKnight, the same fellow who owned the Santa Rita copper mines, had a part interest in the gold mines at Guadalupe Y Calvo. He was the one who hired Kirker. But it wasn't long before the Mexican government called Kirker back to Chihuahua City. This time they promised him a lot more money for each Apache scalp."

"So Black Dove went with him?"

"For a while. When Kirker and the men got to Chihuahua City with the scalps, the governor told them he could pay only ten percent of what he had promised. Black Dove was furious. The legend has it that he painted half his face red and half black. Then he marched into the governor's office brandishing his tomahawk. Black Dove threatened to scalp the governor—and I imagine he would have."

"Our pal Black Dove didn't have much respect for human life."

"The governor gave Black Dove the mules and horses that were his due. Then Black Dove left Kirker. Some of the Indians stayed with Kirker until his death, the records show. But Black Dove went back to Guadalupe Y Calvo and again hired himself out to protect the gold mines. We don't have any records, but Dr. Oldham was told that Black Dove died and was buried there."

"There ought to be records of Black Dove's burial in the church cemetery," Garth said.

Kitt shrugged. "Dr. Oldham wasn't able to get any. And if the town hasn't even progressed to the wheel, they might not have kept many records. Although . . . even very old churches usually have something . . ."

"We could call—"

"I doubt there'd be phones."

"Write."

"Go ahead, Garth. But I can guarantee you're not going to be able to get anything more than Dr. Oldham did. He's the best there is at digging up records."

"You respect him a lot."

"Yes, I do. He's efficient and careful. He wouldn't miss something like that. Besides, I saw all his notes. There are no records of Black Dove's death."

"Of course there aren't. Because he's buried in the Muddy Flats cemetery in New Mexico."

"Oh, Garth!" Kitt felt a chuckle well up in her chest. He was smiling at her, his hair rustling over his forehead.

"The facts are clear, Dr. Tucker. On the one hand, you have a very distinctive-looking Indian named Black Dove. He was tall, he had a Roman nose—and he had two gold teeth. A fact that is mentioned by more than one contemporary source. Most important, you have no records of Black Dove's death. On the other hand, you have a mighty suspicious-looking skeleton with two gold teeth."

Kitt swallowed. "He was an Indian, too... Dr. Dean told me yesterday afternoon after he'd finished his examinations."

"Kitt—"

She picked a peony and twirled the stem in her fingers. "Not only that ... Dr. Dean told me the man was tall and physically fit even at an old age. He had lots of healed bone fractures. And he was handsome."

"Why didn't you tell me?"

"Why would someone like Black Dove ever have come to Muddy Flats, New Mexico, Garth? Why? Just answer that one question and I promise I'll take up your challenge. I'll find out what really happened to Black Dove."

Seeing him start to respond, she quickly added, "And you can help me."

Garth grunted and tossed a stick into the river. He broke a second stick and tossed the pieces into the rushing water. Kitt was trying to be skeptical, he knew that. But she was losing the battle. She wanted to find out about Black Dove as much as he did. And not just because it was a fascinating little story. It would mean working with him—sorting out clues, time in the library... time together.

He glanced at her. She was thumbing through his file, her dark brows drawn together. Dressed as she was in a feminine white blouse and pale pink shorts, she might not be taken too seriously. But he knew that clever mind of hers was working over the facts—and probably more efficiently than his had.

Why had she kept the report about the skeleton's Indian features to herself? There could be only one reason. She wanted to go on the scavenger hunt badly—but alone. Yet, she had told him of the clue in the end. She had let him in.

"I think I know why Black Dove came to Muddy Flats," Garth said.

Kitt's dark eyes pinned him. "Why?"

"He was a man on the run. He joined up with Kirker in the first place because he was an outcast. The white man had taken his land. He'd been humiliated by his chief. He felt like a failure and he didn't care if he died hunting down Apaches. He didn't have anything to live for."

Garth had hooked one arm over his knee and was absently tapping a long stick into the folds of the blanket. Tension rippled the muscles beneath his navy T-shirt.

"It was kind of like when I left you, Kitt." His voice had that raspy, low quality. "I was a wild man. I thought your love for me had died with the baby, you know?"

He looked at her, his blue-gray eyes rimmed with red. Kitt reached out to touch him—to tell him to stop talking. He didn't need to tell her this. She wasn't sure she was ready to hear it. But he took her hand in his and began to stroke each finger.

"I knew if I left, your parents would take you back home. You'd be happy again. You'd be where you belonged. You could have the life you deserved. I...I didn't want to live without you, Kitt. But I knew you didn't want me anymore. I knew how much you resented me for what happened. We'd made a mistake and you got pregnant. And then you thought you had to marry me. Your parents disowned you. You cried so hard about that. And even though things were good between us, when the baby died inside—"

"Garth—" There was a note of panic in her voice.

"I'm sorry, honey. I won't talk about it." He hung his head for a moment, and Kitt saw the little boy again. "I stayed with my uncle in Amarillo for a while after I left you. I drank a lot. I tried to find a job. I tried to rodeo. Nothing worked. I mean—I just wanted to die all the time. So I enlisted. I didn't have any college or anything so they sent me straight over to Vietnam. The war was nearly over, but I saw some combat."

He looked at the river and his face was far away in steaming green jungles. His fingers were laced through Kitt's...holding tight.

"God..." he said, shaking his head.

"Garth." She felt as if she were crawling deep inside herself. "I never hated you or anything like that. I never blamed you for what happened."

"Maybe not. I sure thought so, Kitt." He gave an ironic laugh. "Well, I didn't die in Vietnam, anyway. I had to keep on going. I guess that's probably what happened to our old buddy, Black Dove. The Apaches couldn't do him in, and he actually got good at his job."

"So why do you think Black Dove came to Muddy Flats?"

Garth turned Kitt's arm over on his thigh. He ran his thumb up her soft skin and stroked the inside of her elbow. "I imagine Black Dove had had about enough of trying to get himself killed," he said.

"You think he was heading off to start a new life for himself?"

Garth looked into her brown eyes. "I think he was going home."

# Chapter 6

The motel blanket felt suddenly too small for both of them, and Kitt got to her feet. She waded through a sea of sunflowers down to the riverbank. Crouching she dipped the tips of her fingers in the icy water. A silvery trout hung motionless in the shadows.

She heard movement in the sunflowers. Glancing to the sandy shore beside her, she saw Garth's running shoes appear side by side on the damp bank.

"Wish I had my fishing pole." His voice above her revealed a strange wistfulness.

She picked up a dried yellow aspen leaf and set it in the river current. It washed downstream a few yards, then hung up in a dam of fallen logs and driftwood.

"So, did I answer your question?" he asked.

She stood. "About Black Dove's motivation for being in Muddy Flats? I suppose it's a possibility that he was on his way home to Ohio. But most of the Shawnees had been run out. There wouldn't be much reason for him to go home."

"Maybe he wanted to find out what happened to his people after he left . . . And if he was headed for Ohio, he might have passed through Muddy Flats. There *was* a town there in the 1870s, wasn't there?''

"Barely. The village itself didn't come into being until 1875. But a few settlers had come.''

"So if Black Dove was passing through, he might have stayed. He might have lived in Muddy Flats for a few years and then died there.''

"That's a huge leap of supposition, Garth. It's remotely possible, I guess.''

"You agree we might have found Black Dove's grave?''

"It's unlikely, but maybe.''

Garth flipped a stone into the river. "So, are we going to work together on this?''

Kitt shoved her hands deep into the pockets of her pink shorts. "I could do the research by myself, and send you the materials for your story.''

"I could do the research by myself, and send you the materials for your book.''

Her eyes darted to his. "But I'm going to follow the clues, Garth. I feel I have to. It's what I do.''

"It's what I do, too.''

His eyes roamed over her face, attempting to read the messages there. She had that stubborn little set to her jaw. Her nostrils flared slightly. She was hardheaded, all right. But those dark brown eyes held a tenderness she couldn't hide. He had seen the soft side of her only moments before. He knew he had glimpsed her soul.

It hurt to go over old memories. It hurt her...and it hurt him. But it was right, too, to fill in the gaps. She hadn't known about Vietnam. She hadn't known why he left her in their little trailer that day. She hadn't understood for fifteen years. Until now.

Kitt's eyes left his and her focus drifted around his shoulder. "Look, Garth. There's a little walking trail. Come on, let's see where it goes.''

Without waiting for him to respond, she took off like a rabbit eluding a fox. He followed her with his eyes as she crossed the redwood bridge, her long bare legs widening the distance between them. The flash of pink shorts vanished around a rock outcrop, then reappeared at the base of a scraggly pine.

"Kitt—damn it!" Garth tore after her, his rubber-soled shoes hugging the rough terrain. "You didn't give me an answer!"

Catching sight of Garth's navy T-shirt just below her on the path, she gave a little shriek and began scampering higher. The path narrowed as it wound among a stand of towering juniper, cedar and pine trees. Her sandals slipped along the thick layer of fallen needles as she ran. She had started with a good lead, but now Garth was almost right behind her.

"Come back here, you . . ."

"You can't force me into things, Garth. I won't be pinned down like that. Cornered . . ." She darted behind the gnarled trunk of an alligator juniper and rejoined the path after leading him off in the wrong direction.

She ran on in silence, aware that he was searching for her somewhere in a thicket of yellow-green cedar bushes. The scent of piñon was heavy in the crisp air. She tilted her head back, letting her hair flip against her hips as the path took her alongside a gurgling tributary. Sunlight, yellow and thick as butter, filtered down through the pine branches to make patches of gold on her face.

"Gotcha!" A massive form leaped out from behind a trunk and swung her gently to the ground. "Can't pin you down, huh? Can't corner you, huh?"

"Garth!" She laughed, pushing at his huge shoulders. "These pine needles are poking into my back."

He grinned at her. One hand was propped on either side of her head. His long body lay just to the side of hers. "Too bad."

"They're sharp as nails."

"Think of yourself as a swami."

She pursed her lips. After her run up the mountain they looked delicious and red. A flush spread from her cheeks down her neck. Her breasts rose and fell, their tips just brushing his T-shirt.

"Okay, Dr. Tucker. The moment of truth. Will we work together or not?"

"Is this how it would be—you bullying your way around and cornering me?"

"It doesn't have to." He brushed a strand of hair from her cheek. "You could give a little, Kitt."

He lowered his chest gently to hers and let his lips drift across her mouth. She sighed raggedly and he could sense the fight still inside her. Placing her hands on his biceps, she gave a push. But her lips were open and her dark eyes beckoned.

"It could be like this between us, Kitt," he murmured. They waited, looking into each other's faces, each allowing the other the opportunity to back away. And then, as if a silent plea had passed between, they reached for each other.

He rolled her against him, holding her tightly. Her open mouth met his, hungrily searching to fill the emptiness. Their lips crushed together. Their tongues tangled, tasting the long-lost nectar of their passion. They explored each silken crevice, each remembered hollow. His teeth found her lower lip, caressed it. She licked and teased and bit at him, aware of the growl deep in his chest.

When his lips moved across her cheek and found her ear, a shiver curled deep into the pit of her stomach. With a damp sensuality, he nuzzled the outer shell of her ear, then flicked the lobe between his teeth. He wound his fingers through her hair, holding her neck to his mouth as he moved down it.

With each ministration of his tongue, the shriveled-up little prune inside Kitt began to swell and grow liquid. A warmth slid down her thighs and settled in the tips of her toes. A molten river shot into the tips of her breasts, making them tingle and ache. She felt hungry, like a child too long deprived of nourishment. This man was a feast.

She ran her fingers up his spine, across his massive, solid shoulders. Up through the soft curls at the back of his neck. Into the thick mat of warm, golden brown hair on his head. Lost somewhere in the past and somewhere in the present, she couldn't think beyond the moment. Her mind swam with pleasure, her body felt driven.

Garth dropped one knee between her thighs. He hadn't expected her response, her heedless plundering of him. Even now, she was tugging his T-shirt from the waistband of his jeans. Her warm fingers sang on the bare skin of his back. He grazed his mouth across her neck, dipped his tongue into the hollow at the base of her throat. She arched upward as he drew a wet line down the center of her chest toward the V of her blouse.

Her breasts, so much fuller than he remembered, blocked his view of her body. They were encased in that prim white blouse. And beneath, he imagined one of those filmy little bras. She had drawn his shirt up. Her nails raked his back, sending shivers of pleasure down his body.

He stroked her hips and pulled her tighter to him, settling his hardness against her thigh, letting her know what she had done to him. She sucked in a breath. He began nudging open the buttons of her blouse with his teeth. The fragile white cotton fabric parted easily.

Beneath, as he had pictured, she wore a skimpy white bra. Its narrow straps barely supported her. Under the satiny fabric, her nipples jutted up like hard little buds. He lowered his mouth and touched the satin. First one and then the other. The fabric dampened, became transparent. The dark circles of her areolas taunted him.

Her breasts, so long untouched, were ultrasensitive. As his tongue made little journeys across her bra, she felt herself swell to meet him. Each nipple strained outward, sending sharp, sweet tugs into the pit of her stomach. She slipped her fingers through his hair and reveled in the warmth of his scalp. His head moved over her, his tongue working the top of her bra down. Her back ached with a pleasure that warmed the inner planes of her thighs and made her knees weak.

One nipple eased over the edge of the fabric. Garth groaned. Taking it between his lips, he pulled and suckled until she thought she would cry aloud. Pressed against her, his body felt like a rigid brand of fire. And as she lay, weak and wanting in his arms, it came to her that she would make love with him. Right there on the forest floor. Right there on the pine needles. She had known him again for less than two days—and she would, without thought of consequences, make love with him.

Garth lifted up on his elbows. His mouth was damp with her. His eyes caressed her face, reading her thoughts.

"Kitt," he murmured. "It's that power between us."

"I know."

He closed his eyes and laid his head between her breasts. She held him close. The pine trees overhead dripped sunlight on them. Kitt knew what he was thinking. This was a mistake. Another of their mistakes. There was a power between them—but, in the end, it was a destructive power. It was too much, too strong. It had consumed them once before.

"I don't ever want to hurt you again, Kitt," he said. His breath was warm on her skin. "I don't ever want to make you cry like you cried when your parents turned away from you. I don't ever want to make you die inside again, like you did when our baby..."

He was afraid of what could happen between them. She was afraid, too. Half of her wanted him to stay, to take her body with his to the heights of passion. The other half wanted to run. Run as far away as she could get. She knew which half was the sensible one. He knew it, too. Right now, the sensible half of her was winning out.

He rolled to her side and stared into the pine branches. They were both silent for a long time, letting the heat subside, trying to make sense of their thoughts. Kitt pulled her clothing together and folded her hands across her stomach.

"I don't think normal divorced people act this way around each other," he said.

Kitt smiled. "So, who says we were ever normal?"

"I feel like I used to up on the hay bales in the barn."

"The pine needles are sharper."

He chuckled. "Damn. You've always pushed me past my limits."

"You know this isn't going to work, Garth."

"I know."

"I mean, if we work together on this Black Dove business, things would probably just get into a real mess between us."

"It might be fun."

"Not in the long run."

He glanced at her. She was talking to him with her eyes closed. Her dark lashes lay like fans on her cheeks. The damp circles on her bra were starting to dry in the sunshine. But her nipples were still hard.

"I'm going to follow those clues, Kitt," he said.

"So am I." Her eyes were still closed.

"Together?"

She watched the patterns on the insides of her eyelids. The future could hold nothing for them. She knew that. There were too many barriers. Too much pain. Yes, they desired each other. But primal body drives could be kept under rein by two professionals, couldn't they? Surely they could.

"Together—but with rules," she said.

"I know the rules. The same ones we had when we were kids."

Kitt's eyelids flipped open. "No! Not those!"

Garth rolled onto one elbow and gazed at her. "Not those rules?" His voice gently teased her. "You don't think it would work to take ourselves just as far as we could go..."

He flipped back the edges of her shirt. One finger slipped beneath the silk of her bra. One fingertip brushed roughly over one nipple. She bit her lower lip. He leaned down right next to her ear.

"We could just play with each other...lots of touching and kissing and tasting..."

She caught his neck suddenly and crushed his lips to hers, wanting one last taste. She was still so hungry for him. Their mouths parted, their tongues fenced and danced. They devoured one another. She sucked the tip of his tongue. He bit at her lip. His hands roved over her body, kneading her breasts, running up the legs of her shorts.

And then, just as swiftly, she pushed him away.

"You see," she said, gasping for air. "The old rules were lousy, Garth. They didn't work back then. And they sure wouldn't work now."

He groaned and fell back on the pine needles. She could see the swell beneath his jeans and knew she had been unfair. But it was all unfair. They couldn't play with each other. Their lives had not been some sort of game. It had been all too real, the consequences deadly serious.

And it wasn't just the baby. She had to acknowledge that. Their hunger for each other had torn them from their families. It had made them reckless. Unwise. It was still unwise.

"Okay, you win." He flicked a pine needle into the air. "We did a hell of a lousy job obeying the old rules, anyway. Let's make some new ones."

Kitt watched a wisp of cloud drift overhead. She imagined God looking down on them and shaking His head. The same two kids—lying on pine needles instead of hay. The same two kids, playing with fire. Making up rules. Pretending they had control of their own destinies. These kids had made a lot of mistakes. They'd paid for them. They'd grown and learned. And here they were again. Lying side by side. Making up rules. Heading back into the fire as if they hadn't learned a thing.

Kitt thought about arguing with God. It was really Black Dove they were interested in. It was a circumstances beyond their control. But she knew the argument didn't hold much water. It wasn't really Black Dove. She and Garth were still drawn together like magnets. Somehow their lives were woven into a circle. The circle had begun fifteen years ago, and had been broken. Now, it was time to complete what they had started. They would finish their circle. Tie up their loose ends.

And then they could go on with their separate lives. She told God that. But He still shook His head. Two kids. Lying on the pine needles. Making up rules.

"Okay," she said. "The new rules are going to be strict. We'll work together in a professional manner. Associates. This Black Dove thing shouldn't take long to resolve anyway. While we study, we'll speak to one another as co-workers. Not as former marriage partners. Nothing about the past, Garth. No playing around, either."

"No physical stuff."

"No."

"But we'll be friends."

Kitt considered. "Colleagues."

"What steps do you think we should take in our research?" Garth glanced at her. She had closed her eyes again. A spot of sunlight shone on the tip of her nose. Long pine needles tangled in her hair. She didn't look anything like a professor or an anthropologist. She looked exactly like Kitt Culhane, his wife.

"To begin with, we'll go over everything in Dr. Dean's report on the skeleton. I'll call Dr. Oldham in Albuquerque and ask him to send me his files on Black Dove."

"I've already done that."

Her brown eyes flicked open. "When?"

"I called him yesterday evening. Nice guy. But he's not going to send his files."

"Why not? That doesn't sound like Dr. Oldham." She felt slightly betrayed that Garth had already contacted her old professor. It was as if he had gone behind her back. Yet, she had to admit she had willingly concealed the physical anthropologist's report from him for a while.

"Dr. Oldham was really skeptical about the whole idea that Black Dove could be buried at Muddy Flats," Garth said. "Called it a wild-goose chase and referred me to the paper he wrote with you. He insists Black Dove is buried in Mexico. I don't think he believes you're in on this with me."

"I'll call him myself. Dr. Oldham is very protective. That's why he's so good. He taught me to protect my sources, my research—and above all my sites."

"Okay, we'll compare Dr. Dean's notes on the skeleton with Dr. Oldham's research on the actual Black Dove. What next?"

"We'll go to the museum at Catclaw Draw and talk to the historian. He knows just about everything there is to know about Muddy Flats."

"And after that?"

"What do you think? What would you do next?"

Garth studied Kitt's face. She was asking . . . but she already knew. Hadn't they talked about it a hundred times in the high school library? They'd picked out their favorite New Mexico heroes. Billy the Kid. Geronimo. Kit Carson. John Chisum. They'd followed their lives in the history books and the encyclopedias. But they'd always talked about their grandest dream of all . . . the ultimate . . .

Garth smiled, remembering. "I'd follow Black Dove's trail," he said.

In a way, it was the method he used when he tracked down stories for the Affiliated Press. And he imagined Kitt probably used their concept a little in her own work with the Bureau of Reclamation. But he'd never had the chance to do exactly what they'd dreamed of in the musty library at Clovis High.

"I'd go every place Black Dove went," Garth said, repeating the plan they had evolved so long ago. "I'd walk in his footsteps and I'd touch the things he touched. I'd find out where he lived, what he ate, what he wore. I'd look up every scrap of paper in every file that had ever been kept on him. I'd relive his life in the West. From the beginning.''

"The beginning." Kitt repeated the words. "Santa Rita. The copper mines at Santa Rita.''

The Catclaw Draw Historical Museum occupied one of the oldest houses in town. Its imposing Victorian facade trimmed with wooden curlicues and fanciful gingerbread, the house loomed over a vast green lawn. An American flag fluttered in the afternoon breeze. Kitt had spent hours there researching the Muddy Flats cemetery with the curator before she started the project. It felt almost like coming home.

"The house is constructed of a type of artificial stone," Kitt explained as she and Garth climbed the wood steps to the porch. "The stone was manufactured in the early years of this century. Several homes in Catclaw Draw were built of it, but most of them have been terribly neglected. It's just a shame to see how run down they are.''

Again Garth was struck with the incongruity. Kitt's professional voice and far-ranging historical knowledge—and her slender brown legs, long and sleek beneath those pink shorts. He'd better get used to it. She might look like a mere girl of twenty, but she thought of herself as she really was. Mature, intelligent, accomplished. She expected him to see her that way, too. They had made an agreement.

On the ride into town they had worked out their plan. This Saturday afternoon they would start their research at the museum. Sunday, each would be on his own, finishing up paperwork. Monday and Tuesday, Kitt would wind down her project out at the site. And Wednesday, they would head for the western mountains of New Mexico—and the copper mines.

"Garth Culhane, I'd like you to meet Charles Grant." Kitt was looking up at a burly redheaded fellow with a full beard. He stood at the foot of a long, blue-carpeted staircase. "Charles runs the museum. Garth's a reporter with Affiliated Press.''

Garth stuck out his hand. "We're trying to track down some information on a Shawnee by the name of Black Dove. Might've spent some time at Muddy Flats."

Charles Grant was a strange mixture of the Jolly Green Giant and Dicken's Ghost of Christmas Present. If he'd chuckled a deep, "Ho, ho, ho," Garth wouldn't have been a bit surprised. But when Charles began to talk there was no mistaking this man for a caricature.

"Black Dove." His voice rumbled. "Rings a bell. Let's take a look at my files."

They worked their way through the rooms of the house—past glassed shelves filled with antique teacups, tiny button boots, crocheted gloves. They skirted the kitchen that still bore the implements of a bygone era. Iron corn-bread molds, corn drying hooks, coffee grinders. The museum smelled of old things—faded wallpaper, dried-up leather, dusty velvet Belter chairs—like somebody's great-grandmother's house that had been shut up for years.

Garth and Kitt were directed into two old oak chairs in Charles's small office. Their host spun across the floor in a wheeled metal chair that looked like it had lost most of its springs. He whirled around, pulling out drawer after drawer. He stacked files on top of files. Books on top of books.

"Now, Muddy Flats is lush and fertile in the 1800s," Charles began. Garth noticed right away the historian spoke in the present tense, as though Muddy Flats were still a vibrant community. His big freckled hands moved as if he could see and touch what he was telling them about. "Muddy Flats is at the juncture of seven rivers, see. They're not dried up, like these days. They're flowing—I mean, really flowing. Oliver Loving and Charles Goodnight pass this way on their trail ride to Fort Sumner. The trail later is called the Goodnight-Loving trail. They're attacked by Indians along the way. But that doesn't stop them. They open up the trail and the cowboys start to follow."

"When does the first settler arrive in Muddy Flats?" Garth suddenly realized he was speaking in the present tense, too.

"Well, there's a Mexican settlement when Goodnight and Loving pass through. But it's not until 1867 that a fellow by the name of Reed—Dick Reed—establishes a ranch and trading post at Muddy Flats. Then old Tom Gardner comes on the scene and starts a small ranch and farm. That's around 1870."

"Around 1870." Kitt looked victorious. "So there *are* people at Muddy Flats. If Black Dove passes through, there are people here."

She was back in the previous century, too.

"There's really no village, though, until five years later. By the 1870s at least thirty men and their families are living at Muddy Flats. Texans, mostly. Some are ex-Texas Rangers. They're all rugged frontiersmen types. In the mid-1870s the population's up to three hundred folks."

"What does Muddy Flats look like?" Garth asked. It was hard to imagine three hundred people living and farming in a place where no one lived now. A place that was semi-desert land, crawling with rattlesnakes and scorpions.

"Muddy Flats is quite a little town," Charles said. "Most of the homes are made of adobe brick. There's a saloon. A general store. A saddle and boot shop are run by a fellow from Germany. A guy named Jim Woods does the horseshoeing and blacksmithing. Dee Burditt is the pharmacist and drugstore owner. Another family runs the hotel and restaurant. The post office is established in June of 1877. There's even a stonecutter. You know about him, Kitt."

"He carved a lot of the headstones out at the cemetery, Garth."

"What about a doctor?" Garth asked.

"No doctor. Kind of hard to imagine, isn't it? All those people. No wonder you have so many babies in the cemetery. Supplies are brought in from Pecos City, Texas, or from Fort Sumner. A round trip by ox team to Fort Sumner takes six weeks. They only go once a year."

"Do you have a list of all the people you mentioned?"

"Well, Kitt's put something together. The lists are scattered throughout a lot of references." Charles dug around in a file. "Here's what Kitt came up with. I think she's been very complete. 'Course, there are a lot of people not mentioned, I'm sure. No census is ever taken in Muddy Flats before the town dies."

"What kills it?"

Charles shook his head, almost as though he could feel a physical ache over the death of the little village. "Overgrazing. Erosion. In 1882, Muddy Flats is the second largest settlement in southeastern New Mexico. Five years later there's a terrible drought. Two years after that there are devastating floods. Cattle are drowned by the hundreds. By 1890, artesian water is discovered to the north around Catclaw Draw. Wells are drilled. A new county is formed—but Muddy Flats is not chosen as the county seat. People start moving out of Muddy Flats. The grass dies. Brush, mesquite, catclaw and greasewood move in. The rivers dry up. That's it. Muddy Flats is dead."

The three of them sat in silence. Kitt felt the watching presence of the past. Muddy Flats had been alive for a few minutes while Charles talked. She had almost been able to see the blacksmith's fiery forge, to hear tinny music in the saloon, to smell bread baking in the restaurant.

Garth was reading over the list of Muddy Flats residents she had compiled. A pine needle stuck out of his metal shoelace rivet.

"What about Indians?" he asked. "Any of them around this area?"

"Indians are stirring up trouble for thirty years. Fort Stanton is built in 1855 to help control the situation—but the Apaches are raiding cattle from the 1860s to the 1890s. Nobody can stop them, not even John Chisum, who's a huge cattle baron out here. He can't stop them stealing his cattle. Nobody can stop the Apaches. They're fearless. And damned tricky."

"Apaches."

"Mescalero Apaches. The place is crawling with them in the 1800s."

"Any record of Fort Stanton calling in an expert to help eliminate the problem?"

"You mean someone like James Kirker and his scalp hunters? No. No record of anyone coming for that purpose."

Kitt glanced at Garth. They were thinking the same thing.

"I suppose Black Dove *could* have moved to Muddy Flats to help control the Apaches," she said. "He was an expert.

Probably the only one left. Kirker was already dead. He'd died out in California almost twenty years earlier.''

"Fort Stanton would probably have a record if they'd brought in someone like this Black Dove," Charles said. "I've never seen anything on it."

"I'll call them on Monday morning and see what I can find out." Garth pulled out his reporter's notebook and made a memo.

Kitt took the list of residents from Garth and scanned the names. "Obviously, some people buried in the cemetery weren't mentioned in my list. We've got so many unmarked graves, now."

"The old Muddy Flats area has been ranched for years, Kitt," Charles explained. "You can't expect every grave to be marked. Plows'll go by and turn over a stone. Cattle come along. I told you about those scouts who went out to clean up the cemetery a few years back."

Kitt rolled her eyes. It was hard to tell what devastation those twelve-year-olds had wrought. "Good intentions, I guess... Okay, let's see, now. We have an Indian with two gold teeth who's supposed to be buried in Mexico. He was a scalp hunter, accustomed to hunting down Apaches. Apaches were causing a lot of trouble around Muddy Flats. Buried in the Muddy Flats cemetery is the skeleton of an Indian with two gold teeth. But Black Dove would have been nearly fifty by the time he came to Muddy Flats. Pretty old to go around scalping Apaches."

Garth watched as Kitt took careful notes and checked things off. Her little notebook was propped on her knees. Her hair fell like a brown satin sheet over her shoulder.

"Kitt told me she had to be cautious not to offend any next of kin living in the area," Garth said. "Is there anyone around here whose family lived at Muddy Flats? Anyone we could talk to who might know something?"

Charles rubbed his rough red hair. "You've got some distant relatives around. A bunch of folks ranch up in the mountains near Ruidoso. But they've all written down their stories. It probably wouldn't do you any good to talk to them. Let's see... around Catclaw Draw, you've got a few families. I can give you some names. Most of the old folks have been in to talk to me. We've tried to get written transcripts of what they remember. You can go through those files if you'd like.''

Garth nodded. "Any artifacts?"

"If you can believe it—not a thing. It's like the whole town vanished. Took everything with them. A few years back one woman called me to say she had a plate from the old Muddy Flats village. But when we had it analyzed it turned out to be modern delftware from Holland. The foundations of an adobe house used to stand out there by the river, but somebody went and plowed them under. You wouldn't believe how hard it is to protect historical sites.''

"Yes, I would," Kitt said.

Charles grinned and slapped his huge palms on the desk. "Well, gotta close up, now. Garth, you come on back Monday and we'll go over those transcripts. But as to anyone really old..." He frowned for a moment and tugged on his thick beard. "Come to think of it, there is one fellow. Lived around Catclaw Draw all his life. Most people think he's a little loco. But the fact is, he's as straight as you or I. We talk a lot. He's been searching for an old gold mine his papa took him to see when he was a kid. It's up on a mountain somewhere, near a pine tree bent in the shape of an L. But this fellow knows a hell of a lot about Muddy Flats. You'd almost think he'd lived there. Name's Hod. Ever heard of him?''

Garth gave a half laugh and flung one arm over Kitt's shoulders. "Good old Dr. Tucker, here, just ran him off the project site.''

Kitt gave Garth a disparaging look. "He'll be back," she said. "I've tried to run him off before. He just keeps reappearing. He tells me the twilight is coming and he has to be there to see it.''

"The twilight..." Charles let out a low whistle. "No kidding. He tells you that?''

"What? What does it mean?''

Charles lifted his red eyebrows. "It means old Hod's about to find his papa's lost gold.''

# *Chapter 7*

Hod didn't come back. Kitt watched for him all day, glancing at his spot beneath the cottonwood tree as she worked in the sweltering heat.

She hadn't seen Garth, either. Just as he'd promised, he treated her with cool detachment. From the moment they'd gotten up off their bed of pine needles, Garth had assumed the role of a congenial colleague. He spoke to her civilly, but never touched her. He smiled occasionally, but never gave her the look she had seen in his eyes at the street dance. After their trip to the museum, he'd taken her to the motel. And that was the last she'd seen of him.

Saturday night she had eaten alone at a restaurant. Sunday she'd sat through a church service wondering if he'd show up. She had half expected him to walk through the door just like the old Garth—all Sunday spit and polish in a white shirt, black tie and shiny wing-tip shoes. He'd sit behind her with his family, his long legs letting his knees poke into her bottom through the metal folding chair. His loud tenor would ring out behind her, clear as a bell. But Garth probably wasn't a tenor anymore. And he hadn't come to church. Maybe he didn't go to church anymore. Maybe he didn't believe in God anymore, after all he'd been through.

God and cemeteries and Garth and their little baby and the past. Everything seemed to be wound together in a tight, painful little knot that twisted inside her stomach.

Kitt carried a heavy pine box to the trailer bed and set it beside others for transportation to the new cemetery site. The recently constructed coffins were small and square, but each contained every item found in its grave—not only skeletal remains, but scraps of fabric, jewelry, coffin wood, spent bullets. A small fragment of each original coffin had been kept aside for further testing and examination. These slivers of wood would be enclosed in the central historical monument identifying the new cemetery.

The orange sun settled low over the dry grama grass as Kitt dusted off her hands. Dr. Dean was sweeping out his yellow nylon tent. A group of summer students had gathered around him to say their goodbyes. Most of them would leave for their hometowns this evening.

Only three graves remained to be uncovered the following day. Kitt and two students would excavate them. Then she would close down the site. The stakes would be pulled up, the contractor's mobile home would be towed away, the earth would be smoothed over. Within a few months the blue-green water of the new lake would begin to seep up and erase all trace of their work. The desert would be covered by twenty feet of water. Speedboats and skiers would skim across the lake's surface. Muddy Flats would be no more.

"Bye, Dr. Tucker." Sam held out his hand. A breeze ruffled his blond hair. "I've enjoyed working for you."

"Thanks, Sam. You've done a great job. I'll send you a recommendation."

The other young men and women stood awkwardly around her for a moment. They had become like family in the few short weeks of working together. Sharing their excited discoveries, mulling over questions, consoling one another at disappointments. There wasn't one of them she didn't like and respect. As if on cue, they began hugging her, murmuring words of appreciation. And then they wandered away like scattered ducklings, driving their dusty cars through the pink grass.

The phone was ringing when Kitt pushed through the turquoise door of her motel room. At the strident jangling, her heart raced into a pinching tightness that caught in her throat. She heaved her leather purse onto the bed and flipped on the light as she hurried across the room.

"Kitt Tucker," she said. The receiver felt clammy in her hand.

"Kitt, how's it going down there?" It was Dave Logan with the Bureau. She berated herself for wishing otherwise, like some schoolgirl with a crush.

"I'm shutting the project down tomorrow. The new site looks great."

"Good job, Kitt. Dr. Dean's had nothing but praise for the way you've handled things."

Kitt felt a sense of satisfaction at Dave's words. She had always been appalled at the normal method by which cemeteries were moved. Usually a relocation contract was awarded to some operator who came in with shovels and backhoes. The graves were transferred swiftly, with no thought for next of kin or archaeological significance.

"Muddy Flats is special. I'm proud of the way we've handled it, Dave," she said. "We've completed everything on time and we've learned several rather interesting things."

"I saw the story Affiliated Press did on you. Nice photo."

Kitt felt a chill creep down her spine. "I didn't know a story had been written yet."

"I've got it right here in the *Journal*. Fellow by the name of Garth Culhane wrote it. Came out in yesterday's paper."

"How did the story sound?"

"Good . . . There's only one thing."

Kitt sat on the chair. Her boots felt heavy. "What's that?"

"Well, it's nothing much. But a man named . . . let's see . . . Oldham. Dr. Frank Oldham—retired history prof at NNMU. He called me yesterday. He tells me this Culhane fellow is trying to track down that skeleton with gold teeth you mentioned a couple of days ago. Dr. Oldham says Culhane claims to be working with you on some kind of project. He says Culhane thinks you may have found Black Dove's grave, and he's requested Dr. Oldham's research notes. What's going on, Kitt?''

Kitt sagged back into her chair. She hadn't been able to reach Dr. Oldham on the phone the day before. Now Garth's bulldog tactics had upset him, and had gotten the Bureau involved as well. Thanks, Garth.

"Don't worry about it, Dave," She began unlacing her boots. "Everything's under control. The skeleton has some interesting similarities to the description of Black Dove. I'm planning to look into it. Culhane insists on following the leads, too. He thinks he's got some kind of story." She paused, wondering what information Garth had chosen to reveal to the public. "Did the article mention the skeleton with the gold teeth?"

"No." A silence was followed by the sound of Dave letting out a long breath. "Kitt, are you planning to work on this research with Culhane?"

"Just during my vacation—"

Three rapid knocks on the door drew Kitt's attention. Garth's figure, tall and shadowy, was outlined against her curtains.

"Hang on just a second, Dave. There's someone at my door." She set the receiver down and headed across the room. Garth's back was to her when she opened the door.

"Moon's out," he said. Turning, he smiled at her. The grin seemed to settle into the pit of her stomach. "Mind if I come in for a minute?"

"I'm on the phone."

"I'll wait." He shouldered past her and eased into the orange vinyl chair by her bed.

"Dave, just don't think twice about this thing." Kitt sat and began working her boot off as she spoke. "There's no problem. I'll be able to wrap it all up quickly."

"Well, what if you had found Black Dove's remains? What ramifications would there be for the Bureau? Would we have to reexcavate that skeleton?"

"No. We've got all the information we could possibly need. Dr. Dean was quite thorough."

"There won't be any problem flooding the site then, will there? I mean a bunch of historians won't put up a huge fuss over this, will they?"

"No, Dave. I'm sure you won't have any problems there."

Garth had propped his boots on her bed again, one foot crossed over the other. He wore a yellow T-shirt with the name of a sports shoe company on it. His fingers were laced over his belt buckle. He twiddled his thumbs slowly while he watched her.

"Kitt, um, I know this is really none of my business." There was another long pause while Dave searched for words. "Dr. Oldham tells me that Garth Culhane is your ex-husband."

Kitt dropped her boot onto the carpet. "That's true."

"Well, we—Sue and I—we're just concerned about you, that's all."

Kitt could picture Dave's pudgy little wife, Sue, hovering in the background.

"See, Dr. Oldham said you'd told him about your marriage a long time ago when you were working together. He remembered the name. Apparently Oldham asked Culhane if he knew you, and he admitted you had been married."

"Please don't worry about it, Dave."

"Kitt, if you need any help down there, or any advice or anything—"

"No, Dave. Really."

"Here, Sue wants to talk to you."

Kitt glanced at Garth. She could see the golden halos in his eyes. He hadn't moved. His long legs stretched out across her bed. His body waited, relaxed but alert. She knew he was listening to the conversation. His face was expressionless.

"Kitt, honey." Sue Logan's sweet, almost childish voice came on the phone. It was hard to connect that voice with her plump, fiftyish body. "Now, you just listen to me for a minute. That man hurt you an awful lot—you told me so that afternoon when I had you over for tea, remember?"

"Yes, Sue. But—"

"Now, you told me he just up and walked out on you barely ten months after you were married. He left you alone in that little trailer with no money and no job. And if it hadn't been for your parents coming along and rescuing you and sending you off to school, you'd have been in real hot water, honey. Now, I know you're a mature woman, Kitt. But we all love you here and we just don't want to see you hurt again. When Dave told me you were working on some kind of a project with that man, my heart just went out to you, honey. Why, you know what this man could do? You loved him so much. He'll play on your sentiments. He'll get you to do whatever he wants—"

"Sue, really—"

"Now, that marriage is over, honey. You've done so well for yourself. Why don't you just come on back to Santa Fe and write your book like you'd planned? We'll go shopping. There's a new exhibit at the folk art museum."

"Sue, listen. Please understand. Everything is all right. Tell Dave that I'll be in Silver City for a couple of days at the end of this week and then I'll be home to write my book. We'll go to the exhibit, okay?"

"Okay." The word was a defeated little sigh. "You've always been stubborn. Kitt, honey... be careful."

"I will."

Kitt hung up the receiver and dropped her other boot onto the floor. "Sue and Dave Logan," she said.

"Sounds like they're worried."

"We're friends as well as colleagues. We've known each other a long time."

"I guess I'm coming off as the bad guy."

"There's still time for you to back out and head for Albuquerque."

"My boss is expecting a follow-up story. Besides, I couldn't let you down like that." His mouth curved into the faintest of grins.

"I didn't realize you'd already done your first article."

"It's just a little piece. I'll do something bigger when I have more on the Black Dove angle."

Kitt realized he wasn't about to back down. Not for an instant. "Dr. Oldham called the Bureau. Dave Logan told me he's suspicious of you."

"You didn't get in touch with Oldham yet?"

"He was out when I called."

Garth shrugged. "Oldham thinks I'm some kind of treasure hunter. He's afraid I'm going to stir up unfounded interest in the story and then looters will start destroying sites."

"Treasure hunter? Why would he call you that?" Kitt rubbed the soles of her feet. There was no treasure involved—unless you could call a couple of gold teeth treasure.

"He said he was afraid I'd think there was treasure and I'd go around digging things up. And then when he found out my name, he put two and two together about us... You seem to have a lot of loyal friends, Kitt."

"I do," she said matter-of-factly. "I place great stock in faithfulness."

The curve went out of Garth's mouth, and he looked at his thumbs. That stung. He knew his presence in her room had brought out the old hurt again. Maybe she was right. Maybe he *should* just head back to Albuquerque.

He lifted his head. She was sitting cross-legged on the hardback chair like a contemplative Buddha. Her dusty boots lay sprawled beneath her. The toes of her socks stuck out from under her thighs.

But this was all part of what he had wanted, wasn't it? That was why he had insisted on working with her on the Black Dove project. If they spent time together, the past was bound to come out. He wanted it out. He wanted a healing. But pain had to come with healing. And some of the pain belonged to him.

"I came over to ask you a question, Kitt," he said.

She watched him from her perch across the room.

"I've spent a lot of time today at the museum. And I've talked with a few people." He uncrossed his boots and crossed them the other way.

"I'd like to go to the site with you tomorrow and talk to old Hod."

"Hod didn't come back."

"I think he'll come tomorrow."

"I ran him off, remember?"

"I put out the word in town that tomorrow was your last day. Hod spends a lot of time roaming around the business district. Especially the local bar. I figure if he really does think you're going to find something out there, he'll go tomorrow."

Kitt dropped her feet to the floor. "Garth, did you really have to go spreading the news around town that tomorrow was the last day? I mean who knows who'll show up? I just wanted to finish out those last three graves and wrap everything up."

He shrugged. "Had to get hold of Hod one way or another. So, can I go out and interview him?"

"Why couldn't you just find out where he lives and go to his house?" She got up and walked to the closet, unbraiding her hair with one hand and loosening her belt with the other.

"Nobody could tell me where he lives. They think he lives out west of town, but no one's ever been there. So, can I come to the site?"

"Persistent, aren't you?" She rifled through her closet and picked out a clean shirt and pants.

"Persistence is a quality I value."

Kitt turned and looked at him. He was smiling again.

"Persistence. Faithfulness. They're pretty much the same thing, aren't they?" He swung his feet off the bed and propped his elbows on his knees.

"No."

"I think they are." He stood and gave a muscle-flexing stretch. "So, are you undressing in front of me because you always used to, and you remember how much I like it? Or are you undressing in front of me because you want to drive me crazy as punishment? Or is it because you finally feel comfortable with me—"

"I'm undressing because I'm getting in the shower."

"You know, I was noticing how really dusty a man gets down here on the desert—"

"Garth." Kitt lifted her eyes to the ceiling. "You can come to the site tomorrow since we're basically finished. I'll put you in charge of running off all the interested citizenry who show up thanks to your townwide broadcast."

"You've got yourself a deal, lady." He moved across the room toward her, his boots catlike on the carpet. He saw her finger stop midway down the long braid. She placed her hands on her hips. He leaned against the frame of the bathroom door, blocking her path. "So, do you think I'll be able to get anything out of old Hod?"

She tilted her head to one side, a wry smile tickling the corners of her mouth. He wasn't going to make any of this easy, was he? She studied his big body for a moment, his shoulders nearly filling the door frame, one hand hanging loosely at his narrow hips. A wisp of sun-gold hair had fallen across his forehead and was brushing the top of one eyebrow. She felt an urge to reach up and tuck it in place.

She glanced down at her half-unbuttoned shirt. He was right, of course. She had begun undressing without even thinking about it. It seemed natural having him in her room, his deep-set eyes watching her as she took off her clothes. That had been one of their pleasures.

"All I've been able to get out of Hod is a lot of rambling nonsense about gold mines and twilight and a tree bent in the shape of an L," she said, keeping her tone light and indifferent. "If Charles Grant thinks Hod's lucid, maybe he is. You'll just have to see for yourself, if he shows up tomorrow."

"I wonder what he thinks you're going to find out there at that cemetery." Garth slipped his palm beneath Kitt's braid. "He doesn't think his father's gold mine is out there. He told you that."

With a gentle tug, he drew her toward him as he spoke. She came, a little hesitantly. It had been so damned hard to stay away from her. For three days he'd listened to her movements through the thin motel wall. He'd watched her leave for church, for meals, for her work. All the time, he'd imagined that she was glad he was leaving her alone, as he'd promised.

Finally, unable to stay away any longer, he had thought up the excuse of asking her permission to visit the cemetery—even though he'd planned to go whether she agreed or not. When he'd knocked on her door, he had been half afraid she wouldn't even want to let him in. But the moment he had seen her face—that look of relief and desire all mixed up in her brown eyes—he had known it was going to be all right.

"Oh, I think Hod's just a curious old man," Kitt was saying. She had jammed her hands into her jean pockets while he fiddled with her braid. "I had quite a few people wander out at the beginning of the dig. Hod was the only one who kept coming around."

"Persistent, huh?" Garth ran his thumb down her hair, loosening the long brown plait. She must have braided it wet after her morning shower. Her hair was all crinkled and wavy, each curl picking up glints of light from the lamp on the table. He sifted it through his fingers, arranging it around her shoulders. His hand trailed lightly down her breast. It was soft and full beneath the cotton fabric of her shirt.

"Garth," she said. Her brown eyes were luminous. "I need to get in the shower."

"Don't let me stop you." He moved slightly to one side.

She knew he wasn't going to leave until he understood her. Until he knew what was on her mind. "You know, I have figured out one thing since you appeared at my door the other night."

"Oh, yeah, what's that?"

"It doesn't matter what happens, because I'm never going to be able to forget our past, Garth." Her voice was soft. "It doesn't matter whether we have long, heart-wrenching talks. It doesn't matter if we have huge fights. It doesn't even matter if we get to be friends. I just...I just can't forget it all. The past has become a part of me. It made me into what I am today." She leaned against the door frame opposite him. "I mean, you can take me on a picnic and wind up kissing me on a bed of pine needles. Or you can come into my room and tease me into actually considering taking a shower with you like we used to."

Garth nodded, his blue eyes shadowed. "I can hear a great big but coming."

"But the truth is—no matter how much we might have loved each other once, and no matter how much we might idly think about the physical side of it—the truth is, the past is always going to be there. And it's more than just that you hurt me or I hurt you. It's that *life* hurt us, you know?"

"Death hurt us."

"Every time I look at you, I remember it all, Garth. You're locked up with that part of my life. The only way I got over it was to erase you."

"Now that I'm back, you feel all the pain again." He ran his fingers down her cheek. "That means you didn't erase me, Kitt. You just put me and the baby on a shelf and chose not to look at us."

Kitt focused on the towels in her bathroom. "I guess I don't know how to erase. I don't know how to forget. And the only way I'm going to get back to being me is when you go and climb on your shelf again where you belong."

Garth stood silently for a moment, watching her fight to compose herself. She looked fragile in the yellow light, and he ached to take her in his arms. Instead, he took both her hands in his and held them loosely. They leaned, their backs against the bathroom door frame, their toes almost touching.

"When I was in Vietnam, I had a lot of time to think it all over, Kitt," he said. His voice was a shade deeper, and it seemed almost to echo from the bathroom tiles. "I knew I could never forget it, either. I knew what happened would always be a part of me, too. I realized that there were two ways I could look at what happened to us. Either we were *meant* to be together—but our parents and our youth and the death of our baby forced us apart. Or we weren't meant to be together in the first place, and we'd just gone along and forced fate off in the wrong direction."

"Which did you decide was right?"

"My brain decided we weren't meant to be together in the first place. It had all been a mistake from the beginning. But the sickness in my heart all those months in Vietnam tried to convince me otherwise. In the end my brain won. I finally accepted that you and I had twisted fate, and had paved our own road to hell. I put you on a shelf, too."

"Well, I guess you were right, then. And so was I. You can't really ever forget the past. Especially when you've blown it as badly as we did. So you just put it away and go on."

"That's what you do."

They looked into each other's eyes. Garth squeezed her hands, his thumbs pressing against her palms. Then he straightened and walked away from her toward the front door. She locked her hands together as she watched him leave. He turned the handle and pulled the door ajar. She turned and started into the bathroom.

"The thing is, Kitt," he said.

"What—" She swung around, a note of unconcealed hope in the word.

"The thing is, I think I was wrong back there in Vietnam." He shrugged and backed out the door. "I think I'm beginning to see that we were meant to be together after all."

The door shut and she was left standing, open-mouthed and open-hearted, in the middle of her motel room.

"Here he comes." Kitt gestured with the tip of a trowel in the direction of the old cottonwood tree.

A battered pickup, minus a windshield and trimmed with rust, rumbled up the dirt road and pulled to a halt. The door creaked open. Old Hod settled his felt hat lower on his forehead and slid to the ground. As he ambled through the grass, Kitt imagined his legs, scrawny and as thin as a sparrow's beneath his wool trousers. He pulled out a yellowed handkerchief, lifted his hat and mopped his forehead.

"He's definitely seen a few years," Garth said.

"Dr. Dean thinks he may be nearly a hundred. I'll try to talk to him."

"Let me. He might think you want to run him off." Garth loped off from the pit Kitt had been excavating since just after sunrise. He had enjoyed the time with her, even though she was quiet and a little restrained. As she worked, she had explained the process of exhuming historical remains, as well as the technical and legal aspects of her work. His appreciation of her skills had deepened. She had even let him dig with her a little, dusting the top of the caved-in coffin lid they had uncovered.

He brushed his palms on his jeans as he approached the old man.

"I ain't leaving." Hod crossed his arms across his chest. He was wheezing from the exertion of his walk. "You tell that Dr. Tucker Miss Priss that I'm here to stay today."

"You can stay. It's all right. She's just finishing up."

The faded blue eyes crinkled with pleasure. "Good." He pushed Garth aside with one hand and tottered forward.

At the lip of the pit where Kitt was working, Hod paused and bent over. "I'm staying."

"That's fine today, Hod." She shaded her eyes from the midday sun. He seemed to be smiling, his few teeth poking askew from his bare gums.

"I'll watch right here." He hunkered at the edge of the crumbling ground and peered down at her back.

Garth knelt beside him. "Dr. Tucker tells me your name is Hod."

"Right."

"Hod . . . Hod what?"

"Ain't that good enough for you?"

"That's good enough for me."

The old face assumed a solemn glaze as Hod watched the lid of the coffin come slowly into view.

"Lived here long, Hod?" Garth asked.

"Long enough."

"I hear you know more about Muddy Flats than just about anyone."

"Who told you that?"

"Charles Grant over at the museum. Says he's a friend of yours."

"Muddy Flats died about the time I was born."

"So you were born here?"

"Not here." Hod scowled, his bushy white brows drawing together. "This here's a cemetery. You don't born babies in a cemetery. No, sir."

"Were you born in Muddy Flats?"

"Over there." Hod pointed west with his chin. "House I still live in."

"Did you know a lot of the people who lived in Muddy Flats?"

"You sure are an all-fire nosy feller." Hod blotted his forehead with the old handkerchief.

"Just curious."

"Curiosity killed the cat."

Garth sighed. Kitt was carefully removing the coffin lid. It had fallen in in the center, as she had told him all the coffins did. There was not much dirt underneath. He could see the top of the skull.

Then Hod surprised him by answering his question. "I did know one citizen of Muddy Flats. My papa. I knew him for ten year before he died. He's the one that showed me the gold mine.''

"I've heard about that gold mine of yours."

"Papa took me up there one fine day," Hod said. He spread his gnarled hand across the sky. "Blue as a robin's egg. Big, rocky mountain. We climbed all day, see. Got there late in the afternoon. My papa said, 'Boy, remember this tree in the shape of an L. Don't you forget it now. I'll write you down the directions.' But, hell, I was just a kid. I went down in the mine with him and saw all the gold. Sure enough—you don't believe me?''

"I believe you."

"Bars on one side. Raw nuggets in saddlebags on the other side. All piled up in a long skinny room of that cave."

"Cave? I thought you said it was a mine."

"I did."

"Well, was it a cave or a mine?"

"It was a cave."

Garth scratched his head. Kitt was picking at the skeleton with her trowel and chopsticks. The skull was completely free of dirt. The bones showed now, too. She dusted a little bit, dug a little bit, then sat on her heels and studied the skeleton.

"But I didn't pay no heed to that mine of my papa's. I just went on playing and fooling around like a boy will do. I was tossing rocks down a hillside and watching them roll along until they hit the bottom. You know how a boy'll do."

"But he left you directions to the place?"

"Not that I could ever find. Papa up and died one day not too long after. He lay there in the field and held my hand and he said to me, 'Boy, I know you'll be all right. You got that gold mine. It's all I got to give you, but it'll keep you rich and healthy all your life.' It was then I realized that I couldn't remember where the mine was, see? And I didn't have no directions. But Papa had passed on."

"So you started searching for the mine?"

"'Course I did. Papa had wanted me to have it. It was all that he had to give me in the world. I wanted to find it again not so much for the gold as for the fact that Papa give it to me. That house and that gold mine. It was all he had to give. I kept the house, but I lost the mine."

A tug of sadness pulled at Garth. He could picture the little boy, holding his father's hand as the old man lay dying. It was plausible that Hod had spent his whole life searching for the lost legacy.

"Didn't your mother remember where the gold was?"

"Mama died when I was born." Hod sniffed and looked away. "Never knew her, myself. Papa told me she was the prettiest damned sight he ever saw. Tiny little ankles. Wide-spaced green eyes. Finished off his roving days right then and there. 'Son,' he told me. 'Find you a good woman like your mama was and don't you never let her go. You hold onto her no matter what troubles come your way.' 'Course I never did find me no woman. I know I never saw my mama in real life, but I got a picture. Weddin' picture of her and my papa. I never knew her, but I loved her all the same."

Garth nodded. For all his rambling, old Hod did sound pretty sane. "Do you remember seeing the smelting furnace down in your papa's mine, or outside on the mountain slope?"

"Smelting furnace? What's that?"

"That would have been where your papa melted out the gold nuggets and formed it into all those gold bars you saw. There would have been a big furnace and piles of cinder slag all around."

Hod pulled at his chin, his blue eyes narrowed. "Nope. No furnace. Papa didn't mine the gold right there in that cave, see. He brung it there. Brung it in on mules. He stashed it there in the cave."

"So it wasn't really a mine after all. It was a cave." Garth felt a twinge of excitement.

"That's what I told you. Why don't you listen, boy?"

"Garth—" Kitt's head appeared over the lip of the pit. "Hand me that screen. Help me do some sifting, would you? I've found the most interesting thing down here."

# Chapter 8

Garth climbed into the pit and handed Kitt the sifting screen. The skeleton was completely exposed now, but he could tell nothing more than that the person had been fairly short.

"Look at this, would you?" She crouched in the dirt at the foot of the grave.

"What is it?"

"Beads! Hundreds of them." She lifted a handful of dirt mixed with shiny, multicolored seed beads. "They're beautiful."

Garth knelt beside her. "What are they made of?"

"Glass, I think." She rolled the beads around in her palm. "They must have been sewn onto her skirt. Can you imagine the work?"

He picked up a few and rubbed the dust away. "I'd guess there are more than a thousand here."

"This is by far the most beautiful thing we've found. And take a look at this."

She crawled over to the spot where the woman's hand had rested on her breast. A gold ring set with an emerald encircled one tiny bone of her left hand. Garth couldn't help feeling that the whole thing was a little morbid. This had been a living, breathing woman once. But Kitt seemed to be concerned only with its archaeological significance.

"This is the most valuable jewelry on the site," she was saying as she carefully picked away the dirt with her chopstick. "Look at the size of her emerald."

"You're sure it was a woman."

"Oh, yes. Look at the facial structure." She paused and gazed at the skeleton for a moment. "She was beautiful. Someone loved her very much to have given her that ring. And her dress must have been costly, too, with all those beads."

Suddenly the detached scientist had evaporated. Kitt's voice was full of melancholy, now. Garth began to realize he'd been mistaken. She brought more than just a trained eye to her work. There was a tenderness, too. A feeling and empathy for who these people had been and what their lives had meant.

"I can't believe she didn't have a headstone," she said softly. "We didn't even realize this grave was here. It was completely unmarked."

"How did you find it?"

"After we excavated all the known graves we did a lot of trenching. We found quite a few unmarked sites. But they were generally the graves of men. By the number of bullets we found in the fill dirt, you could imagine that they were men who had just been passing through Muddy Flats. They'd probably gotten into fights in the saloon, or something, and been shot. Some didn't even have coffins."

She turned to the ring and stroked it for a moment. "But this woman. Someone really cared for her. Look how she was buried with her hands folded over like that. And she has on the prettiest shoes. Not even boots. See, this is patent leather. You can tell they were high-topped shoes with heels."

Garth picked up another handful of beads. "I wonder why she didn't have a headstone."

"Nobody would carve one for her." The voice came from above them at the top of the pit. Kitt and Garth lifted their faces into the late afternoon sun. Hod was gazing at the skeleton, his face lined with sorrow. "She had a wooden cross once. I guess somebody stole it. Or maybe it just rotted away. But nobody would carve the stone for her."

Kitt glanced at Garth. He was staring at the old man. Hod folded his handkerchief and brushed it beneath one eye then the other. He took off his hat and held it in his lap for a minute, turning the brim around and around.

"Hod," Garth said gently. "This grave. Is this...is this—"

"The twilight has come." Hod settled his hat on his head and gingerly rose to his feet. "And now the night will follow."

With that, the old man ambled away.

Garth looked at the skeleton at his feet. A chill prickled up his spine. He felt like he was standing on hallowed ground.

"Did I hear him talking about..." Kitt's words faltered. She knelt on the dirt.

"I have the feeling I should go after Hod," Garth said. He heard the pickup cough to life and begin chugging away into the distance. "I think this is his mother."

The Bureau of Reclamation truck sped down the highway toward Catclaw Draw. Garth stared out the window while Kitt drove in silence. She had handed the excavation assignment to her assistants. Dr. Dean would photograph the remains, then set the skeleton on a tray to measure. Then he would sift the soil to retrieve each and every one of the thousands of seed beads.

"You really think you should have left the site, Kitt?" Garth angled his head toward her.

"I don't think I can go casually digging up the remains of someone's mother and then just leave it at that." Her fingers were wrapped tightly around the steering wheel. If only she'd known that was why Hod had been loitering around the site. She would have spoken with him more seriously; she would have taken his feelings into greater account.

"Well, when you're relocating a historical cemetery, you hardly expect to find a survivor just one generation removed," he said. "I mean, it is a historical site. You would automatically assume that the remains would be those of distant ancestors."

"I should never have assumed anything. Dr. Dean guessed Hod was old enough to have known someone buried in the

Muddy Flats cemetery." She shook her head. "What did Hod tell you about his mother? I was concentrating on the dig."

"He said he never knew her. She died giving birth to him."

Kitt gave him a quick glance, then swallowed. "Dr. Dean will be able to tell us whether the remains fit that description."

"How?" It seemed highly unlikely that much at all could be told from a collection of disjointed bones.

"If the woman died in childbirth, her pelvic girdle will be expanded. Dr. Dean will be able to give us that information. He can also tell us her approximate age, her height, a composite physical description, and her general physical fitness. That should give us a fairly good idea whether she was Hod's mother."

"What are you planning to do when you find Hod, Kitt?" Garth could see the pain etched in her face as she drove. She wasn't just seeing an old man's suffering. She was seeing a young woman giving birth—a young woman with wide-set eyes, a gold and emerald ring on her finger, and a skirt embroidered with a thousand glass beads. She was seeing a tiny baby—alive. A beautiful mother—dead.

"I'm going to talk to him," Kitt said. "I feel I should go over the Bureau's policy again, and I feel I need to make an apology... Hod was acting so strange. All that about the twilight and the gold mine. I'm uncomfortable about the whole thing."

"He told me he still lives in the house where he was born. It's somewhere west of Muddy Flats. Should we try to find it?"

"Let's look for him in town first. He may have gone to see Charles Grant."

"His father died when Hod was ten."

"After showing him the gold mine?"

"Turns out it's not a mine after all. It's a cave. Hod's father brought the gold in on mules and stored it there. There was no smelting furnace or anything. Part of the gold was in bars and part of it was in nuggets."

"So you believe Hod about the gold?" Kitt again glanced at Garth. He was stretched out across the seat, but she could sense the tension in his muscles. His blue-gray eyes scanned the highway.

"I do. I think Hod is telling the story as he remembers it."

Kitt swung the pickup into the museum parking lot. "The question remains how well Hod remembers anything."

Charles Grant stood on the porch, fumbling with keys as he locked the museum. At the sound of the truck, he turned and waved.

"Any sign of old Hod around here, Charles?" she called.

He shook his head. "Try Mi Rincón down on Main. It's the local tavern where he hangs out. Should be there by now."

"Any idea how we could get out to his house if he's not there?"

"What's going on?" Charles headed down the sidewalk toward them.

"He was acting strange at the site," she explained carefully. No need to mention the grave. "I'd feel more comfortable if I could talk with him."

"He lives in an old adobe house out west of town's all I know. Take Prickly Pear Road and head in that direction. You'll probably see his old truck. Need some company?"

"That's okay. Thanks anyway." Kitt gave Charles a little smile before pulling onto the street.

Mi Rincón sat on a shaded lot at the edge of Catclaw Draw. Though it was just after five, cars and trucks already lined the street in front of the small tavern. Sure enough, Hod's old pickup had been badly parked at the side of the bar. Kitt heaved a sigh of relief and glanced at Garth. He gave her a thumbs-up sign and climbed out of the truck.

Curly wrought iron covered the windows of the flat-topped little building. A neon beer sign flickered in one window. A bouquet of faded plastic flowers peeked over the sill of the other. The tavern's name had been painted across the white stucco wall in shades of blue and pink. From inside, the jumbled sound of a poorly recorded mariachi band filtered into the yard. A skinny dog with big brown eyes lounged on the front step.

"Mi Rincón," Garth said softly as they stepped through the door. "My hideaway."

Kitt leaned against a cool white wall for a moment, waiting for her eyes to adjust to the gloom. The smell of heavy Mexican beer mingled with the scent of lemons, cigarette smoke and perfume. A bar lined with patrons stretched from one end of the room to the other. Waitresses in white peasant blouses and flower-embroidered red skirts wandered back and forth chatting with customers, enjoying their work. Two couples danced sinuously in one corner, keeping a beat with the blaring *rancheros* music.

"There he is," Kitt whispered, elbowing Garth in the ribs.

Hod was slouched in a far booth, alone. His hat sat forlornly on the table beside an empty bottle. His eyes were trained on the bottle of beer he was twisting around and around in his palms. Garth and Kitt wound their way among the tables and slid into his booth. He didn't look up.

"Hod," Kitt said softly, leaning across the table. "Hod, it's Dr. Tucker from Muddy Flats."

Hod kept turning his beer bottle.

"Talk louder," Garth whispered, leaning against her.

She cleared her throat and began again. "Hod, it's Dr. Tucker from the Muddy Flats cemetery. Could I talk with you for a moment?"

"She sewed him up, see," Hod mumbled. "Her being a seamstress and all. It was a natural thing."

Kitt glanced at Garth.

"He come into town with that wound, but nobody'd touch him. 'Course they wouldn't. Scared to death of him. Always was. But not her. She wasn't scared. Took him in and sewed him right up."

"Hod—"

"It was her as sewed them beads on the dress. He told me that. I do recollect that. He brung the beads to her, see. As a present for sewing him up. She wouldn't take no payment."

"Are you sure your mother was buried at Muddy Flats, Hod?" Kitt asked.

"Papa buried her, all by hisself. 'Course I forgot where the grave was after somebody stole the wooden cross. Or maybe it rotted away. I forgot just where it was he put her, see. Just like I forgot where the mine was. I do recollect a good many things. But them two things I forgot. I forgot where it was Papa put her, and I forgot where it was he took me that day."

"But you do remember her burial was at the Muddy Flats cemetery?" Kitt wished Hod would at least look at her. The empty bottle on the table attested to the fact that the old man was already pretty well fortified, and it was going to be hard to reach him.

"Only place around in them days was the Muddy Flats cemetery," Hod said. He took another swig of beer. "Muddy Flats town was about gone by then. Papa said she didn't care. Her family took off West and left her without even a fare-thee-well. She didn't care. She was happy with my Papa, see."

"Hod, by tomorrow we should have a fairly good physical description of the woman in the grave. If you'd like, I'll be happy to share that information with you. I want to apologize for not consulting you more closely in this situation. If you'd mentioned that your mother was buried in the cemetery, I'm sure the Bureau—"

"She loved him in spite of everything," Hod said. He shook his head. "Oh, Papa told me they had their hardships all right. Him so old and her just a girl, really. Him a stranger and her a hometown gal. Her family disowned her, see. Booted her straight out of the house. But she and my papa got married anyway, so it was all right."

Garth studied Kitt's face as she listened to Hod ramble. Her brown eyes had gone deep, shadowy. She slid from her place beside Garth and slipped in next to Hod. Her braid fell over her shoulder as she took the old man's hands.

"Hod, I'm having new headstones carved right now in Carlsbad. The ones for the unmarked graves will read, Unknown. But if we can show that the woman in the grave is your mother, I'll be more than happy to have her name inscribed. And if you have any more information as to her birth date—"

"I was borned—" Hod took another swig "—out in that big house. Papa told me he done everything he knew how to do for her. She was just a tiny little thing, see. Like a little bird. Not near big enough to have a baby. I guess I killed her."

"No, Hod." Kitt squeezed the old man's hands. "You didn't kill her. It wasn't your fault that she died."

She felt strange and detached suddenly. The music seemed to be pounding in her head. Garth reached out and touched her arm. Hod sank down in the seat, his body heavy against hers.

"If I could have found that gold, see, I'd have been okay. It was my Papa's gold that he brung with him when he come to Muddy Flats. He had it when he met my Mama. He was going to take care of her. But she died. And then he died, see. And I forgot where everything was."

Hod set his hands on top of Garth's and the three of them sat there, hands clasped across the narrow table, waiting, listening. The mariachi record ended and a country-western band started up. More people filtered into the bar, men in straw cowboy hats, women in tight jeans. The sky outside the iron-barred window had darkened to cobalt.

"I do think—" Hod began speaking again "—we could carve her a headstone... 'Sweet intercessor 'twixt God and man, gone on wings to plead for us there.'" He hung his head and sighed. "Papa always wanted one for her. 'Course he never had one neither. I never knew where exactly they buried my papa. They took me away. Gave me to some family in Carlsbad to raise me. But I come back to our house, see. As soon as I could get away, I come back to our home. I ain't never been gone again—'cept to look for the gold mine."

Hod's head swayed as he spoke, finally coming to rest on Kitt's shoulder. He closed his eyes. She gazed down at the wreath of wrinkles lining his face. His eyelashes were white. The yellowed handkerchief lay on his lap, forgotten.

"Kitt." Garth whispered her name. She lifted her eyes. Their three hands, stacked cuplike, still lay on the table, Hod's on top. "Is he all right?"

"She sewed him up, see," Hod mumbled. "She was a seamstress."

"I think he's passing out..." She looked around the tavern. One of the waitresses was leaning against a pole, smiling at the three in the booth. Kitt smiled back, a little uncertainly. Black-haired and buxom, the woman lifted her shoulders from the pole and sauntered across the room.

"Drunk?" she asked.

Kitt shrugged. "I think he may be asleep."

"He's drunk." She grinned and clucked her tongue. "Every night, same thing. Two beers and he's out. We usually drag him to the couch over there and let him sleep it off. He gets up sometime in the night when he's sober again and drives home. You want I should call Juan?"

"No," Garth said. "We'll take him home."

"You friends of his?"

"Sort of. He comes here every night then?"

"Every night, regular as clockwork. Sits right in that booth. Reads the newspaper. Drinks two beers. Falls over on the table and we drag him to the couch. He's too old to be drinking, you know. And you should get his windshield fixed, if you're his friends. He's too old to be driving a truck like that."

"How old do you think he is?" Kitt asked quietly. Hod was snoring softly against her shoulder.

"He's over a hundred. We have him a party every year around Christmastime. Let's see . . . I think he told us he was a hundred and five last Christmas. But with Hod, hell, you can't be sure. Everybody likes the old guy, you know. He's kind of cute. But he tells some stories—I mean some real stories. So, how you know old Hod?"

"I met him out at the Muddy Flats cemetery," Kitt explained. "I'm relocating the graves there."

"No kidding? I heard about you. So, you want a beer or what? We got margaritas and everything. You name it."

"No, thanks. We'll just take Hod home. Any idea how to get out to his place?"

"Hell, nobody ever goes out there. Everybody thinks it's kind of haunted, you know. Like ghosts and everything. The stories that old guy tells—I mean like his papa was some kind of traveler who married this young seamstress and when she died he went crazy with grief. It's like everybody Hod knew died some strange way or something. But he just keeps on living and living." She leaned down close to Garth. "Hod says he's not allowed to die until he finds his papa's gold mine. You ever heard that one, huh? He ever tell you that story?"

"Not that one."

The waitress threw back her head and laughed. "I guess he's gonna go on living forever. Because he sure ain't having much luck finding that gold mine of his papa's." She shook her head and chuckled again. "So, you sure I can't bring you a drink? We got nachos, too. With jalapeños."

Hod slept on Kitt's lap while she drove through the darkness, west toward the last remnants of sunset. Garth followed in Hod's truck, eating her dust through the open windshield. Prickly Pear Road dwindled into nothing more than a rutted track. Thick dry grass swished against the sides of the Bureau pickup. A barn owl lifted into flight from a fence post.

Kitt followed the trail until it came to a fork. Guessing the more traveled ruts might indicate the way to Hod's home, she turned south. Before long the silhouette of a flat-roofed adobe house appeared like a wraith out of the darkness. No lights shone, and she might have driven past it but for the moonlight glinting on the glass pane of a window.

As the two trucks pulled up in front of the house, Kitt realized it was much larger than she had at first imagined. A long wooden porch wrapped around it on three sides, and it seemed to ramble on and on in a disorganized fashion as though no one had thought it through before building it. Grass had grown up all around. A honeysuckle vine hung over the steps, nearly cutting off the entrance to the porch.

"I'll carry him," Garth whispered, appearing at Kitt's side. She slid out and he gently eased Hod into his arms. "He's as light as a feather. I bet he doesn't weigh much over a hundred pounds."

Hod snuggled up against Garth's broad chest, burying his cheek in the corner of the younger man's arm. Kitt pulled the honeysuckle to one side and Garth bent low as he stepped onto the porch. Two old rocking chairs sat on either side of the open front door.

"See if there's a light," Garth said.

Kitt ran her hand over the rough adobe wall in the entry hall of the old house. There was no switch. But she did find an oil lamp and a book of matches sitting on a pine table beside the door. The lighted room revealed a long, flagstone-floored hallway, lined on either side with stacks and stacks of newspapers and old books.

"This place is a fire waiting to happen," Garth murmured as he carried Hod down the hall. "Take a look at this living room, Kitt."

Holding the lamp aloft, she sidestepped between the rows. The living room was a portrait of chaos. An old ruby velvet couch, an upright piano, an elaborate étagère, and two dusty chairs were half buried in pile upon pile of faded, yellowing newspapers. Maps lay in heaps like old wood shavings. Books formed mountains on the floor. The one bookcase in the room had been completely buried, as though someone kept trying to put books on the shelves even after there were no more shelves in sight.

"I'll bet there's some really valuable old stuff in here," she said. Garth nodded, his eyes appraising the old newspapers. "Come on, I'll help you find the bedroom."

They passed room after room in the sprawling house, and each was filled almost to bursting with reading matter. Kitt saw at once that Hod's home was valuable for more than just the materials he had collected over the years. The furniture belonged to another era—and though covered with dust and cobwebs, it appeared to be in fine condition. Beautiful dishes lined the kitchen cabinets. Tea sets etched with gold. Darkened silverware. Creamy white pottery. But then there were newspapers stacked in the sink, and only one leg of the table was visible beneath another mountain of paper.

The bedroom, oddly enough, was neat as a pin. A massive brass bed stood at one end, weighting down a pink and red flowered hooked rug. Tables lined with old photographs in silver frames marched along the walls. In one corner, a vanity with flower-printed drapes seemed to be waiting, untouched. Silver-backed combs and brushes and mirrors had been artfully arranged. Perfume decanters and atomizers—their contents long evaporated—sat in two tidy rows.

"Do you suppose this is his room?" Garth asked, as he settled Hod on the intricately patterned quilt. "It looks more like some kind of a shrine."

"I think he sleeps here. Look, his clothes are in this wardrobe. But he obviously does most of his living in the rest of the house."

"Obviously." Garth studied Kitt as she wandered mesmerized around the room. She looked like some sort of a ghost herself, with that lamp. She drifted over to where Hod lay slumbering peacefully on the bed. Kneeling, she set the lamp on a table and began unlacing his worn leather shoes. She pulled them off and placed them side by side, their heels just even with the side of the bed. Then she loosened Hod's collar and drew two old quilts over him.

"Let's look around," Garth said.

"Maybe we shouldn't. This is his home, Garth. I feel like I'm trespassing."

"Come on, Kitt. You're letting sentiment take over your professional curiosity. I want to see how old some of these newspapers are."

Kitt nodded, her eyes still on the old man. "Look how the wrinkles on his face have sort of relaxed and smoothed out. He seems younger now." She reached out and stroked the lock of white hair on his forehead. He was beautiful, in an odd way. A living link with the past, with a time long gone.

He had been born in another century, and in a strange way he had held onto his past—a house with no electricity, probably no plumbing. A house filled to the brim with the passage of time, with records of the first automobiles, of the first washing machines, of electric typewriters, of men walking on the moon. He had lived through four American wars, a depression, flappers and hippies . . . it was hard to imagine the rapid changes the old man must have witnessed.

Garth had lit another lamp. Kitt could see lights and shadows through the doorway as he wandered from room to room. She felt connected, somehow, as though in the tavern with their hands laced together, she and Garth and Hod had formed a sort of bond.

Picking up the lamp by the bed, she walked slowly around the room, gazing into the faces of Hod's past. There were old lithographs, daguerreotypes, faded photographs. No children. Only adults—women in long white dresses with leg-of-mutton sleeves, men in starched white collars and checkered suits. Who were they?

Kitt turned the frames over, looking for inscriptions. Those she found shed no light on their identities. They were written in black ink, in a beautiful, feminine hand. "Aunt Rose in the garden." "Cousin Sylvia having tea with Catherine." "Anna Emaline's twenty-first birthday." "Uncle Andrew outside his new law office."

"Kitt, come here!" Garth appeared in the doorway. He had on a silk top hat and a flowing black wool cape. He looked like a phantom.

"What are you doing in that outfit?"

"Come here and take a look at what I've found. It's an anthropologist's dream!"

He vanished with a swirl of black rustling fabric. Kitt grinned and glanced down at the frame in her hand. It was a small picture, tinged with the sepia tones of an old daguerreotype. Kitt held it close to the lamp.

A small-framed woman with beautiful deep-set eyes stood beside an old man in a chair. One hand, slender and pale, rested on his shoulder. Oddly, the man and woman were smiling—almost unheard of in these old, stern photographs. It was as if they had pulled off some sort of grand joke. Kitt studied the writing at the bottom of the picture. The words had been printed in a different hand—bold and masculine.

"Wedding day," it read. "August 13, 1876."

"Kitt—are you coming?" Garth poked his head in the room.

"I found a wedding picture," she said. "But it looks like a father and daughter."

"Maybe it is."

"Didn't Hod say his mother was young but his father was old when they married?"

"Yes."

She set the photograph on the table. The woman might be Hod's mother. She would have to contact Dr. Dean about the results of his tests—he might even want to take a look at the picture. She glanced up. Garth had disappeared again.

"Where are you?"

"Down here."

She headed for a pool of lamplight at the far end of the hall. When she stepped inside the room, she caught her breath. Looking like a boy who has just discovered Santa's workshop, Garth sat amid stacks of of antique clothing, utensils, books, furniture, trunks.

"You won't believe this stuff!" he said with a laugh. "It's enough to fill a small museum. And the quality—I mean this is really fine furniture. Take a look at this dress."

He held up a gown of turquoise silk, heavily embroidered and encrusted with tiny silver beads. He shook it a little, and a fine powdery dust cloud drifted out and settled onto his lap.

"Hod must have moved most of the house's contents in here as his piles of newspapers grew." Kitt waded into the room. She felt like she was walking into someone's private treasure trove. A huge buckled trunk stood in one corner. She stepped over the stack of framed photographs that Garth was sifting through. The trunk's leather straps had deteriorated, but she gently unbuckled its heavy green lid.

"Oh, Garth," she said in a whisper. The trunk had been filled with women's clothing—beautiful dresses and skirts, artfully embroidered chemises, delicate cotton petticoats. Each was tied with a blue ribbon. A scrap of paper had been pinned to the ribbon. "Mrs. Samuel Whiting," one read. "Eliza Morgan." "Nellie Wirth."

"This was her sewing trunk, Garth," she murmured. "These were her customer's names. Look at all the different colors of threads in the bottom. And here's a pattern she made out of a butcher paper. Oh, Garth—here are her scissors."

Kitt held up the tiny silver sewing scissors molded in the shape of a stork. "I think we should go home, Garth. These are Hod's things."

He nodded. "I'll tell Charles Grant about it. He might want to talk to Hod. It's a shame to let everything just deteriorate like it is."

Kitt carefully buckled the trunk and moved to kneel at Garth's side. "I wish there were something we could do for Hod. He seems so alone."

"We could look for his gold mine."

"He's been looking for ninety years. I doubt we'd find it—even if it does exist."

"He could die in peace if we found his gold for him."

"You really believe everything, don't you? The gold, the stories he tells."

Garth's blue-gray eyes fastened on Kitt. He took her hand and settled her shoulder against his chest. "I guess I'm just a fool for love," he said. His voice was almost inaudible. "A man and a woman battling the ostracism of society. Building a home of their own. A dream home, filled with nooks and crannies and the little knickknacks of their lives. Creating a child..."

They sat in the silence of the cluttered room, neither speaking. Kitt studied the folds of the black silk cape draped across Garth's thigh. His fingers lay on her arm, tracing a little circle around and around. It was as though they had stepped into a timeless place where the past had become the present. Everything seemed certain and right. Old Hod asleep down the hall. Garth holding her. She nestled against him, where she belonged.

He picked up an oversize ostrich feather hat lying at his knee. It was fashioned of black velvet with huge white plumes circling the brim. With a smile, he settled the hat on her head.

"Feels good in here," he said quietly. "Kind of makes me forget about computers and fax machines and wars and people running amok in post offices or fast food restaurants shooting everyone in sight. Although I guess the old days had their own worries." He gave a little laugh. "Look at this fellow here. I wouldn't want to run into him."

He pulled a silver-framed daguerreotype from the pile on the floor. It was of a man with arms crossed over his chest in a pose of supreme confidence and defiance. Face turned slightly to one side, he stared at the world with beady-eyed malevolence.

Kitt shuddered slightly. "Not in a dark alley, anyway. Those eyes—if looks could kill... Look, someone's scratched his name down here at the bottom." She lifted the lamp from the floor and held it close to the picture.

Garth bent close, trying to make out the swirling hand. "Don Santiago Querque, it says. He doesn't look Spanish to me."

"He's not." Kitt turned to Garth. Her mouth felt dry. "Don Santiago Querque was the name his men gave James Kirker, the white scalp hunter. Black Dove's boss. The scourge of the Apaches. The king of New Mexico."

# Chapter 9

"Why would Hod have a picture of James Kirker?" Garth voiced the question they were both wondering about.

"Well, there are an awful lot of pictures in this house. More than you'd think for the historical period."

"The Kirker picture is just piled in with the rest of these frames, as though it weren't important."

"Maybe it wasn't. Maybe someone in Hod's family collected daguerreotypes—sort of a hobby." Kitt turned the frame over and over. "But all the pictures in the bedroom were inscribed by the same hand. It's as if the owner knew the subject in each frame."

"Maybe Hod's father was a photographer by trade. An itinerant photographer. Maybe that's why he was traveling through Muddy Flats."

"With a wound so bad he needed sewing up? Photographers don't usually get shot at or stabbed."

"Good point. Well, maybe Hod's mother collected the pictures. But why would she have one of James Kirker?"

"Back to square one. Kirker *was* famous in early New Mexico. But this is obviously a one-of-a-kind shot. I mean, James Kirker wasn't the sort of person who was going to appear on postcards that you'd send your Aunt Sally. This is a daguerreotype. Kirker must have sat for it somewhere and it ended up in this collection. But how?"

"And why?" Garth reached up and fingered one of the white plumes on her hat. "Doesn't it strike you as a little weird that we've been talking about this Black Dove and wondering whether he's buried in Muddy Flats—and then his boss's picture shows up in this old house?"

"A little weird, yes. But there could be a very simple explanation for it. We'll just have ask Hod."

"Not tonight."

"No." She smiled. "It's going to be awkward talking to him about this, you know."

"No problem. We'll just say, 'Oh, by the way, Hod, we brought you home the other night and decided to go poking through all your old stuff while you were asleep. We opened your trunks and put on your ancestors' clothes. That was right after we dug up your mother's grave.'"

"Garth, that's not funny."

"No, it isn't. Hod's whole situation is really pretty sad. Let's go on back to the hotel. I need to get an early start for Carlsbad in the morning."

He turned to Kitt. She was aware of him suddenly, as if the room and their invasion of it had faded. His eyes were shadowed, deep-set in the lamplight. She could imagine him living in Kirker's time—his body was tough and lean, as though made for driving cattle across windswept plains. He could have done it, too. He had practically lived on a horse when he was young. The honed, taut musculature had stayed with him. Even his face, it seemed, had been carved by the wind into sharp angles and rugged planes.

Her eyes traced the contours of his features. His lips, straight and masculine, moved with an almost honeyed sensuality when he spoke. His eyelashes were tipped with a gold that seemed to reflect the halo circling their blue-gray centers.

"Don't look at me that way, Kitt." His voice had dropped to a whisper.

She glanced at her hands. It had felt natural to study him, as she always had. She hadn't even realized she was doing it. Uncomfortable, she took off the hat and set it on the floor. She got to her feet and started for the door without speaking. In the hall, she leaned against the cool wall and closed her eyes. She could hear the sounds of his movements as he straightened the room—trunks shutting, picture frames sliding across each other, dresses rustling. And then there was a new sound—slow, hollow music.

Curious, she retraced her steps and peered inside. His back was to her as he thumbed through a pile of shiny black records stacked beside a battered upright phonograph. She didn't recognize the song, but it clearly belonged to a forgotten time when big bands played lazy, melodic music.

"It's a Victrola," he said, turning to face her. He still wore the cape and top hat. "Care to dance, Miss Kitty?"

"Oh, Garth." She found herself grinning. "We've got to be going. Come on."

He waded through the jumble of furniture toward her. Along the way, he picked up the ostrich feather hat. "One dance?" he asked.

Without waiting for an answer, he settled the hat onto her head and pulled her into his arms. Unable to move much around the trunks and scattered items, they simply turned in circles to the lilting music. Kitt felt Garth's hand slip to her waist, his thighs brush hers. Neither spoke, but their eyes met and locked as they moved through their slow-motion dance.

One part of her wanted to reject it all—the unreal aura of the room, the unexpected warmth of Garth Culhane, the strange turn her life had suddenly taken. And yet she continued to dance with him, letting it happen, putting aside sane, rational arguments and welcoming the misty, pulsing magic of the moment.

They spun and Garth drew her closer. His lips touched the side of her neck. Her fingers found the soft curls at his collar. More of the frozen block inside her began to melt, and she felt a liquid fire flow down to her knees and make them weak. She put her cheek on his shoulder, breathing in the scent of his skin. With her eyes closed, she absorbed the smells of him...laundered cotton, fresh air, suntanned skin, a trace of dust from the day's work, another trace of spice...

"Mama?"

Kitt stiffened and she focused on the room. Hod stood in the doorway, his clothing and hair rumpled from sleep, his head tilted down in confusion.

"Mama, is that you?" he asked, his voice timid and confused like that of a little child awakened from a deep sleep.

"Oh, Hod. No, it's just—"

"Papa?" Hod rubbed his eyes. "I can't find it anywhere, Papa."

"What have you lost, Hod?" Garth spoke gently, as if he were talking to a small boy.

"I've lost the gold mine, Papa. I've looked and looked, but I just can't find it."

Garth took Kitt's hands as he walked toward the old man. "It's okay, Hod. You don't have to find the gold mine anymore. You can stop looking now."

"Are you sure, Papa?"

"I'm sure, Hod."

Hod rubbed his eyes again and started to cry. "Papa, where did you bury Mama? I forgot that, too."

"Come, Hod. Let's put you to bed," Kitt said softly.

The three of them padded slowly down the hall, Garth and Kitt supporting Hod between them. He continued to sniffle, dragging his feet like a tired toddler who wasn't sure where he was. Kitt settled him onto the bed, and Garth drew the quilt over his shoulders.

"We'll be going now, Hod." Garth bent and kissed him gently on the cheek. "Good night."

"Good night, Papa." Hod closed his eyes and yawned. "Good night, Mama."

An envelope had been taped to Kitt's motel door. She tugged it free and flipped open the letter inside. The light over the door cast a yellow glow on the paper.

"It's from Dr. Dean," she said. Garth shoved his hands into his pockets. He stood in the darkness, just beyond the ring of yellow light.

"What does it say?"

"It's the results of his examination on that skeleton. The one with the beads. A woman, he says. Petite—around five feet tall. Age eighteen to twenty-one. Probably very pretty with wide-spaced eyes and high cheekbones. She had a delicate nose, and a small gap between her two front teeth. Found in the grave: approximately fifteen hundred beads, high-topped patent leather shoes, small brooch at neck, eight matching buttons." Kit glanced at Garth. "It was very rare that all the buttons matched."

He nodded.

"It says she had a gold and emerald ring on the third finger of her left hand." Kit read the words in silence then looked up.

"What is it, Kitt?" He moved into the circle of light.

"It says her pelvic measurements indicate she would have been unable to successfully bear a child—and that her pelvic girdle was separated at the time of death. Possible cause of death, childbirth."

Garth leaned against the motel wall and studied his shoes. The flicker of neon from the motel sign turned them red, then yellow, then red again. He knew what he wanted to ask, but he wasn't sure Kitt was ready. She was looking fragile again, despite her boyish button-fly jeans and rugged leather work boots. It was as if the ostrich feather hat had transformed her into one of those pale, genteel Victorian women who fainted easily and needed lots of tender care.

The image wasn't accurate, of course. Kitt was still tough and rational. But since he had come back into her life, he had watched her slowly change. The hardened facade she had worn at the beginning had begun to bend and sometimes lift. He wondered what the softening of Kitt Tucker would lead to—and he wasn't certain he was willing to be the cause of the disintegration of her hard-won veneer.

Still, if they were going to work together and solve the riddle—more important, if they were going to resolve their past—they would have to take some painful steps.

"Kitt," he ventured. She looked up from the letter, her brown eyes fathomless. "If the woman's pelvic girdle was too small, and if she did conceive and attempt to bear a child, and if she died in childbirth—wouldn't the child have died, too? Wouldn't the child have died . . . have died inside her? I mean, it doesn't make sense that Hod could be her son."

Kitt's shoulders were rigid as she thought. "Unless somebody removed the baby immediately after the mother died," she said evenly. "I suppose Hod's father could have performed a sort of Caesarean section after he was certain his wife had passed away. It would have been a real act of courage."

"And love."

They both stood in silence, thinking about life and death. Garth watched his shoes change color. But he wasn't seeing his tennis shoes. He was seeing Kitt, sitting on that brown-and-gold checkered couch in their little trailer.

"Garth," she was saying, "I haven't been feeling the baby move lately." She was sitting there in that white shirt of his, her stomach spread out almost to her knees and a look of panic in her eyes. "I think we should go to the doctor," she was saying.

And then another picture formed. Kitt was lying on the doctor's steel table, her arm over her eyes while the doctor listened to her stomach with the stethoscope. Her long brown hair had draped over the edge of the table and spilled almost to the floor. The doctor was looking at them with sad gray eyes and saying, "I can't hear a heartbeat, Mrs. Culhane. We'll need to run some tests, but I'm afraid . . ."

"Good night, Garth." Kitt took hold of the doorknob. "I'll see you Friday afternoon."

"Kitt—" He reached for her. She slipped past him into her room and shut the door behind her.

Nobody actually lived at Santa Rita. The town itself had been razed nearly twenty years earlier to make way for the mile-wide, thousand-foot-deep open-pit copper mine. Friday afternoon and evening, Garth and Kitt drove from the southeast corner of New Mexico to the southwest corner, with plans to stay in Silver City.

Needing both cars so they could go their separate ways after the trip, Kitt followed Garth's gray compact car in the Bureau of Reclamation pickup. They climbed through the Sacramento Mountains to Alamogordo. They skirted the White Sands National Monument with its vast stretch of crystalline gypsum sands, climbed the southern end of the San Andres Mountains and ate dinner in Las Cruces. Late at night they continued west, passing the little town of Deming and the

City of Rocks State Park until their two-car caravan pulled into a motel in Silver City in the Mogollon Mountains.

It had been a long while to drive alone, but Kitt felt a certain relief to have the time to think. Her last three days in Catclaw Draw had been packed with work from sunup until late in the night. She had filled out all the necessary government forms to complete the project; checked twice on the monuments in Carlsbad; gone over all the notes with Dr. Dean before seeing him off at the airport; and finally she had worked hours writing up a preliminary report on the findings at the Muddy Flats cemetery.

She would have to stop back through Catclaw Draw after her vacation to make sure the monuments were set up properly and that the final details were taken care of. But the project was all but complete, and she was able to leave Catclaw Draw with a sense of satisfaction.

She had seen nothing of Hod since the night at his home. Garth had not called, even though he had been only a twenty-minute drive to the south. She felt thankful for the respite from both of them.

One evening she had finally reached Dr. Oldham and explained the situation to him. Though skeptical, he had agreed to send the notes from his research to her address in Santa Fe. He speculated that the Muddy Flats skeleton belonged to another man entirely, and that certainly more than one person could fit the description of an Indian with two gold teeth.

Dr. Oldham's familiar voice, his stalwart logic and his reasonable doubts made Kitt wonder all over again what she was doing driving to Santa Rita behind Garth Culhane. Like Dave and Sue Logan, Dr. Oldham expressed loving concern for her well-being.

The more she thought about it, the more she felt sure she had been carried away on a wave of emotionalism. From the moment she had seen Garth, she had done any number of uncharacteristically flighty things—trailing an old man into a bar, dancing in the street, trespassing on someone's property and looking through his personal possessions, kissing her ex-husband in a pile of pine needles.

She wasn't behaving at all like Dr. Kitt Tucker, head anthropologist-archaeologist for the federal Bureau of Reclamation in the tri-state area. Time to get with the program, Kitt.

"Smell that fresh air!" Garth stretched his arms as Kitt climbed out of the truck.

She shouldered her purse and passed him with a smile, unwilling to let herself be taken in by the sight of his biceps bunching beneath the green cotton T-shirt he had on. He tucked the shirt back into his jeans and followed her into the office.

"Two rooms," she said to the sleepy-looking clerk. "Tucker and Culhane. I reserved them three days ago by phone from Catclaw Draw."

The old man scratched his head and ran his finger down the list of registrations. "Who'd you talk to? Me?"

"I don't know. It was a male voice."

"Probably Gene. Damn. He's only put you down for one room. It's under the name Culhane."

Kitt felt Garth brush up behind her and lean over her shoulder. "Problems?"

"They've only reserved one room."

"That's okay by me."

"Of course it's okay by you. It's reserved under your name," she said wryly. "But I intend to have a room of my own."

The clerk glanced from one to the other. "You don't want to stay together?"

"It'd be fine with me," Garth said.

Kitt observed the grin tilting up the corners of his mouth. He was enjoying this. "No. We need separate rooms," she explained.

"I think I got some vacancies. Let me see... Okay, no problem." He wrote her name beside the number of an empty room. "That Gene. I gotta talk to that boy. He's always doing this to me."

In a few minutes they had registered and settled into separate rooms. As Kitt climbed into bed, she realized she was listening for the murmur of Garth's television, the hiss of his shower, the thump of his headboard against the wall. But

Garth and his comforting sounds were in a distant room, across the empty expanse of the motel swimming pool.

As Kitt knocked on Garth's door, the sun peeked over the edge of the motel roof. The scent of mountain pine, piñon and juniper hung in the crisp morning air. She waited a moment and knocked again. The door opened. Garth smiled at her. He was wearing only a white motel towel wrapped around his waist. The dark hair that swathed his broad chest glistened with beads of water.

"I thought this was your vacation," he said, widening the gap in the doorway. "You used to sleep till noon on Saturdays."

She stepped past him into his room. "I guess a person can change a few habits in fifteen years."

He shut the door and padded across the room to the bathroom. His bare feet made damp indentations in the carpet. Taking a towel from the stack held by stainless steel rings, he rubbed his hair. In the mirror, he watched Kitt glance from the rumpled bed to the single chair piled high with his bags. Gingerly, she settled on the edge of the bed.

"I bet you'd sleep till noon if you could ever learn to relax," he said.

"I'm relaxed." Her bottom barely met the edge of the bed. Her back was ramrod straight.

A subtle smile stole across his lips. "So, Kitt. How'd you sleep?"

"Fine." She glanced at his back. His shoulders formed the top of an upside down triangle that ended with his narrow waist and tight buttocks. She could tell they were damp beneath the white towel.

"I don't know. My bed seemed a little lumpy." He walked across the room and sat beside her. His weight caused her to slip and she was forced to ease her hips onto the bed. Aware of his wet shoulder against hers, his taut thigh pressing hard against her leg, she knitted her fingers.

"My bed was fine."

"Not lumpy?"

"No."

"Feel this." He leaned back on the bed and ran his hand across the sheet. "There's a big lump right here."

Kitt turned, her eyes grazing the coarse masculine hair that covered his thighs and calves. She stroked the sheet with one palm and shook her head. "I don't feel a thing."

"Guess I'm just like the prince who slept on a pea that nobody else could feel."

"It was a princess who slept on a pea."

"The same princess who let her long hair down from that tower so the prince could climb up?" He lifted the swath of brown hair that had fallen over her shoulder. Putting his nose into it, he took a deep breath.

"That was a different princess. You're thinking of Rapunzel."

He looked into her eyes. "That's not what I'm thinking of."

She met his gaze. She knew what he was thinking about. His masculinity was oozing out of every pore. She could feel his muscles ready to spring, pantherlike. He reminded her of a wild caveman. His tousled, damp hair curled on the ends. His jaw bore a dark unshaven shadow that she knew would be raspy to the touch. With a bearskin instead of a white motel towel, he might have made the perfect Neanderthal—and she almost wished he were. A primitive male cave dweller probably would be easier to handle than a half-naked, damp-skinned Garth Culhane.

"What are you smiling about?" he asked.

"Just picturing you in a bearskin."

"Oh, yeah? Care to elaborate?" He hooked the handle of his bag with a bare foot and dragged it across the floor. Rummaging around, he came up with a wood-handled brush and began running it through the tangle of curls on his head.

"You were talking about Rapunzel and everything, and it occurred to me that you look more like a Neanderthal than a prince right now."

"So how do you feel about Neanderthals?"

"I don't feel one way or the other about them."

"Are you sure about that?"

"I'm sure."

"You mean you don't want to be dragged around by your hair?" He pulled the wooden brush through her hair from her ear to her waist. The bristles stroked her chin, over the crest of her breast and dipped to her thigh.

"No, I don't want to be dragged around by my hair."

"Because I'm sure I could accommodate that fantasy."

"I'm sure you could."

"What about a prince? You ever wanted a prince, wooing you from one knee?" He slid to the floor and knelt at her feet. As he spoke, he drew her hair over her shoulders and ran the brush through it. Again and again, down her chest, over her breasts, stopping at her thigh. "I think I could be a prince, if that's what you wanted. Or maybe you've always dreamed of a cowboy. That's what I used to think when I was a kid. I thought you wanted a cowboy and that's why you fell in love with me."

"Garth, get up off that floor."

"You did fall in love with me, you know."

"Would you get dressed?" She felt unbalanced again. And it was all due to this man kneeling at her feet, running a brush through her hair. She could feel every shaft on her head tingling as the brush pulled each individual hair down and down. Every bristle pressed the skin through her blouse.

"You know what I was thinking about, Kitt?"

"What."

"Remember how we used to take showers together in the old days? Remember how small the shower was in our little trailer and we'd get in there together, both of us barely fitting. And then you'd get the soap and rub it all over my back and my chest. Then you'd hand the soap to me and I'd rub it across your shoulders and down to your waist."

With the brush, he drew gentle circles first around the tip of one breast and then the other as he spoke. Her hair tangled in the bristles. Her eyelids felt heavy, her lips moist.

"I do remember that," she said, her voice sounding far too low in her ears.

"Remember the time we turned out the lights in the bathroom and took a shower in the dark? There was nothing but your soapy body and mine, all curves and muscle and the sweet smells of our loving mingling in with the sound of the running water."

"Garth." Kitt ran one finger down his neck and over the hard hill of his shoulder. "You're breaking the rules, you know."

"I don't see how you can say that, Kitt. I'm not breaking any rules. This brush, maybe. I mean, this brush just seems to have a mind of its own. Look at the way it keeps circling around and around. You're just about to come right out of that skimpy little bra you have on."

Kitt gave a slight smirk.

"You do have on one of those little bras, don't you, Kitt? I'd better check." He reached for the top button of her blouse.

"What are you now—the underwear inspector?"

"Kitt!" He looked at her with mock surprise. "You have fantasies of the underwear inspector? You do have a vivid imagination."

"*You* made up the prince and the cowboy—"

"You made up the caveman." He unfastened the last button. "Actually, I like reality a lot better than fantasy."

"I'm a reality woman myself." She watched his long fingers part the edges of her blouse and heard the audible intake of his breath as he confirmed she was not wearing a bra. Her nipples seemed to swell and tighten beneath his gaze. Rosy and flushed from the strokes of his brush, they tingled with a life of their own.

She shook them slightly and sat forward, bringing her breasts almost directly in line with his mouth. "Don't break any rule now, Garth." Her voice held a note of teasing, and it felt good to turn the tables on him.

"Damn." He shook his head. Slowly he leaned toward her and opened his mouth, covering but not touching one nipple. He breathed warm air over her skin. She shivered. Then he cupped the other nipple and warmed it with his breath. Kitt arched forward, willing him to take her between his lips. Her thighs parted and she felt his chest slide between them.

He paused and stiffened, as if remembering something.

"We're never going to get to Santa Rita by nine o'clock," he said suddenly, coming to his feet. "Hate to run, Kitt, but you know how it goes."

Dazed, she watched him stride across the room to the closet. There was a huge vacuum. A blank of cool air where once his warm, vibrant body had filled the empty space. She sat stiffly on the bed, unmoving while he shut the door to the bathroom.

She looked down at herself, spread wide to him—ready and willing once again to become a part of the man she had vowed over and over to forget. Her shirt was gaping, and her breasts felt as if they were throbbing with life and desire. Her legs were parted for him, and she felt the damp hunger between her thighs.

What harm could there be in making love with him? The thought swung through her mind like a Scottish reel. What harm? She wanted him. That was obvious. He wanted her. That was equally clear. What harm then?

Some half-buried animal instinct for self-preservation reared its head. What harm? Take a look at the harm you reaped once before, Kitt. Take a look at the consequences of your heady passions. What would you gain from a moment of pleasure with Garth Culhane? You'd only want more of him—like you did before. You'd only want to be with him again, to share in his life. He's heading off to Beirut, Kitt. Or Bogotá. He's not going to be around long . . . just as he wasn't around long before.

She licked her dry lips and fumbled for the buttons on her blouse. He left you, Kitt. No matter what he says about his despair and Vietnam and wanting to die without you—he left you. All alone in that battered trailer with an empty crib and an empty heart.

Sure, you're drawn together. There's an animal mating instinct between the two of you. But most animals don't mate for life. Keep apart, Kitt. Keep separate, or you're going to be hurt again. This time it won't be so easy to put back the pieces of your shattered life.

Garth ran the razor over his chin. A pillow of white foam gathered beneath the blade. Water ran from the faucet into the sink, drowning all noise but itself.

Damn. He ran the razor under the stream of water. Damn, what had he been thinking about? She'd walked into his room in those tight jeans and that turquoise blouse, and suddenly all he could think about was teasing her into wanting him. One look at Kitt Tucker and he might as well be a Neanderthal in a bear skin.

Frowning at himself, he scraped the skin at his throat. Was she like that with other men? Damn it all! Why was he thinking about Kitt with other men? She wasn't his wife anymore. He didn't have a claim on her. Hell, if she wanted to sleep with a different man every night of the year it was her prerogative.

Of course, Kitt wasn't the type to do something like that. The truth of the matter was, she hadn't changed as much as she wanted to believe. He'd always been able to tantalize her. And she'd kept him in a state of perpetual arousal from the moment he laid eyes on her in the hall of Clovis High School. He'd run after her like a dog with its tongue hanging out. There had been no other young men for Kitt once Garth took her on that first date. And he hadn't had a flicker of interest in any other girl.

Not that they'd completely lost their senses. They'd both had friends—male and female. But it had always been Garth and Kitt. Garth and Kitt. Garth and Kitt from the very beginning.

He threw the razor into the sink. What the hell had happened to tear them apart? And if it happened once, could it happen again?

He buried his face in a towel and shut his eyes. There she was again. Not the Kitt with sparkling eyes and laughter on her lips. Not the Kitt who bounced into his waiting arms.

It was that other Kitt. Sitting in the white rocking chair in the living room of their trailer. Rocking. Rocking. Eyes straight ahead, dull brown, glazed. Rocking. Rocking. Not saying anything. Not eating or taking a bath or brushing her hair. Not even looking at him. Just rocking and rocking. Her stomach huge with their baby inside. Their little baby who had died inside her. Rocking and rocking and waiting for their dead little baby to be born.

When Garth came out of the bathroom Kitt was sitting in the chair by his bed reading the newspaper.

"I like the story you wrote about the project," she said softly.

He sat on the bed and pulled navy socks over his bare feet. He had put on a pair of clean, pressed jeans and a red polo shirt. He'd brushed his wet hair neatly back from his forehead. The dampness made it look darker, all the blond streaks almost brown. He smelled subtly of male cologne.

"You left out the part about the skeleton with gold teeth," she said.

He shrugged. "I have to get the whole story. Don't want anybody to scoop me."

He pulled on his white running shoes. Kitt observed his long brown fingers as they formed the lace into a bow. Had she ever told him how much she had loved the shape of his fingers? His nails were blunt and white and strong. His hands bore a subtle power in every movement.

"I need to write a follow-up story pretty soon. Of course, I guess Burton could do that."

"He's well?"

"Yeah." Garth turned to her. "I talked to the chief last night. Burton wants to take over the Black Dove story."

"I see."

"The chief told him what was going on. Burton would like to interview you."

"What about you?"

"My territory is the north. Albuquerque. Crime stuff. Government. Didn't you ever see my byline?"

"I don't read all that government stuff in the paper. I get my fill of government with all those forms I have to complete."

"That's my beat anyway. Exciting happenings."

"So, after this trip and whatever you find out, you're going to turn the story over to Burton?"

"That's my assignment." Garth studied Kitt's face.

She carefully folded the newspaper, unable to say the words forming in her throat. Stay, Garth. We'll work together. We'll figure it all out. Not just Black Dove. Us. We'll understand what happened to us and make it all come right again.

"I guess we'd better head out to the copper mine," she said.

# Chapter 10

"It reminds me of an amphitheater," Kitt said in a hushed voice.

"Or the Forum in Rome."

The enormous pit carved into the earth gaped before them in shades of rust, gold and taupe. Tier upon tier of terraces marched down, narrowing into a crudely shaped bowl. Innumerable roads curved through the bottom of the pit, circling water-filled crevices. Steam shovels and huge trucks crawled along the roads, digging ore and transporting it to the reduction mill at the southwest of the pit.

"It's like something from outer space," she commented. "It just doesn't seem to belong in the middle of these mountains."

Garth nodded. "I wonder if it was as huge and unearthly in Black Dove's time."

"No. Back then, narrow shafts were driven down to the copper veins. The open pit wasn't dug until around 1910."

At the sound of rocks crunching on the shelf of the observation point, Kitt turned. A middle-aged woman wearing sturdy walking shoes, a flower-printed dress and a blue scarf tied under her chin lifted a hand in greeting.

"I'm with the copper mining museum. My name's Mrs. Lujan. Can I help you?"

"I'm Dr. Kitt Tucker with the Bureau of Reclamation and this is Garth Culhane with the Affiliated Press. We're working on a project and we were wondering where we might find the oldest records of the mine's history."

Mrs. Lujan joined them at the double metal rail overlooking the mine. "You're going to have trouble there, I'm afraid. The Kneeling Nun Mine has changed hands so many times. Some of the companies took an interest in the history, and some didn't. A lot of the old records have been destroyed."

Kitt's heart sank.

"But we do have a nice recording of the mine's history. You just go up to the museum and press that little red button on the panel by the door." Mrs. Lujan smiled contentedly.

"Actually, we're interested in the very early history of the mine. Back when James Kirker was here."

"Oh, James Kirker!" Her dark brown eyes sparkling, Mrs. Lujan looked at Kitt and nodded. "Now I see you do know your history, Dr. Tucker. The Kneeling Nun copper mine was first claimed in 1800. Later the Mexican government operated a penal colony here. They built a triangular fort prison with round towers at the corners and thick adobe walls between. Indian slaves and Mexican convicts mined the copper. But I'm telling you, it was bad in those days."

She chuckled and shook her head. Kitt began to think perhaps Mrs. Lujan could help them more than she'd thought. The woman had that love of history—that sense of its vitality and immediate presence—that Kitt often had felt in kindred spirits.

"The slaves worked in dark, cramped tunnels digging out the ore and lifting it up in baskets." Mrs. Lujan leaned against her shoulder, as if giving her a great secret. "When they were digging the big open pit almost a hundred years later, they found artifacts and skeletons down in the shafts, you know. Some of those poor slaves had been buried alive."

Kitt grimaced. "The shafts had collapsed on them?"

"*Claro.* I'm telling you, the slaves had these old leather bags to haul up the ore. And they used to climb up notched poles called chicken ladders. It was a pitiful situation."

"And the copper was carried out by trains of horses to Chihuahua?"

"Burros. Burro trains carried the copper to Mexico to be minted into coins. Then in 1837 a fellow named John James Johnson did a terrible thing. We've got two or three legends about it, of course. But I'm telling you what most people think happened. John James Johnson, who was a part-time scalp hunter, got this brilliant idea of how to kill Apaches. He invited all the braves, squaws and children to a big feast in the fort. They filled up with food and liquor. Then Johnson told them they could go into the courtyard and take away all the ground corn they could carry off."

She paused dramatically.

"So what happened?" Garth asked.

"John James Johnson had buried a big cannon in the middle of the food pile. While all the Apaches were grabbing the food, somebody lit that cannon and blasted all those people with nails and bullets and metal shot. The Apaches who weren't killed tried to run away—and Johnson's men fired on them with muskets."

"Sounds like a massacre."

"More than three hundred murdered. Women and children, too. Evil and shameful, if you ask me."

"No doubt the Apaches began to attack the copper trains even more ferociously than before."

"*Claro que sí!* I would be angry, wouldn't you?" Mrs. Lujan pushed a tendril of glossy salt-and-pepper hair firmly into her scarf. "So when the Apaches attacked again and again, the owners of the mine had to call James Kirker and his boys to kill and scalp them. Do you know how they used to scalp somebody?"

Garth glanced at Kitt. She was looking a little green around the gills.

"You cut a circle at the crown of the head," Mrs. Lujan began, sounding for all the world like she was right there watching the grisly deed. "Then you sit down with your feet resting on the shoulders of the dead man. You grab a handful of hair, lean back and push forward with your feet until you hear a loud *pop!* Then you sprinkle the scalp with salt to preserve it and you tie it onto a scalp pole.

"Damn." Garth felt like rubbing the top of his head just to make sure his hair was still firmly attached.

"That's what James Kirker and Black Dove and the others did?" Kitt asked, the reality of the situation sinking in. Black Dove—for all his bravado and mystique—wasn't much more than a murderer. And a pretty gruesome one, at that.

"You didn't know that, after the paper you wrote with Dr. Oldham?" Garth asked her.

"Not quite so vividly."

"We are talking about brutal people here," Mrs. Lujan explained. "Of course the Apaches were brutal, too. They kept attacking those poor burro trains and killing everyone and stealing the copper. It's hard to say who started it first, and who was the most cruel."

"Did the mine keep records of the hiring of Johnson and Kirker, and all their activities?"

"Well, they have a few things over at the mine's main offices in Hurley. But you aren't going to find anything that's not written down in the history books. They already pitched out the stuff that they decided wasn't important." She frowned at the huge mine.

"Are the records at the main offices open to the public?"

"Some are, some aren't. But like I say, lots of it was thrown away." She sniffed. "Come to think of it, a few years back I went through and picked up some of those old papers they were throwing out. I thought the museum might want to have them, you know. But then I put them away somewhere and to tell you the truth, I never thought about them until this minute. I figured they couldn't be worth much or they wouldn't be throwing them out."

Kitt's pulse sped up. "Do you suppose we could have a look at those old records?"

"Oh, my, let me think now. Where did I put those boxes?" She closed her eyes and tapped her chin. "Where, where, where?"

Kitt felt like she was at a football game, willing a touchdown with her whole body and her entire power of positive thinking. She leaned forward on the rail, as if she could push the memory of the salvaged records into Mrs. Lujan's mind.

"Probably in the back room," she said. Her dark brown eyes flashed. "You want to see?"

"Yes!" Garth grinned victoriously at Kitt.

The Kneeling Nun Mine museum was little more than an outpost perched near the edge of the vast open pit. Mrs. Lujan pressed the button on the little panel she was so proud of, so that her guests could listen to the already familiar recounting of the mine's history. For several minutes she rambled around in her back room, clucking over the piles of unmarked boxes and wondering aloud where, where, where she had put those old files.

"Got it!" She emerged at last, triumphantly carrying a torn cardboard baby-food carton full of tattered file folders. "It was beside the drinking fountain under my knitting. I bet I've looked at it every day for three years!"

Kitt and Garth descended on the box like a pair of vultures. Mrs. Lujan crossed her arms over her ample breast and watched in satisfaction as they flipped through file after file.

"I have a bunch of old medical records from the 1930s here," Kitt said.

"This one is full of medical records, too. Looks like it's from around the turn of the century."

"Was there a hospital here, Mrs. Lujan?"

"We had a mission near Santa Rita for a while. Nuns, you know. I guess they took care of the sick. And then there was a small clinic for a few years. People came here when they had breathing problems. There was a sanatorium at Fort Bayard. Lots of people came here for their health. Still do. Most of the mine workers went to doctors in Silver City for treatment."

Kitt shuffled disappointedly through more files. There appeared to be nothing more in the box than medical records. Garth stuffed two folders in the carton and took out another.

"Medical records," he said, lifting his eyes. "Was this the only box, Mrs. Lujan?"

"It's the only one I saved. They had a bunch of them to throw out, you know. They didn't want me to take even one box, but I told them I was from the museum. One fellow and me, we really had a scuffle over it. This was the only one I could grab before they made me leave."

Kitt grinned, picturing the stout little Mrs. Lujan waging a tug-of-war with some burly maintenance man over her file box. It never failed to appall her how little understanding most people had of the value of historical artifacts. Yet there always appeared to be someone like Mrs. Lujan, someone with a grasp on the ephemeral nature of history to act on its behalf.

"Hang onto these files, Mrs. Lujan," Kitt said. "Somebody's going to put them to good use one day. I'm sure your fight to save them was worth it."

"They don't have anything you want?" A note of disappointment hung on her words.

"I'm afraid not. We're looking for employment files. Records of James Kirker's stay at Santa Rita."

"There are some good books on Kirker, you know," Mrs. Lujan said in a helpful tone.

"Actually, we're trying to find out about one of Kirker's men. A fellow by the name of Black Dove. He was a Shawnee warrior."

"Black Dove. I've heard of him. Two gold teeth?" Mrs. Lujan touched her own teeth.

Kitt nodded. "Well, shall we head over to the mines offices, Garth? Maybe they'll let us see what they have."

Mrs. Lujan waved them off, her blue scarf drifting around her face.

Hurley lay fifteen miles from the Kneeling Nun Mine. The offices were scattered over several blocks, and it took a long time before they were able to find the public relations department. The officer kindly referred them to two books on the mine and one on Kirker—all of which Kitt and Garth had already read. The records were closed to the public, the woman said apologetically, but all the important historical information had been culled and given to historians to put in their writings. The rest of the early records had been disposed of a number of years ago. She suggested they speak with the director of the Silver City Museum.

Disappointment almost palpable in her mouth, Kitt rode with Garth the fifteen miles to Silver City. They ate a quick lunch then drove to the red brick building with its cupola and

Victorian mansard roof. The local museum was a treasure trove of Victorian furnishings, as well as Southwestern artifacts.

"We're looking for early mine records," Kitt heard herself repeating to the museum director. "We are specifically interested in James Kirker and his scalp hunters. Black Dove in particular."

The woman shook her head. "I'm afraid the mine owners destroyed most of the records. You might try the library."

The head librarian walked them through stacks of journals and periodicals that mentioned the mine—most of which were recent and nearly all of which Kitt had read. He offered to let them borrow the historical books on the mine, but Kitt already knew she would find nothing new about Black Dove.

"Well, thank you for your time," she said.

"I'm sorry I couldn't be of further help. The Kneeling Nun Mine has changed hands several times. The owners destroyed many of the old records."

"Yes," Garth concurred. "We know."

They nodded to the librarian again and started for the door. From a small office beside the check-out desk a young woman ran toward them, a scrap of pink paper fluttering in her hand.

"Dr. Tucker?" she called in a stage whisper that drew frowns from several patrons. "Sir, are you Dr. Tucker?"

Kitt swung around. "I'm Dr. Tucker."

"Thank goodness." She paused, out of breath, and unfolded the pink note. "Mrs. Lujan from the Kneeling Nun Mine museum called. She was really agitated because she'd called everywhere trying to track you down. She told me to look for a woman with long brown hair and a handsome blond man."

Garth straightened his shoulders. "Well, that must be us."

Kitt rolled her eyes. "So what did Mrs. Lujan want?"

"I'm not sure. The message got kind of garbled because she was going on and on about how long it took her to find you. But she kept repeating she had found it, she had found it. She wants you to go back to the museum."

"All the way back to the mine?"

"That's what she said."

Kitt turned to Garth. "It's only medical records."

"She must have found something she thought we'd be interested in. Come on. Let's go."

The sun seemed to perch just over a mountain as they drove the winding road to the Kneeling Nun Mine. They had just turned into the parking area of the museum when Mrs. Lujan burst through the front door, waving her arms with excitement. She had forgotten her blue scarf and her neat bun threatened to fall apart as she ran.

"You came! Thank goodness." Huffing, she caught Kitt's arm, dragged her out of the car and began to haul her toward the museum.

"Mrs. Lujan, what have you found?"

"You wouldn't believe the trouble I had to find you. First I called the mine office in Hurley. They told me they had told you to go to the museum. Then I called there and you had already left. I thought I would never find you!"

Garth leaped to open the front door and Mrs. Lujan barreled through, Kitt in tow. "So, what did you find?" he asked.

"At the museum, they told me they had sent you over to the library. I called over there and all I got was this young girl who sounded like she didn't know anything. The librarian was busy guiding people around, so then I just gave up and left a message to tell you to come back here if the girl saw you. I can't believe you're here!"

"Here we are, Mrs. Lujan." Kitt leaned across the neat desk with its guest register and donation jar. "What have you found?"

"I got this!" She swept open the top drawer of the desk and held up a tattered file folder just like the others they had already been through.

"What's in it?" Kitt tried to sound excited.

"It's the medical records from those years when Kirker was guarding the Kneeling Nun Mine. The 1830s!"

"Really!" Kitt glanced at Garth, still unable to imagine there could be anything of value in the folder. "Do they mention anything interesting?"

"I got your man right here. Black Dove."

Kitt and Garth lunged for the file at the same time, but Mrs. Lujan whisked it away. Setting the folder on her desk, she carefully turned through the yellowed, crumbling papers.

"After you left, I got to searching through the box," she said. "I got to thinking that I should know what was in there, in case somebody else ever came looking. You said someone might, and I thought it would be a good idea to know what I had, just in case."

Garth hung over the edge of the desk, practically salivating while Mrs. Lujan primly turned page after page.

"Here." She slapped the paper. "It says right here that the Shawnee Indian, Black Dove, was a patient of a Dr. Miller in August of 1838. He was nineteen years old, six feet four inches tall, weighed two hundred pounds. *Dios mio!* A big fellow."

Garth put his arm around Kitt's shoulders. He could feel the sense of relief and pleasure flowing through her as Mrs. Lujan spoke.

"Black hair, it says here. Dark brown eyes. Doesn't say one thing about two gold teeth. How about that? It's all you ever hear of Black Dove. But this doctor doesn't even mention the teeth."

"Why did Black Dove go to the doctor?" Garth asked.

"Dr. Miller must have written this part. It's hard to read— you know how doctors always have that terrible handwriting?"

"Yes."

"He says Black Dove was brought in on horseback after an Apache raid on the copper train. He had one spearhead and part of a shaft impaled in his thigh. The thigh bone was broken, it says. The doctor wrote that he was able to get the spearhead out of the thigh and close the wound. He plastered the broken leg."

"So Black Dove wasn't invincible." Kitt suddenly felt a sense of reality about the warrior. He was no longer just the stuff of legend. She understood the work he did—the actual killing and scalping of other human beings. And she knew that at least once he had been badly wounded.

"There's one more thing here," Mrs. Lujan said, squinting at the paper. She held it up to the light. "Oh, yes. Black Dove had a knife tip broken off in his scapula. What's the scapula—some embarrassing part we shouldn't talk about?''

"It's the shoulder blade, Mrs. Lujan."

"The knife was buried two inches deep in the bone of the scapula, Dr. Miller writes. He tried, but he couldn't get the knife tip out of the bone. I guess he must have left it in. Can you imagine going around with a knife tip stuck in your shoulder?''

Mrs. Lujan lifted her head and smiled. "So does that help you?''

Garth was squeezing Kitt's shoulder so tightly she could barely breathe. "That helps, Mrs. Lujan," she said. "That helps a lot."

"I still can't get over it." Kitt strolled beside Garth down the streets of Silver City's central historic district. Sturdy brick Victorian homes stood in the lamplight, like old ladies waiting for a dance. The moon hung white and full over the cusp of the mountain range surrounding the city.

"What can't you get over—that you're walking along in the moonlight with your handsome husband?''

"You're not my husband, Garth."

"You don't really believe a little piece of paper can sever the marital bond between two people who loved each other, do you?''

Kitt glanced at the tall man beside her. She could hear the teasing tone in his voice, but it made her uncomfortable that he would speak of their marriage as though it were still vital.

After leaving Mrs. Lujan at the museum—photocopies of Black Dove's medical record in hand—they had returned to their motel to clean up for dinner. Somehow out of the cloth sport bag he hauled around, Garth had managed to extract yet another pair of freshly pressed blue jeans and a white shirt. A pair of tan roper boots and a fancy buff-colored Stetson completed the outfit. Now more than ever, Kitt had the sense that the old Garth walked beside her—the old, familiar Garth mingled with the new, far more exciting man he had become.

"I suppose if a small piece of paper can link two people together in marriage," she mused, "another piece of paper can just as easily break the bond."

"But you don't really believe that."

"Why would you say that?"

"You haven't gotten married again, have you?"

"I just haven't found the right man."

"Until now. It took a while for me to find you again."

"Garth, please." Kitt shook her head. How long was he going to keep this up? "You weren't even looking for me when you found me. Now let's get back to the subject at hand."

"You and me."

"Black Dove. I just can't believe he could be in that grave at Muddy Flats. I mean, it just doesn't fit. And yet, all the pieces are there. The skeleton has two gold teeth, it's that of an Indian, it matches the height and build description in Mrs. Lujan's report. And there's that knife tip in the scapula. It has to be Black Dove's grave!"

"So what's the problem?"

"He's buried in *Mexico*, Garth."

"Did it ever occur to you that your beloved Dr. Oldham might have been wrong just once?"

"But you don't know Dr. Oldham. He wouldn't make a mistake like that. It's too obvious. Someone somewhere told him that Black Dove was buried in Guadalupe Y Calvo."

Garth studied Kitt's face. She had that familiar stubborn set to her jaw. Her dark eyes practically flashed in the moonlight as she spoke. Again there was that fascinating incongruity about Kitt—she spoke in the clipped, professional tone he had grown used to; she held her body almost rigidly under control, back straight, chin high; she hardly gestured when she talked.

And yet over that thirty-two-year-old woman-of-the-world suit of armor, Kitt wore a cloak of softness. Her long hair swung gently at her waist with the smooth flow of her movements. A full denim skirt fell almost to her ankles and was cinched at the waist with a heavy silver concho belt. Her almost fragile shoulders were clad in a puff-sleeved turquoise blouse. Turquoise-colored flats on her feet seemed to whisper on the sidewalk.

He wanted to draw her to him and hold her tightly to his chest. Yet he knew that if he pressed too far, held her too close, the sharp spikes of her protective armor would pierce him through her outer softness.

Once in Vietnam, Garth's commanding officer had found him sitting alone in his tent while the other men played cards in the main barracks. After a brief talk, the officer had instructed him to speak with the company chaplain about "that gray cloud he carried around."

The bearded chaplain had given Garth a foam rubber ball and told him to squeeze it as tightly as he could. But when Garth began to wad the ball up in his palm, an open paper clip buried deep inside the foam poked into his hand. "Be like this ball, Culhane," the chaplain had told him. "Moldable, adaptable and sensitive to others. But keep a point at which you start to push back. Wear some protection underneath, and you'll be a lot better off."

At the time, Garth had thought squeezing a foam rubber ball a sorry excuse for help to a young man who had lost his marriage, his wife and his child. It had taken a few years, but he had grown his own steely core after all—and so had Kitt.

"If Black Dove is buried in Mexico," Garth said slowly, on the lookout for spikes, "then who is buried in the Muddy Flats cemetery?"

"I don't know. I just can't figure it out."

They wandered past an Italianate red brick home and stopped at a tall archway. "Big Ditch Park," the sign read. From the arch, a long wooden bridge stretched across what looked exactly like a big ditch. Victorian-style lamps lit the expanse, casting a yellow light on large green trees and the well-groomed lawn leading down to the ditch.

"This ditch used to be the main street of Silver City," Garth said as they started across the bridge. "At the turn of the century, a series of floods washed the street away along with most of the homes."

"How did you know that?"

"I read the sign back there on the post."

Kitt had to laugh. "Here I am admiring your vast knowledge."

"Admire away. No telling what else you'll walk right past without me to guide you."

"I've made it around fine for fifteen years."

Garth paused and leaned on the wooden rail of the footbridge. "You're walking right past all the signs about Black Dove."

"I just want to be careful, Garth. Allow me that."

Kitt rested her elbows on the rail and followed the curve of the ditch with her eyes. Garth took off his hat, running the brim across his palm. The yellow lamplight coated the round muscle of his shoulders, and carved deep shadows in his face. She could see his tanned fingers rotating the hat, and she could feel his mind working. Part of her wanted to know what he was thinking—and part of her already did.

It was their last night together. Somehow they had been brought together, and within a few hours they would be pulled apart again. Funny how at first, she could hardly wait until he left. Now she wasn't ready for this moment. Things needed to be said. Ends needed to be tied up. Yet she felt afraid of all that—as if in finishing up their past she would have to lose him once and for all.

She knew she didn't want him; at least she didn't want to start something that could hurt her even worse. She also knew she didn't want to let him go again. Not just yet.

"What are you planning to do, Kitt?" he asked. His voice had deepened, roughened.

"About what?"

"Tomorrow."

Out of the corner of her eye she saw him pick up a tress of her hair and begin stroking the end of it through his fingers.

"I'm driving to Santa Fe in the morning," she said. "I have to finish all the reports for the relocation project, plus I need to wind up my book. My editor wants it in three weeks. What about you?"

"I'm due in Albuquerque Monday morning. The governor's holding a press conference there. Education, teachers' salaries, all that. There's something going on about animal control, too. I'll have to take a look at that."

"I'll have to start watching for your stories in the paper."

"Yeah."

Kitt picked at a splinter of wood. At the moment, she felt she could probably tear down the whole bridge splinter by splinter for all the tension shooting through her arms and back. Garth just kept stroking her hair.

"I have a dog," she said, trying to fill in the uncomfortable silence.

"What's his name?"

"Apollo. He's incredibly unintelligent."

He laughed. "You got him from the pound, didn't you?"

She nodded.

"Remember that dog we used to have? You got him at the pound, too."

"Joker. He died about five years ago."

"You kept Joker?" He turned to her.

"Of course I did. He was our dog."

Garth gathered Kitt gently to him. She came, her body still stiff and distant. He could feel her defenses, but he wanted to be near her anyway. *You don't just go off and leave a dog because you're having a little trouble.* He could almost hear her thinking the words. *You don't just go off and leave your wife, either.*

"Thank you for taking care of Joker all those years," he murmured into her hair.

She closed her eyes and leaned her forehead on his shoulder. He was going to say sweet things—she could just feel it. And if he said tender words, she was going to melt all over the place again. She was going to forget all the hurt he had brought her. She felt torn in two, wanting his gentle words and his loving touch, wanting to run away and hide from him.

"Garth," she began. She lifted her head and looked into his blue-gray eyes. But he didn't say the tender words she had expected.

Instead, he drew her body up against his and kissed her. His lips moved over hers with the fierce hunger of many empty years. His hands wound through her long hair, squeezing and caressing it as if he could not get enough.

She caught her breath as his overpowering masculinity poured over her. His breath, his taste, his touch, all bore the indelible stamp of man. Not Garth, the teenager, fumbling and out of breath with desire. This was the new Garth—moving against her with the control of a panther on the hunt, willing her every response, beckoning her with each touch of his hands, each brush of his lips.

He pushed her hair aside and bent to kiss her neck. His mouth moved down her skin, his breath warm and moist. His tongue made delicious little circles that sent shivers of desire deep into the pit of her stomach. How could she resist him—he was the man she craved.

# Chapter 11

Hardly aware of the trickle of water beneath the bridge or the rustle of birds settling in the trees for the night, Kitt knew only the trace of Garth's breath in her ear. They were alone, no passersby at this late hour. She slipped her hands up his back and ran her fingers down the valley of his spine. His shirt felt soft, the heat of his skin warming her fingers through the cotton fabric.

Her body had sprung instantly to heightened awareness. She could smell the subtle scent of his cologne. His smoothly shaven cheek pressed against hers, cool and firm. His fingers tightened in her hair, cupped her neck, drew her head back so that he could take her mouth more easily.

Momentary curtains of restraint descended over her and she kept her lips closed. But his tongue stroked across them, willing them apart. She opened her mouth then and took him in, reveling in the familiar taste and the sensual way he sought each silken fold and hidden crevice. Their tongues tangled and danced. Kitt felt consumed.

She pushed her hands into the back pockets of his jeans, feeling the hard curve of his buttocks. His long body holding hers to the wooden rails of the bridge was urgent against her, his thighs rigidly pressing hers, his belt buckle jammed against the silver concho at her waist.

"Kitt." Her name escaped like a low groan.

He wrapped his hands around her shoulders, aware of the round fullness of her breasts against his chest. She smelled of flowers, and he breathed deeply of her skin. Dipping his head, he ran his tongue over the delicate bone at the base of her neck. She caught her breath and tilted her head back. Tasting her skin on his lips, he moved lower, his mouth warming the rise of her bosom.

Slipping her fingers through his hair, she held his head against her breasts. Through the fabric of her blouse he nuzzled her until she grew pebble-hard against his tongue. He wouldn't hurt her—ever again. But he wanted her as badly as she wanted him.

Taking her hand, he pulled her along the bridge away from the yellow glow of the lamplight and into the deep black privacy of a giant juniper tree. She came willingly, her hand stroking the planes of his chest, her head tucked against his shoulder.

The summer grass felt soft and cool against Kitt's legs as she settled down beside Garth. Nothing mattered but this moment, this man. His mouth moved across her cheek, his tongue burning hot circles in her skin. She looked into his eyes, shadowed by darkness, as she slowly unbuttoned her blouse.

"Kitt…" He reached behind her and flicked open the clasp of her bra. The clothing slid from her shoulders and as she lay back in the grass, moonlight dusting her breasts with a silver glow. Silently, he took first one then the other between his lips. He ran his tongue over their tips, tight as little rosebuds.

With a tiny cry of pleasure, she reached for his shirt. The buttons seemed to fall apart beneath her hungry fingers. Rolling against him, she lifted onto her elbows and buried her nose in the mat of crisp hair on his chest. She found his flat nipples and teased them with her tongue. Then she drew a wet line down to the smooth skin of his belly. Her fingers worked at her belt, drawing out the thick leather, parting the brass buttons of his jeans.

Unable to control himself with this wild, hungry woman whose hands even now fondled him so deftly, he drew his fingers up the silky skin of her bare legs. Her denim skirt gathered beneath his arms until he touched the flimsy fabric of her panties. Dainty laces and bows. He cupped her hips and pulled her against him, kneading her smooth flesh. His mouth suckled hers. Their tongues caressed, teeth gently nipping at lips and ears.

Sliding his hand across the taut curve of her stomach, he coaxed aside the fabric of her panties and drew his fingers through the soft curls beneath. Kitt tensed, waiting breathlessly while his hand stroked her, moving closer and closer. Then in one liquid movement, his fingers parted her and began playing within the damp, burning depths of her body.

Feeling as if she were about to come apart in a shivering, frenzied explosion, Kitt lifted her hips to his touch. Her hands moved across his bare back, stroking and pulling him against her. With a life of their own, her breasts seemed to swell toward his chest, her nipples burying themselves in his hair. His fingers teased the tiny pearl between her legs, pushing her onward and upward, until she was sure she was completely powerless in his arms.

It was more than a hunger, more than desire. She knew it with certainty, as Garth pulled her panties past her knees and gently parted her thighs. At this moment—if not at any other—they belonged together. She pushed his jeans down and slipped her fingers beneath the band of his underwear. His hardness filled her hands.

They did belong together, as they had so many years ago. The moment of passion that had taken them away that clear summer night had been hardly different from this—the same two people, the same insatiable hunger. Only the consequences had broken them apart.

Consequences.

A flood of feelings washing over her like a chilling wave, Kitt suddenly grabbed Garth's shoulder and pressed her face against his neck. He stiffened at the sudden change in her. His hands slipped up to her waist.

"Kitt?"

"Consequences," she breathed.

He lay rock still, his body driving him onward, but his mind trying to fathom what she was saying. "Consequences, Kitt? Talk to me, honey."

"Last time . . . last time we did this, look what happened."

"Kitt, you can't believe we aren't meant to be together. You want me as badly as I want you."

She nodded, biting her lower lip.

He stared into the black branches of the juniper tree. He didn't even have to ask. Suddenly he understood her fear. Neither he nor Kitt was protected against the chances of another baby forming inside her—the seed of their lovemaking. This moment under the juniper tree might reap the same consequences as that first night of their loving. That night when both had been so consumed they had lost all restraint. One night of loving. One baby.

Closing his eyes and clenching his jaw, Garth willed the heat inside him to subside. He could wait for her until the time was right. He held Kitt tightly to him, arms wrapped around her shoulders, nose nestled in her hair.

"Do you remember the first time we made love, Kitt?" he murmured, trying to even his ragged breathing.

She nodded.

"Your parents had told you they were sending you away to boarding school in Virginia. Remember that?"

She pressed her shut eyes against the curve of his neck.

"You came to me that night—walked all the way out to the farm—and knocked on my bedroom window," he said. "It was raining a little. You were wet and crying. I climbed outside and we held hands and just walked and walked through the dark mist. I didn't even know where we were. You told me about the boarding school and how angry your parents were that we wouldn't break up. Remember?"

"I don't want to remember."

"But you do remember. We felt like we weren't ever going to see each other again . . . just like tonight."

It was all true. They had held each other as if their world were coming to an end. Their kisses had changed swiftly to caresses. Garth touched her where he never had before. The rain stopped and the night sky seemed to light up. Ravenous, they tumbled to the damp ground. Kitt felt there was nothing in the world more important than that moment—that boy in her arms. They had made love, then, with all the fervor and pent-up desire in their young bodies. It had been wonderful, painful, wonderful again. Above all, utterly necessary.

"And then you found out you were going to have our baby." Garth's words brought out the finality of the situation. "We both wanted that baby more than anything else in the world, didn't we, Kitt?"

"Yes." She heard the quiver in her voice and swallowed hard to erase it.

They had wanted the baby. They had wanted each other. But the baby had died and something inside Kitt had died, too. Everything fell apart. Now here they were, beneath an old juniper tree, risking it all again.

Garth smoothed Kitt's skirt down her legs. "Let's go back to the motel, honey."

"I plan to see you again, Kitt." Garth leaned against the motel door frame looking much as he had that first night in Catclaw Draw.

"I don't think it's a good idea, Garth. We're just bad luck together."

"Hell, that isn't true." His voice held a note of belligerence.

"How do you know?"

"You take a risk."

"Look what happened when we took the last risk." She shook her head. "Oh, Garth. All those silly rules and things. We might as well face the fact that when we're together we get out of control. We don't think."

"We can make sure you don't have another baby, Kitt. Modern medical advances have taken care of that pretty well."

She had to grin. "I'm aware of that. But modern medical advances haven't done a whole lot for healing human hearts. That's what I don't want to get torn up again."

He settled his hat on his head and crossed his arms over his chest. So, he was just supposed to walk away and let her go again? Just like that? Was she really able to turn aside from him so easily?

No, she wasn't. He could see the wanting in her eyes.

"I need to interview you again," he said. He'd leave one foot in the door, no matter how hard she tried to push him out of her life.

"What for?"

"For the story on Black Dove."

She straightened in the open doorway. "I thought you said Burton—"

"Why do you think I came all the way to Silver City? I'm going to write up our findings."

Kitt's eyes widened. "Are you going to write that Black Dove is buried at Muddy Flats?"

"I plan to give all the evidence we unearthed. I don't suppose we'll ever really know where he was buried."

"I feel that story would be premature, Garth. We still have absolutely no motive for Black Dove being in New Mexico. And we *do* have a reason he was in Mexico. We also have reports stating he died and was buried in Guadalupe Y Calvo."

"What else could you do to get evidence, Kitt? Go to Guadalupe Y Calvo yourself?"

She shrugged. "I need to think it all over. That's how I work. I want to review all the findings at the cemetery. Then I want to go over my original paper, as well as Dr. Oldham's notes. I'd like to talk with him as well. I'll probably even read over the primary texts relating to the period and see what I can find. I have to be careful."

"Sometimes a person can be too careful, Kitt. So careful she might miss the opportunity of a lifetime." He touched her chin. "You know what I mean?"

She read the personal message behind his words. But she and Garth had separate lives now. As much as they wanted each other physically, there could be nothing more between them.

She realized she was afraid of Garth Culhane. He held a power over her heart that no man had ever held. She could so easily lose herself to him again. But she had worked too damned hard to find herself. And she had no guarantee that Garth wouldn't do the same thing to her again. When the going got rough, he might just walk out on her once more. He wasn't made of the stuff of commitment and marital permanence. At least—she didn't think he was.

"I was seventeen years old, Kitt," he said. He could read the walls rising between them. She was distancing herself even as he studied her face in the moonlight. "Seventeen. I'm thirty-three now."

She glanced away, her eyes filling with tears for the first time since she'd seen him. Yes, he was thirty-three. But so little had changed between them. In a way, they were still exactly the same two kids—so ready to make the exact same mistakes.

"Garth," she said carefully. "I loved you once. And you loved me. Please let that be enough."

Without looking at him again, she turned and shut the door behind her. She stood in the darkness, fingertips pressed against her eyes, letting go. Letting go.

"You came back, Dr. Tucker!" Mrs. Lujan beamed with pleasure as Kitt entered the little museum early the following morning.

"I just wanted to say goodbye and thanks again. You really added a lot to my study with your find."

The truth was, Kitt wanted to walk through the museum one last time before she left for Santa Fe. It was here that Garth had held her so tightly, here that they had been united and joyful for the last time—no pain, only the pleasure of discovery and the fun of being together.

"I hope you've stored those records away safely."

"*Claro!* I already put them in a fireproof filing cabinet." Mrs. Lujan hurried around the desk, craning her head toward the window. "Where's your young man, Dr. Tucker?"

"Garth. Oh, he left for Albuquerque some time this morning."

"You were not together?" Mrs. Lujan knocked her head lightly with the heel of her palm. "Sometimes I am *loca*, you know? You made such a nice match with that young fellow, I thought you belonged together. He seemed to like you a lot."

She lifted her eyebrows hopefully. Kitt smiled and walked toward the huge picture window. "We're friends from many years ago."

"I see." Mrs. Lujan edged to Kitt's side, her sturdy leather shoes squeaking a little as she walked. She had on another flowered dress, this time pink. Her bun was knotted neatly at the nape of her neck.

"The mine looks almost pretty at this time of day. All those shades of color."

"Did you see our kneeling nun?" Mrs. Lujan pointed to a nearby outcrop of rock. "You were so busy with Black Dove yesterday, I think I forgot to tell you the story of the kneeling nun. Do you see her there on the hill?" Mrs. Lujan had not taken her eyes from the rocky mountainside.

Kitt focused in the direction of Mrs. Lujan's gaze. Perched on the side of the hill sat a strange stone formation. In silhouette, it appeared to be the figure of a robed and veiled woman, kneeling on one knee. The nun gazed upward into the sky in a mixture of rapture and sorrow.

"That's where the mine gets its name," Mrs. Lujan explained. "Isn't she sad?"

Kitt nodded, feeling a little like her own face mirrored that of the nun.

"Do you know how she came to be made of stone?"

"Tell me, Mrs. Lujan."

"She was the youngest in the order of good sisters who ran a little hospital not far from here. One day a wounded soldier crawled into the adobe courtyard of the hospital. He was nearly dead and in terrible pain. The sisters brought him inside and began to tend his wounds. The youngest of the nuns took care of the poor soldier very tenderly for many days until his wounds began to heal and his thirsty body came back to life. The soldier began to talk with the little nun, and he told her that he had been on a patrol. The Apaches had ambushed the men and killed all but him. Him they left for dead in the hot sun."

"That is a sad story."

"But that is not the whole story. The little nun began to support the soldier as he walked around the courtyard to regain his strength. He told her he was from the east, a beautiful land of tall green trees and fertile farms. The sister also had grown up in the east, not far from the soldier's home. Gradually, without intending it, the soldier and the little nun fell in love. The soldier begged her to go home with him—back to the east where they both belonged. But she shook her head. How could she leave the church? It would be too painful. She let the soldier go away and rejoin his troops who were gathering just over the ridge.

"That evening when the moon rose, the little nun could not bear it any longer. She left the hospital and set out over the desert toward the ridge. But when she got there, the troops had gone. She could see the cloud of dust as they rode away. The little nun knelt to pray without the strength or the heart to return to the hospital. She knew she had broken her vows. She continued to pray through the night and into the next morning. Gradually, her shoulders, her arms and then her whole body turned to stone. And there she kneels, year after year, our little nun with the broken heart."

Kitt stared at the silhouette in the distance. "Do you think she should have gone with the soldier when he asked her to, Mrs. Lujan? Even at the cost of such great pain and sacrifice and uncertainty?"

"What do you think, Dr. Tucker?" Mrs. Lujan reached out and laid her brown fingers over Kitt's hand. "It is for each of us to decide."

Her little adobe home on a Santa Fe side street beckoned Kitt more than she had ever remembered. Though it was summer, the night was chilly. One of her neighbors had lit a fire, and the musky smell of piñon smoke hung in the air. Kitt drove the Bureau truck into her driveway and began unloading her bags.

Wandering through the empty house, she felt a sense of comfort at its solidity and familiarity. She had carefully decorated with a soft mixture of Southwestern and Victorian prints. Muted shades of peach, turquoise and gray formed geometric designs on her sofa, chairs and the wallpaper borders that ran throughout the home. Antique lace antimacassars covered tables and hung from lamps. The fragrance of cinnamon drifted around clay pots filled with potpourri. In a niche over the fireplace, a collection of silver bowls and trays gleamed softly.

Kitt turned on some music and poured herself a glass of red wine. Her back felt stiff from the hours of driving. Her head throbbed. She'd had too much time to think. Too much time to remember the way Garth's mouth curved higher on one side than the other when he smiled. Too much time to think of the way his hands had touched her in the darkness beneath the juniper tree. Too much time to dwell on every single thing she had once liked about him—and to find that in spite of everything, she still liked him as much as ever just for who he was. More than ever.

But that was over. Kitt opened her leather portfolio and took out the paperwork she still had to compile. Rows and columns of typed letters swam before her eyes. She stared at them blankly. Why was it suddenly so quiet in her house?

She jumped to her feet and turned up the music. She poured herself a little more wine. Stretching out on the couch, she thumbed through the stack of paper. She could always work on the Black Dove information. Dr. Oldham's notes should be in the pile of mail her landlord had stacked on the hall table while she was away.

She stared at her ceiling. It looked blank and empty. She felt exactly like a little, broken-hearted nun. Turned to stone for fear of taking the risk of love.

Garth's article on Black Dove didn't show up in the Santa Fe newspaper. Kitt searched for it every morning while she sat at her kitchen table in her robe. She saw his byline on the governor's visit to Albuquerque series. She read every word. His upbeat style of writing made politics sound almost interesting. He also wrote a recap of the legislature's latest laws and the effects their passage had had on northern New Mexico. She read all of that, too.

A week of her vacation went by and Kitt spent every spare minute finishing up the last details of her project report and completing her book on the white scalp hunters. The blue light of the computer in her office gleamed night and day. The hum of the printer rattled through her scant lunches and carry-out dinners.

Dave and Sue Logan invited her over one evening, but she declined. She just had too much to do, she told them. Sue dropped by and asked her to go to the new exhibit at the folk art museum. Kitt said she was sorry, but she was really too busy. Sue left with a perplexed expression on her face.

Dr. Oldham had sent his notes, accompanied by a scrawled message of concern. He wanted to meet for lunch one day and discuss the Black Dove research. Kitt stuffed the notes in their envelope and left it on the hall table. Why had Black Dove seemed so important anyway? He played such a small part in her book. She could leave him out entirely and there would hardly be a dent.

In Catclaw Draw things had gotten completely confused. That was all there was to it. Things that should have been important weren't. And things that shouldn't have mattered at all suddenly had seemed crucial. She had lost her balance momentarily. But that was expected. It wasn't every day one ran into one's ex-husband.

As time passed, Kitt slowly began to feel a little more normal. She went shopping for groceries and cooked herself a roast so she'd have food for a few days. She accepted a dinner invitation from the Logans. She finished the project reports. One more trip to the new cemetery site, and that part of her life would be over. She took out her notes on the new ditch project. It was time to focus on the future.

Kitt pulled into her driveway, feeling a little full on Sue Logan's homemade sopaipillas. Though it was a Saturday night, she had turned down an offer of a late movie with one of her colleagues. She planned to take a hot shower and edit the final fifty pages of her manuscript before going to bed.

It had been good to spend time with Dave and Sue. She had laughed, recollecting old Hod and the trouble he had given her by persistently appearing on the site at Muddy Flats. Dave had shared some of the latest foibles with the new dam being built. Sue talked Kitt into going to the folk art museum the following afternoon after church. No one had mentioned Garth, and it was just as well.

Kitt lifted her shoulders and took a deep breath as she fitted the key to her lock. As she walked down the hall, setting her keys on the little table, she noticed that she had forgotten to turn off a light in the living room before leaving that evening. She wandered into the kitchen and filled the kettle to make a cup of tea.

Pulling pins out of the topknot she had worn to dinner, she headed down the hall to turn off the living room light. She was humming one of the new songs she'd be singing with the choir in church the following morning. When she turned the corner, she caught her breath. Around the edge of the door she saw a pair of men's leather loafers and muted argyle socks stretched across the ottoman by her couch.

"Hi, Kitt." Garth's long frame slowly unfolded from the couch. "I waited outside for about two hours and it got a little cold. You'd left that front window open. Hope you don't mind that I came in to get warm."

She stood rigidly in the hallway.

"You really ought to be careful about leaving windows open, Kitt. I mean for all its Old World charm, Santa Fe is a big city. If you're going to go to the bother of locking your door, you probably ought to lock your windows, too."

"What are you doing here?"

It was all she could manage. The balance she'd worked so hard to regain had suddenly slipped askew all over again. Here was Garth—in her living room. He had on a pale blue oxford shirt, open at the collar. Charcoal-gray pleated trousers and an argyle sweater gave him a sophisticated, man-of-the-world look. He smiled at her, his eyes a dark blue in the lamplight. She felt he was looking right through her.

"You had better stop climbing through my windows, Garth Culhane."

"How come you didn't look over Dr. Oldham's notes?"

"I mean it. If you climb through one more window of mine—"

"He's got some interesting stuff here. But not much that we don't already know about Black Dove." Garth tossed the manila envelope onto Kitt's round oak coffee table.

"How did you find me, anyway?"

"I looked in the Santa Fe phone book and there you were. Kitt Tucker."

The kettle began whistling in the kitchen.

"You have no right to read my mail, Garth. Dr. Oldham's letter was addressed to me."

"Where have you been for three hours?"

"None of your business." Kitt walked past him and took a china teacup out of her corner cupboard.

"Did you go on a date?"

"Jealous?"

"Yes."

She faced him and saw the deadly serious expression on his face.

"Excuse me, I have to make my tea."

Walking by him again, she went down the hall. Her head felt light. Again she was torn. Her heart pounded heavily as she poured boiling water over the bag of Darjeeling tea. He had come back. He had looked for her and found her. Garth had come back.

But she didn't want him. She'd made a second break—and even that had required some healing. If he kept coming back, she would have to keep breaking from him. Wouldn't she? But he *had* come back!

"Do I get a cup of tea, or am I being punished for climbing in your window?"

Kitt swung around. Garth Culhane was in her kitchen. He looked like he belonged there, leaning against her refrigerator like that. He looked comfortable. The diamonds on his cardigan complemented the geometric print in the wallpaper border. He blended.

"Get a cup, if you want some tea."

She walked toward the refrigerator to get the milk. Garth leaned on it, not moving.

"You look beautiful tonight, Kitt."

She reached for the pottery milk jug. "Are you going to get a cup?"

He watched as her slender, tanned arm lifted the heavy jug. Her silver bracelets clanked together. She was beautiful. Her hair draped down her back. A colorful cotton belt cinched the dark purple dress she wore. The full hem of her skirt swayed around her ankles.

He knew she hadn't been on a date. The calendar in her office was clearly marked with the dinner invitation to her boss's house. He'd enjoyed walking through her house, looking at her things. She decorated like she dressed—tastefully, but with a touch of the exotic.

Snooping was one of his best assets as a reporter. Garth could tell more about a person by studying his or her house than most people could in a two-hour conversation. Kitt, he had learned, was organized, punctual and a little rigid. Her endless rows of books revealed eclectic tastes. She didn't like to cook. There was a sad-looking, half-eaten roast in the fridge, along with a couple of yogurt containers and a wilted salad.

It had interested him to see that she had only a single-size bed in her master bedroom. She had shoved it off in one corner and covered it with pillows, as though she had little room for sleeping and other bedtime activities. The rest of the room had been turned into a second living room—two loveseats, a potted palm and an Indian rug on the floor.

"Well, if you're not going to get a cup, I don't see why you asked if you could have some tea." She was stirring an inordinate amount of sugar and milk into her tea, making it a light sand color.

"I just had to watch how you did that. It's sort of tea-flavored milk now, isn't it?"

"I like it this way. You can have your tea in whatever manner you wish."

Not looking at him, she walked out of the kitchen into the hall. He followed her and got himself a cup from her little collection in the corner cupboard. She was acting distant—almost angry. But he knew it was a cover. Kitt had always been an open book to him. He could sense the mixture of hesitation and relief in her eyes.

"I like the way you've done your house, Kitt." He settled back onto the couch with his tea.

"Garth, this is my home and my space. I'd have preferred it if you had been able to respect that."

"But I had to come here."

"Why?"

"I told you once, I'd come if you needed me."

"I don't need you."

"Yes, you do."

"I needed you when I was seventeen and you were my husband. That's when I needed you."

"I'm beginning to think what you really needed at seventeen was just what you got. Time to grow up. Time to find out who you were. I think I needed that, too, even though I didn't realize it."

"And now that I'm grown up and independent, you think I suddenly need you again?"

"Yes."

Kitt stirred her tea. She felt all at odds with him here in her living room. Why did he have to look so good on that sofa? She had bought it for herself. But he looked just like he belonged there, his long legs stretched out on her ottoman.

"I've been doing a lot of thinking, Kitt. And the truth is, when you're as young as we were, the only kind of love you can really have is a needy love. We needed each other like two empty teacups. I needed you to fill me and you needed me to fill you. But the truth of it was, we were both empty."

"I don't think we were empty."

"We were empty of what we needed to make a marriage—maturity, levelheadedness, goals, a sense of self. Now that I know myself and feel like I really don't need anybody, I think I'm just about grown up enough to make someone a pretty good companion for life."

Kitt took the first sip of her tea. It was lukewarm going down. She set the cup on a side table and observed her fingers for a full minute. What Garth was saying was right, of course. She had needed to grow up. So had he. But was she ready—now—to let someone walk beside her as she followed her own path in life?

"Why did you come here, Garth?" she asked.

She expected some philosophical answer about needing and wanting and growing up. But he silently reached inside his sweater and took a small envelope out of his shirt pocket. "I came to bring you a present."

"What is it?"

"Open it."

She took the envelope and pulled back the loose flap. Inside lay two airline tickets. She drew them out and read the name of the destination on the typed itinerary. Guadalupe Y Calvo, Mexico.

# *Chapter 12*

Guadalupe Y Calvo. Kitt knew what the tickets meant. They represented an offer from Garth. He hadn't written the story about Black Dove, as he'd told her he would. Now he was giving her one last shot at finding out the truth about the man buried in the Muddy Flats cemetery.

But there was more. Kitt lifted her head and met Garth's even gaze. These tickets would bring one more chance for them to be together. One more chance to work through their past. A last opportunity to learn what a future might bring.

"I'm not going to walk away and leave you again, Kitt," he said. "And I'm not going to let you walk away, either. I'm going to keep finding ways to see you until we work it out."

"Until we work it out," she repeated. "And after we work it out, *then* you can walk away?"

"No."

"Then what? What's the point, Garth? What are we working out, anyway? We both know what happened to our marriage. I think we even understand now why it happened. So tell me what you want out of this. What do you want out of me?"

"I don't know yet." He turned the teacup in its saucer. "I just know that when we're together, good things happen. I feel right. Don't you?"

"No. Yes. I feel confused. I find that I can enjoy being around you. But on the other hand, you turn on a lot of negative tapes in my mind."

"Well, I'm glad I turn you on one way or another." Grinning, he stood and stuck his hands in his pockets. "You're going to have to erase the tapes, Kitt."

"That's not possible."

"I think it is. I'm erasing mine."

"How?"

"I'm recording over them. New stuff. Better stuff . . . with you." He walked past her, his leg brushing the side of her chair. "Got to run, Kitt. I need to finish up a story before we leave. I'll see you in the morning."

"Garth." She jumped up from her chair and followed him down the hall and out the door. "What are you talking about? I'll be at church in the morning. I'm singing in the choir, for heaven's sake. I'm not going to—"

"Our flight leaves at ten. It's the only one I could get that would connect with the puddle-jumper taking supplies into Guadalupe Y Calvo twice a week."

"Puddle-jumper . . ."

"See you at nine, Kitt." He lifted a hand as he headed down her driveway toward his little gray car. "Sing your hymns for me on the flight. I could use some religion."

"Garth Culhane! I have a lot of work to do—"

"No, you don't. You've finished your project and your book. I checked in your office. Very efficient, Kitt."

He was almost shouting at her as he got farther away. She could barely see him through the darkness. His car door slammed shut. "I am not finished with my book, Garth," she shouted back. "I still have—"

"Finish it tonight," he called out the window as he drove off. "See you at nine!"

Sometime in the middle of the night as she was nursing her printer, Kitt realized she did have a choice. Just because Garth was bullheaded and insistent—just because it had always felt

good to do what he wanted because she knew he loved her—
she suddenly saw that she still had a choice. She could go on
the trip or choose not to.

She studied the tickets lying on the chair where she had
dropped them. The flight was open-ended. How characteris-
tic of Garth. She would have felt a lot more comfortable
knowing how many days to expect to be there. She wanted life
tidy. Finishing up her book and the cemetery project would be
a neat piece of work.

But Garth wasn't something she could tie up in a neat
package and be done with. She did have a choice, however. She
could refuse to go to Guadalupe Y Calvo. She could refuse to
ever see him or speak to him again. She could go on with the
life she had made for herself as if the past weeks had never
happened. Erase *those* tapes, instead.

The life she had made for herself. It had always seemed good
enough. Maybe not happy, maybe not deliriously passionate
like her marriage had been—but stable and efficient and comfortable. Risk free. That was it. She had chosen not to take
risks anymore.

Garth was a risk.

The printer stopped humming. Kitt slowly set the tickets on
the ottoman where his feet had been. She stood and checked
her watch. Two in the morning. Walking down her long hall,
she turned into the master bedroom. She sat on her bed and
stared at her feet. Then she knelt on the floor, reached under
the bed and pulled out her suitcase.

"You'd really like the view if you could look down." Garth
was looking out the window of the tiny four-seater airplane.
"It's all mountains and tall green pines down there. Just
beautiful."

He turned to Kitt. Back rigid and fingers dug into the sides
of the seat, she was chewing gum like it was her last meal. She
didn't look at him, she just stared at the mesh compartment
divider between the pilot's chair and the two back seats. The
floor between them was littered with baskets of bananas, boxes
labeled with soap and cigarette brands, cartons of wool dyes.
Behind them stood row upon row of full gasoline cans, sloshing their contents as the plane bumped through the clouds.

*"Cerca, señora!"* The sweaty, unshaven pilot leaned past the mesh divider, waving his half-smoked cigar. *"Muy cerca!"*

"He says we're almost there, Kitt," Garth said helpfully.

She turned brown glassy eyes to him, her face white. "I speak Spanish."

"I'm sure Miguel's flown this plane to Guadalupe Y Calvo hundreds of times, Kitt. If you could just relax, it's really not such a bad flight."

Kitt studied the mesh divider, sure she would never forget its tiny knotted pattern as long as she lived. Especially if she only lived another two or three minutes—which seemed highly likely.

Risks, she fumed. Risks! What a great start she'd made at beginning to take risks again. She was riding in an unpressurized flying Molotov cocktail right over the tops of pine trees.

"The Sierra Madres are some of my favorite mountains," Garth was saying, his eyes on the view outside again.

If she'd had the strength, Kitt would have socked him.

*"Aqui está!"* Miguel pointed to the ground below the plane. He stubbed out his cigar on the instrument panel and banked the plane into a severe turn. Kitt shut her eyes and clamped down on her chewing gum.

"It looks like we're going to slide in right between those pine trees up ahead." Garth's voice held a note of excitement. "Damn, Miguel. You'd better go in carefully. Lift the plane up a little bit."

*"No, señor—es como enamorarse a una mujer resistente. Entrar rapido! Aiyee!"* His white teeth flashing at Kitt, Miguel cut the plane through the tips of the pine trees and down toward a tiny strip of cleared meadow on the crest of a mountain.

"What did he say?" Garth called over the roar of the engines. "I couldn't quite catch it."

Kitt opened her eyes into slits. The plane was vibrating so badly she felt like her teeth were going to fall out.

"He said it's like making love to a resistant woman. Enter quickly." A basket of bananas tipped over on Kitt's feet. "He's a man after your own heart, Garth."

As Garth chuckled, the plane bounced onto the ground with a spine-jarring thud, then rose. Seconds later it crashed down again. This time Miguel let out a whoop and braked the plane to a halt just at the end of the grassy airstrip.

"*Bienvenidos a Guadalupe Y Calvo!*" Jerking the safety latch, he threw the door open and kicked down the rickety steps.

Kitt gingerly lifted the bananas from her feet. "If you ever try to talk me into anything like this again, I won't speak to you for as long as I live."

"Come on, Kitt. That wasn't much worse than a good old-fashioned roller coaster ride."

"I've always hated roller coasters. Especially ones that travel twelve thousand feet in the air." She swallowed and her ears popped. "And don't try to tell me you weren't scared, too."

"Scared as hell. That's part of the fun."

She had to smile. "Come on, Marco Polo. Let's go exploring." Heaving up from the seat into which she had sunk, Kitt waded through the boxes to where Miguel, suddenly all gentleman, was waiting to hand her down.

"*Le gusta el vuelo, señora?*"

"*Sí*, Miguel." Kitt stepped out into the chill evening air. "It was a fantastic flight."

At the edge of the airstrip where the mountain seemed to drop off into nothingness stood a squat young man in a straw hat and a brightly colored serape. Six small horses grazed on green grass beside him. The man smiled shyly at Kitt as he rounded up his horses and began leading them toward the plane.

"Where is Guadalupe Y Calvo?" Kitt asked aloud. She turned to find Miguel staring at her with a puzzled expression. "*Donde queda Guadalupe Y Calvo?*"

"*Abajo!*" He pointed over the ledge of mountain.

Down? Kitt waded through the stubby grass in the direction he had pointed. She glanced back. Garth was helping Miguel and the young *caballero* load the ponies with provisions from the plane. He was chatting away in Spanish as though he felt right at home. In tan slacks, boots, brown sweater and an olive bush jacket—pockets heavy with film, camera, notebooks and tape recorder—he looked every bit the intrepid journalist.

She sucked in a deep breath of air. She felt dizzy and a little sick. Altitude, she told herself. She wasn't about to let a roller coaster plane ride and a little thin air get her down. After all, wasn't this what she'd always ached to do? Leave academia and bureaucratic detail behind. Venture into unknown realms. Document uncharted anthropological data. Interview people of other cultures and languages. Put all her learning into practice—not just in the classroom, or on tame domestic digs. See what the rest of the world had to offer.

She stepped forward. Grass thinned to bleak gray rock at the edge of the mountain. She grabbed the spindly trunk of a pine tree and leaned over the side to look down. Covering her eyes, she swung herself back onto firm ground and swallowed. She took another deep breath. She opened her eyes and leaned out again.

Five miles below, in the tiny cup of a valley between the huge Sierra Madres, nestled a village. The descent to it consisted of a series of rocky, shale-strewn ledges. Tendrils of white smoke curled upward from the chimneys of little shingle-roofed houses. Cattle grazed at the foot of the mountains. Cleared patches of earth sported shaggy green gardens of corn and beans.

"Looks like about a forty-five degree angle to me," Garth said behind her.

"I think I'll crawl down on my hands and knees."

"You won't need to do that. Miguel's lined up a couple of horses for us."

Kitt lifted her eyebrows. "Horses? You think we should ride down a forty-five degree rock slide on horses?"

"Pedro is."

She studied the stout little *caballero* perched atop a knock-kneed mount. Well, if he could do it . . .

Without looking back, she marched to the horses and climbed onto the one Pedro indicated. Chill evening air nipped at her cheeks. Thank goodness she'd had the presence of mind to wear khaki slacks and desert boots, along with a turtleneck and a thick cotton sweater. The shaggy brown horse gave a sharp nod as she settled her feet into the stirrups.

*"Vamonos!"* Pedro gave his horse a jab with his heels. The string of mounts headed for the mountain ledge. Kitt gripped the reins with sweaty palms and gave Garth a wan smile.

*"Adios, señor y señora!"* Miguel called from behind.

Kitt thought about looking back and waving goodbye, but at that moment her horse stepped off the meadow onto the rock ledge. With a bouncing gait that left her breathless, the bony animal began trotting along a nonexistent path of scattered shale. She caught her breath and shut her eyes. The horse leaped to a lower ledge, landing neatly and moving straight into his comfortable gait. She glanced behind. Garth flew over the same emptiness with a wide-eyed expression.

"Damn!" he said with a laugh. "This is nearly as good as that plane ride."

"Better, I'd say." Kitt mustered a grin.

She decided the best thing was to let her horse have its own way. Relaxing her hands on the reins, she settled into her saddle.

The sun dipped behind the western peaks, leaving a gold-streaked sky behind. The little village grew nearer. The smell of freshly baked bread mingled with the musky tang of pine smoke. Old men sat in doorways, smoking pipes and chatting. Some children chased a puppy down a street. A baby cried.

The horses bounced down the final ledge almost into a town street. From a nearby shop, an electric light bulb went on. A hefty, elderly man stepped out onto the porch of the shop and waved a pudgy hand.

Garth rode his horse alongside Kitt's. "I bet that's Diego Martinez, the general store owner. Miguel told me he'll be able to help us with a place to stay."

The horses ambled to a halt in front of the store. Señor Martinez waddled down the steps and introduced himself with a wide, congenial smile. No, there was no hotel in the village, he told Garth and Kitt, but he had a back room where they could stay as many nights as they wished. For a small fee, of course.

Garth glanced at Kitt, and she nodded. This was no time to make a big deal about sleeping arrangements. She was too sore to do anything but crawl into bed and fall asleep, anyway.

Señor Martinez had an ample little wife and seven pudgy children, ranging in age from about fourteen down to a couple of months. The *señora* showed her guests to a small, lamplit room at the rear of the wood-frame home. A bed covered in thick gray blankets stood against one wall, three iron hooks protruded by the single window, and a rickety chair leaned beside the door. She told them dinner would be ready in a half hour, and left them in the semidarkness.

Feeling warm and comfortable in the cozy room, Kitt slung her bag onto the cleanly swept floor.

"I'm sorry about the plane and the horse, Kitt," Garth began. "If I'd had any idea—"

"I hope you would have asked me along all the same."

"I would have."

"I know." She rubbed her fanny and sat on the bed. "Thanks, Garth—for the tickets, the trip... It was a good idea."

He studied her face in the lamplight. Wisps of brown hair had come loose from her braid and tickled beneath her chin. Her cheeks were pink from the chilly air. A soft smile played about her lips. Her eyes looked luminous—almost black.

"You're beautiful, Kitt."

She laughed and flipped the braid over her shoulder. "I expect my face was green after that plane ride."

He sat beside her on the bed. He picked up her hand and wove her fingers between his. "It feels good to be here. New Mexico is too close to everything that happened."

"We certainly are isolated here."

"Affiliated Press knows where we are. But I doubt if they'll come looking."

She reached up and touched the strands of gold hair that had fallen over his forehead. Bending toward her, he kissed her lightly. His mouth was warm, gentle. With Garth holding her hand and kissing her, she had a sense that everything was right—just exactly right.

Dinner was a hearty meal of beef, potatoes, fish, bread, tortillas, mangos, bananas and an excellent white cheese. Señora Martinez served heaping bowls of frijoles—refried beans—for dessert. The children ate like they hadn't had a meal in days. Kitt saw where they got their pudgy physiques and fat cheeks.

After dinner, Señor Martinez settled back in his chair with a steaming cup of black coffee. He smiled expansively. "How do you like my light?" he asked his guests in Spanish.

Kitt glanced up at the bare forty-watt bulb hanging from the ceiling by a black wire. She looked at Garth and he shrugged.

"It's very nice," she said.

"Only three electric lights in the whole village of Guadalupe Y Calvo. One is in my store in the front. One is here. And the other is in the school. The electricity comes by gasoline generator. We bring the gasoline on the airplane from Chihuahua. Very expensive."

Kitt nodded, remembering the gas cans sloshing behind her on the ride in. She decided she preferred the orange glow of the nearby fire in its beehive fireplace to the naked glare of electric light.

"So tell me why you have come to Guadalupe Y Calvo," Señor Martinez said. "We have few visitors in our little village."

Kitt briefly explained their search for information about Black Dove—*Paloma Negra*. Señor Martinez scowled and shook his head.

"I have heard of him, I think." He took a long sip of coffee, swirled it around in his mouth and swallowed. "That man was an Indian. He was not trusted, even though he had been hired to protect our town."

"But he was a Shawnee—not an Apache."

Señor Martinez shrugged. "An Indian all the same."

"We hope to find burial records for Black Dove in the church," Garth explained.

"Then you must speak with the padre. He will show you the records. But I cannot imagine that an Indian would be buried in the church cemetery. It would not be thought proper."

"Do you know any of the legends about Black Dove's time in Guadalupe Y Calvo?" Kitt wondered.

"For that, you must speak with old Santiago."

"Santiago? Who is he?"

"Santiago Garcia, of course. The grandson of Black Dove."

A prickle ran down Kitt's spine, and she turned to Garth.

"Black Dove had a family—children—in Guadalupe Y Calvo?" Garth asked.

"You don't think he was going to live here all those years like a monk, *señor*. Of course he had a family. He took as a wife—not a proper wife, but a woman to live with—the daughter of the schoolteacher. They had a baby, a daughter named Maria. Then Black Dove's wife, she died."

"Of what?"

"Who knows? Maybe a woman sickness—but no one would tend her. She was not thought well of by the villagers. She lived with the Indian, you see. At the time Black Dove's wife died, their daughter, Maria, was about twelve years old. The schoolteacher, he came and took Maria away from Black Dove, her father. This man told the warrior he would not be able to care for his daughter in a good way. So she was taken from him. A short time after that, Black Dove was killed."

"Killed? He didn't just die?"

"Killed. By Apaches. You talk to old Santiago about that part. He knows it better. Maria grew up and got married. Santiago is her son. Black Dove's grandson. He lives just two streets over. We'll go tomorrow morning after you talk with the padre. Good?"

"Good," Kitt and Garth said in unison.

Kitt sat cross-legged on the bed, her feet tucked under her. The night air in the little room chilled her fingers as she worked at the clasp on Dr. Oldham's manila envelope. Beside her, Garth held the kerosene lamp at shoulder height.

"I don't remember reading anything in Dr. Oldham's notes to contradict what Señor Martinez just told us."

"You shouldn't have been reading my private mail in the first place." Kitt slipped her fingers into the envelope and pulled out the sheaf of papers. "You sneaked into my house, read my mail, went through my office. What else of mine did you look through?"

"I would have scoped out your lingerie drawer just for curiosity's sake—but I already know I like what you wear under all those layers of functional clothing."

"My lingerie drawer! Now I know you have a sick mind, Garth Culhane."

"Lovesick."

Kitt glanced at Garth. He was grinning. Relaxed. His brown sweater was pushed up at the sleeves, despite the chill. He'd kicked off his hiking shoes and they lay in a tumble beside Kitt's neatly aligned desert boots.

"So what does Dr. Oldham have to say about Black Dove?" he asked.

Shifting her attention from the proximity of Garth's shoulder and the woodsy scent clinging to his wool sweater, she began flipping through the notes. They mostly concerned other members of James Kirker's gang.

"This part tells about Spybuck," Kitt murmured. "He was Kirker's right-hand man. Part Shawnee. What a character he was."

"Here's something about the black fellow named Andy. He fought with Kirker in an attack on Cochise... The stuff on Black Dove is near the end, I think."

Kitt shuffled through a few more notes, scanning each page carefully for mention of the warrior. It warmed her inside to see Dr. Oldham's meticulous work. Each character in the cast of players had been well documented. A thorough bibliography appeared at the end of every section. The whole sheaf of photocopied documents accompanying the research data had been cross-referenced and annotated.

"Here!" Kitt lifted the page labeled, in bold black type, Black Dove. Garth leaned closer, his shoulder behind hers, as they read in silence. "Shawnee Indian; tall; physically fit; two gold front teeth—"

"He doesn't mention the knife tip in the scapula."

"Dr. Oldham wouldn't have had access to the records at the Kneeling Nun Mine. Look right here—he writes that he contacted the mine supervisors with no success."

"This is the part I remember reading last night. It's about Black Dove losing his teeth in the fight with that other kid. Can you believe Black Dove bit the other kid's ear clean off?"

"He had no qualms about tomahawking people and cutting their scalps away. Biting off an ear must have been a piece of cake."

Garth grimaced. "I'm not sure I like this Black Dove—"

"Look at this! It's a footnote," Kitt interrupted. She jabbed her finger on the page and began reading aloud. "In 1842, after guarding the gold mines in Guadalupe Y Calvo, Kirker and his men were called to Chihuahua City by the Mexican government. This time Kirker was promised a significantly greater amount for each scalp. During this period Kirker's men found an abandoned gold mine in the Sierra Madres.

"After routing some Apaches, the men happened upon the ruins of what once had been a lively community. They discovered the foundation of an old church, and the remains of a smelting furnace, a pile of cinder slag, and some copper and silver dross. One of the men found a gold nugget. But they were on their way to Chihuahua City with what they thought was even more valuable—scalp poles lined with Apache scalps. None of the histories mentions this mine again. It may be assumed Kirker and his men never revisited it."

"An abandoned gold mine in the Sierra Madres." Garth shook his head. "Old Hod should hear about this one!"

Kitt stared at the lamplight, remembering the persistent fellow watching her from his spot beneath the cottonwood tree. Poor lonely Hod. She wondered if she would ever see him again.

"I bet Black Dove finally got his new gold teeth from nuggets found at that mine," Garth said.

"I doubt it. Dr. Oldham doesn't think anyone ever went back to the mine."

"Well, if Black Dove eventually moved to Guadalupe Y Calvo to live after he'd left Kirker for good—maybe he did go back to the mine. At least to get some teeth."

Kitt laughed. "Would you get off the teeth business? I'm sure Black Dove had already had those gold teeth made a long time before—he certainly would have had enough money"

"New teeth, maybe. But I bet he got the gold ones from that old mine they found."

"You really think Black Dove would have gone there?"

"Kitt, if you ran across a gold mine and found a nugget, wouldn't you think about going back to it one day?"

"I guess so." Wealth and all its trappings had never held much pull for Kitt. She'd had her share of financial prosperity while growing up with her parents. Money drove people. It had driven her father—it had tormented old Hod all his life. Maybe it had driven Black Dove, too. But Kitt always felt she could do with just enough to be comfortable.

"I'd go looking for the gold," Garth said. She studied his face as he spoke. He was earnest, his brow drawn and his eyes far away.

"Why?" she asked.

"I believe in taking advantage of every opportunity that comes my way."

"If you had gold, people you didn't even know would be knocking on your door for handouts. Treasure hunters would be all over the place trying to find your mine. They'd decimate historical sites, ruin the environment—"

"Okay, okay!" He held up his hand with a laugh. "Never mind. I'll go on being a happy but impoverished journalist for the rest of my life."

"You're not impoverished, Garth."

"Not right now." He touched her cheek with the tip of his finger. She shivered, aware of the closeness of his body on the bed. The sides of their knees touched. She felt the warmth of that one tiny spot more intensely than she felt the gray scratchy blanket beneath her.

Garth fixed his eyes on the plastic end of his shoelace. An almost overwhelming mixture of pleasure and sadness flooded through him. He was here with Kitt. He might lose her again. But he might not. If he lost her, he wasn't sure what he'd do to keep going. If he didn't lose her, he wasn't sure how he'd handle having her in his life.

"I've got everything I need," he murmured, lifting his eyes to her face. "It's good to be with you now, Kitt. All those months in Vietnam, I thought I'd never see you again. I didn't want to see you because I knew you hated me. But the thought of never holding you or touching you . . ."

"I didn't hate you, Garth. I've told you that."

"Then what happened?" His eyes pleaded. "Please tell me what happened to you after you found out about our baby."

"Is this why you wanted to come here with me? To make me talk about things I can't bear to remember?"

"I want to be with you. Those days apart from you were empty as hell. Tell me you felt that, too."

Kitt knotted her fingers, wishing she were good at lying. She didn't want to speak the truth. He had already gotten into some of the places she had shut away. Now he wanted more. He wanted it all.

"I adjusted to my old life after I got to Santa Fe," she said.

Garth sat silently on the bed, staring at the flame in the glass lamp. A fear had crept into his stomach to tangle with the other emotions there. Maybe Kitt was telling the truth and had been all along. Maybe she really didn't need him. Maybe she didn't want him the way he wanted her.

He weighed that thought, turning over in his mind her physical response to him as opposed to what she said. With her words, she was far away. With her body, she was near. Maybe it was only sexual after all. He could have been wrong about her. But if all he evoked in Kitt was a purely physical appetite, that wasn't enough. He had loved more than her body. He had loved her spirit, the part deep inside her that made her unique.

But she didn't seem to love his hidden, inner self anymore. And that was what he wanted from her more than anything.

"I'll make up a pallet of blankets on the floor," he said, rising from the bed.

Kitt caught his wrist. "It's okay, Garth. We can sleep here in the bed together. I'll have my clothes on, and you—"

"No, I don't think so."

"Garth." Kitt stood beside him and turned him to face her. "Please sleep with me tonight."

# Chapter 13

"I used to find it hard to speak my mind, Kitt." Garth seemed to tower over her in the golden light. "Now it's hard for me to stay quiet when I have something to say."

"Say what you have to say to me, Garth."

"Do you love me, Kitt?"

She tried to force herself to breathe but the air wouldn't seem to come. "I used to love you."

"Damn it, Kitt! That's not enough. Do you love *me*?" He jabbed his chest with his thumb. "I'm not seventeen. I'm thirty-three. Do you love this man standing here? Do you love Garth Culhane?"

She jammed her hands into the pockets of her pants and let out a cloud of white breath. "I'm just cold. That's all I know. I just wanted to feel you next to me. I'm not asking you to make love to me, Garth. I'm not asking for eternal commitment, either. Could you just put your arms around me and hold me without turning it into a question of love?"

"All right. Get in bed."

His voice was brusque, almost angry. He bent and blew out the lamp. Not sure she even wanted the warmth of his body anymore, Kitt yanked back the sheet and climbed into the narrow bed. She rolled over facing the wall, her back to Garth as he settled down beside her. For a moment, neither of them moved. Kitt could feel his massive form, hard against the curves of her own body. His chest pressed her shoulder blades. His knees crooked in behind hers.

Then Garth pulled the sheet and blankets over them, and drew Kitt against him. She shivered at the sheer strength of his muscled arms as he curled them across her stomach. His face pushed into her hair and his breath warmed her neck.

She stared at the black wall two inches from her nose. The rise and fall of Garth's chest was labored. She knew he was not asleep. She knew she had hurt him. But dear God—did he really want her to love him again? To love him body and soul, as she had done before. Did he love her that way? Why hadn't she asked him how *he* felt about *her*?

She didn't want to know, that's why. It was too frightening to know that somewhere deep inside herself she might actually love Garth just as she had—no, more deeply and better than she had. And he might love her the same way.

As always, when Kitt thought of loving Garth, her thoughts went to their child. In her mind's eye, she saw him sitting beside her on the bed only minutes ago asking her once again—why? What happened, Kitt?

"The doctors called it a severe depression," she said softly to the black wall. "Lots of people have them. Mine started when the baby died."

Garth's body had stiffened behind her, but he said nothing.

"I kept thinking about our baby being dead inside me. I wanted it to go away. But I also loved it. I wanted to keep it. I felt sick inside. I tried to think where to turn, but I couldn't see any way out. My parents had disowned me. You were so young, and all you could do was stare at me with that look of panic in your eyes."

"You kept rocking in the old rocking chair, Kitt. I didn't understand."

"I couldn't do anything else because the doctors decided to leave the baby inside me until labor started spontaneously. I know that's normal procedure, but for some reason it just paralyzed me. All that time while I was waiting for the baby to be born, I could think only the same two thoughts over and over. There's a dead thing inside me and I want it out. I love that dead thing and I don't want to let it go. I couldn't win. I felt like I was inside a black box with six blank walls. No windows. No doors."

"Why didn't you talk to me about it, honey?"

"I couldn't see outside of myself and the black box. I could only see me and the baby. You seemed far away. I don't even really remember you during that time. I don't remember eating or sleeping or anything. I only remember that when I sat in the rocking chair, my thoughts seemed to have a certain rhythmic order. When I rocked, it seemed like I could wait."

"If I'd known what was happening, Kitt—I'd have made them take the baby out. I swear I would have." Garth closed his eyes in the warm nest of her hair. He felt a painful sense of emptiness, as though he could have prevented the horror that had happened to both of them. But he had been too blind and stupid to see what was going on.

"We didn't understand, Garth. We were kids. You thought I was hating you and blaming you. But really I wasn't thinking about you at all. I was just trying to survive."

"But even after . . . when the baby was born, Kitt—"

"The depression didn't end after the baby was born. I couldn't snap out of it. The doctors said my hormones were all messed up. Post-partum depression, you know. The baby blues. But I knew that was only a small part of what was happening inside me. Everything had been so horrible. The only way I could deal with it was to block it all out. I still don't remember much of that time."

Garth pulled Kitt closer into the protective mass of his body. She had curled into a fetal ball as she spoke. Her arms had stiffened and her fingers clenched his wrists. He knew he should let her go now, let her sleep. But in spite of her pain, she finally had opened up to him. He wanted to know more.

"How did you come out of the depression, Kitt?" he said softly. "Tell me about that. I feel like it's the last thing I don't really understand about you."

She began slowly. "One afternoon, my dad came to the trailer and found me. My mother still didn't want anything to do with me. But my father had heard you were gone. He came over to check on me and saw the shape I was in. He said I looked half dead, but I don't remember it clearly. Then my parents just took over."

"How?"

"They got me to a doctor so that I could start to rebuild my physical strength. Then they set up a series of appointments with a counselor. My mother took care of all the divorce papers while I was still so sick. She thought my depression was all your fault, even though I tried to explain it to her... Slowly, I began to get better. Then my parents enrolled me at the university in Albuquerque. I went to counselors there for about two years." She gave a wry laugh. "Sounds like a long time, doesn't it?"

"Not really. You had a lot to get over." He thought for a moment. "I think it took me two or three years to begin to feel better."

"After I came out of the worst part of the depression, I still had to learn to handle my anger. I was very angry with our baby for dying like that. Pretty illogical, I guess, but that's how I felt. And I was angry that you had abandoned me."

Garth closed his eyes, feeling her feelings, berating himself for his blindness. "So, you finally healed, honey?" he whispered.

"Mostly. I learned to put everything away. When it all came rushing into my mind, I learned to take control and put it on a shelf. I couldn't erase what had happened. But finally, I was able to just stop dwelling on it. I went on with my life and built my career. It's really a good life after all."

Garth kissed the side of Kitt's neck. She uncurled a little. Gently, he took her shoulders and turned her over to face him. The bottom of his chin rested on her head. She wrapped her arms around his waist and stretched out her legs so that she could feel the length of his body.

"Did your counselor say you had done everything you needed to do, Kitt?"

She gave a little sigh. "I was supposed to cry. My counselor kept telling me that if I would just cry about my losses, I could finally finish the grieving process. But I never could cry. Everything was stopped up inside me like a big dam. I never have cried about what happened, and I don't think I ever will."

"Kitt, honey. Can you ever forgive me for leaving you when I did?"

Kitt lifted her head. She could not see Garth's face, but she heard the pain in his voice. "Forgiveness is choosing to let go. I let go a long time ago, Garth."

He lay in the darkness, turning her words over in his mind. If forgiveness was letting go, then he had forgiven her as well. He had forgiven her for what he'd perceived as her hatred of him, her rejection of him. Finally, he had let all of that terrible, confusing experience go.

But he knew he had never let Kitt go. Not the Kitt he had always loved. He had held onto his memories of her, his love for her. In his mind, their marriage had never ended, even though he hadn't believed he would ever see her again.

Kitt's body had finally warmed and relaxed. Garth thought she might be asleep. He knew how much it had taken out of her to dredge up the memories. He knew she needed to rest and just feel the strength of his arms. But there was one last thing he had to understand.

"Kitt," he whispered.

She moved against him, nestling closer. "Yes?"

"When you let go of the past, do you think you let go of me?"

"I let go of the memories that hurt so much."

Garth closed his eyes. "But do you think you let go of me, Kitt? Me. Do you think you let go of me and our love?"

She sighed and her breath on his wool sweater warmed the tip of her nose. She felt too tired to lie. She felt too tired and too wonderful just being with him again. "No," she murmured. "I didn't let go of you."

Waking in the orange half-light of dawn, Kitt stared at the hazy window. This was her favorite time of day. The night, with its darkness and its potential for terror, was over. The full light of day—with all its promise of fulfillment and pleasure—waited only moments away. But right now, in the twilight of the dawn, she could rest.

Garth's body lay heavily against hers. One leg angled over her thighs. His arm, as if seeking to hold and protect her, curved over her stomach, and his tousled head lay on her breasts. She curled her arms around his head, wove her fingers through his hair and gently kissed the warm skin of his forehead.

A strange sense of release had settled over her as she slept. Perhaps it had something to do with her talk with Garth the night before. Perhaps it was related to the fact that he was sleeping with her, holding her close and keeping her warm through the night as he had long ago. Or maybe it was just the fact that she'd taken in a lot of excitement and fresh air. Looking at it one way, she realized, this crazy trip was her first vacation in years. People took vacations to unwind. Maybe she was unwinding.

Garth stirred. Kitt studied his face. How strong and masculine it was yet somehow gentle in sleep. A thick growth of light brown whiskers shadowed his jaw. She tried to picture him with a beard. A smile drifted across her mouth as she thought of the scattered peach fuzz he'd been so proud of at seventeen.

She was glad Garth had grown up. As much as she had loved that gangly boy—she could appreciate the fully adult male more. He talked better, he cared more deeply, he fought harder.

His blue-gray eyes drifted open and focused on the wall. Then, as if he remembered where he was, Garth lifted his head and settled his gaze on Kitt's face.

"I love you," he said.

She closed her eyes. "Garth."

"You don't have to say anything, Kitt. I just wanted you to know."

"Thank you." It was an inane comment, but her mind had suddenly catapulted into confusion. Why was he so honest? Didn't he think what such words could mean? Didn't he think about the future and the past and all the tangled mess their lives could become again?

"I've never seen your hair looking so beautiful, Kitt." His sleepy voice let her know he was saying the first thing that came to mind, with little thought for significance.

She pursed her lips. "Okay, wise guy. I know my hair looks like a rat's nest. I didn't even get it unbraided before I went to sleep."

"I mean it. Something about the way the light is coming in. Makes it look almost red. Auburn."

He leaned toward her shoulder and kissed the shaggy braid. Then he settled his head on her chest, nuzzling between the full rise of her breasts beneath her sweater. His big hand splayed across her stomach began to circle slowly.

Kitt caught her breath at the unexpected flood of heat that surged down her legs at his touch. She lay still, feeling the electrical current running from his hand to the skin just above the waistband of her pants. If she could have, she might have made a move to get up and start the day.

Garth's hand slipped under her sweater. His warm fingertips traced wide circles on her flesh. She willed her breath to a steady pace as his hand rose higher. Turning his head, he rubbed his face between her breasts. The slightly scratchy fabric of her turtleneck sweater nudged the bare tips of her nipples into tight buds of pleasure. She bit her lower lip as Garth slid up higher on the bed and began kissing her neck with warm, wet, languorous strokes.

"I didn't say I loved you, Garth," she whispered in a last-ditch attempt at control.

"I can wait for the words. They're in your heart trying to get out."

"You don't know that."

"I have faith."

The tip of his tongue touched her ear as he said the words. Kitt shivered and turned to him, wrapping her arms around his chest. She lifted her mouth and their lips crushed together. Parting, she took in the full length of his tongue, savoring the familiar, tangy-sweet taste of her husband. As their tongues danced, his hand slipped over her breast, cupping the full, bare flesh and teasing her nipple between his fingers. She cried out softly, aware of the tugging pleasure deep in the pit of her stomach. He took first one then the other hardened bud, pulling and twisting slightly, heightening her pleasure the way he knew she loved. Back and forth, first one nipple then the other until her hips were swaying against his thigh.

She ran her tongue down the side of his neck, aware of his hardness against her legs. Slipping her hands out of his hair, she reached for him, stroking the warmth of his arousal. He groaned at her touch. Imagining the pleasure of his naked body against her, Kitt began to tug his shirt out from the waist of his pants. He lifted her sweater, exposing her breasts to the bare skin of his palms. His fingers rolled over and over the hardened pebbles until her back arched and her hands caught his hips. Leaning toward her, he took one nipple between his lips, suckling and tugging at it.

Her heart hammering in her temples nearly drowned out the quick rapping on their door. But she couldn't ignore the melodic voice that followed the knock. *"Desayuno, señor y señora."* Señora Martinez called softly.

Kitt caught her breath.

"Breakfast," Garth whispered.

"I don't care." The thought of food held no appeal compared with her hunger for the man whose body had tangled with hers.

Garth held her still for a moment as he stared at the door. He thought of all the precautions he needed to take, of the consequences, the pain.

"Let's wait, Kitt."

She shut her eyes against the damp skin of his shoulder. "I don't want to wait, Garth."

He lifted her chin with the crook of his finger. "Let's wait until tonight. Until we're ready."

"I might change my mind. You know how I am."

"You won't change your mind."

"I'm ready now, Garth."

"You'll be readier tonight. Wait and see." With a sly grin, he gave her breasts one last torturing pull with his lips. As she reached for him, he rolled out of bed, leaving her empty-armed and famished.

"There's the padre, over by the candles." Garth took Kitt's cool hand and walked beside her down the stone floor of the church.

Like a miniature version of a European cathedral, the Iglesia del Sangre de Cristo had an aura of holy beauty. Dimly lit, smelling of incense and candle wax, the air wore a musty cloak. The ceiling soared on stone pillars. Carved cherubim and seraphim fluttered among grotesque gargoyles along the tops of the pillars. Niches in the side walls displayed peeling portraits of Christ's long journey to the cross. Rows of worn wooden benches filed down the nave and faced the giant wooden crucifix that hung between two stained-glass windows.

On a back bench, a ragged young man lay asleep with his arm angled across his eyes. His snores mingled softly with the sound of footsteps as Garth and Kitt made their way through the cavernous sanctuary. Near the front, an old woman in a black mantilla rose from her knees. She genuflected in the aisle before passing the visitors without a glance.

The padre, dressed in a black robe, was small and nearly bald. His thin fingers gently straightened rows of half-burned candles. But his bright black eyes were fastened on the newcomers.

*"Bienvenidos."* His voice was almost inaudible as he greeted them.

Kitt felt she should do something in obeisance, but she wasn't a Catholic and she wasn't sure what would be appropriate. As it was, Garth bluntly began explaining their reason for coming to the church, leaving her with nothing to do but wish she had at least worn a hat on her bare head.

*"Permitéme."* The priest gestured toward a wooden door at the side of the apse. His feet invisible beneath his floor-length robe, he glided ahead into a small room containing a table and chairs and the rail to a descending staircase.

"Down there," he said in Spanish, barely raising his voice, "we keep the records of every baptism, marriage and death in Guadalupe Y Calvo."

Kitt glanced at the wooden railing and the chipped stone circular stair. "May we look through the records? It shouldn't take us long."

"I have already looked for the burial records of Black Dove, the Indian. He is not mentioned."

"But we have been told that Black Dove was buried in Guadalupe Y Calvo."

"Not here," the priest said. "He was killed outside the town, the legends tell us. But not buried at the church. I wrote a letter to Dr. Frank Oldham, the colleague of whom you spoke. I told him the legends, and of the veracity of the outlaw's death. He asked me to search the records. I did search, but when I found nothing, I saw no point in further correspondence."

"So all Dr. Oldham knew was that you had said Black Dove was killed near Guadalupe Y Calvo. But you actually found no record of his burial?"

"Not surprising. Do you think we would bury an unrepentant, non-Christian murderer in our midst? Certainly not. It would be a defilement. I believe the Indian must be buried in the mountains where they found his body."

"So they did find his body." Kitt felt that the priest was being evasive.

"That, *señora*, I do not know. I am much too young. I know only some of the stories of Black Dove. For the most accurate story, you will need to speak with old Santiago, the grandson of the Indian."

"Well, thank you for your time—" Garth began.

"Wait." Kit laid a hand on his arm. "May we look through the records ourselves, Padre? Perhaps we will find some mention of his wife and children."

"Maria was not a real wife. They were never married in the church."

"We understand that," Kitt said. "But please—may we just look?"

The priest turned his head and stared at the dark staircase for a moment. "Only the oldest records are kept below. The books are very heavy. They are crumbling. It will be quite difficult for me to bring them up to you."

"We'll go down and look."

The priest shook his head. "That place is not pleasant. In the old days, before the cemetery we now have behind the church, the bodies were placed in the crypts below."

"It's all right, Padre. I'm an archaeologist. I'm used to seeing skeletal remains."

"The crypts form a difficult maze. You will find the records in the first room to the right, behind a metal door. Please do not wander around, I'm not sure I would be able to find you if you became lost."

"We'll just look at the records and come back up."

"Very well." The priest handed them a lantern and a box of matches. "Go with God."

Garth lit the lantern as the priest made his way into the church. "Are you sure we need to do this, Kitt?" he whispered. It had been strange enough watching Kitt uncover the remains of the lady with the thousand beads. But a bunch of skeletons scattered around in a dark maze sounded particularly bizarre. "We could just trust the guy. He is a priest, you know—I doubt he'd lie."

"I know. I believe him. But remember Mrs. Lujan and the Kneeling Nun Mine? I'll never forgive myself for failing to look more closely at those medical records of hers. It was just lucky the way it worked out. You can never be sure unless you check out everything yourself."

Taking the lantern, she started down the steps. A chill colder than refrigerated air-conditioning crept around her ankles and up her slacks. Her fingers slipped down the worn, curved railing. As her eyes adjusted to the darkness, her nose accustomed itself to the familiar smell of age. Old, dank stonework, dusty cobwebs, must, niter. The scent of incense had drifted down and mingled with the other smells, leaving an almost tangible taste on her tongue.

"First door on the right," Kitt said to herself. She could hear Garth climbing down behind her as she stepped onto the damp stone floor. "There must be an underground stream nearby. Look how I'm leaving faint wet footprints. Wow, take a look at these remains. Wouldn't Dr. Dean love this!"

Garth swallowed as they filed past rows of reclining skeletons. He could see the jaunty swing of Kitt's hips and the sway of the lantern ahead of him. She was moving back and forth, holding the light up to the skulls in their niches as if greeting old friends.

"This is just excellent! Look how well preserved they are. We could really learn a lot about the people of this area here. You'd get a real cross-section of the population. I bet there are some Indians buried here. Most of these people have a great deal of Indian blood mixed in with their Spanish heritage— whether they want to accept that or not. You know what I've always wanted to do, Garth?"

She whirled, her brown eyes glowing in the darkness. He hooked his thumbs in his pockets and grinned. "Live in a cemetery?"

"No, silly."

She looked beautiful, at that moment. Her hair had fallen around her shoulders and her face was rosy, full of life. If she hadn't been standing in the middle of a crypt full of dead people, he'd have picked her up, swung her around and given her a big kiss.

"Tell me what you've always wanted to do, Kitt."

"This!"

He glanced around. "Walk around under a church with a bunch of bones?"

"See the world! You wouldn't believe the archaeological and anthropological mysteries no one has ever even thought of exploring. I'd like to do an intensive study of some of the old Latin American peoples who were wiped out by the Spaniards. And there are populations in places like Tierra del Fuego that hardly anyone has studied. And Africa! Now think about that—there are hundreds of tribes. Each has its own language. Its own culture. Some of the languages are still unwritten, Garth. You know what I'd really like to do?"

"Tell me, honey."

"I'd like to take all the legends and oral histories of the tribes in a certain area of Africa—or Latin America, or anywhere. And I'd like to translate them and then compare them. I bet it would be astounding!"

"Mind boggling."

She heard the note of teasing in his voice. "You don't think that would be interesting?"

"I think it would be fantastic, Kitt. Do you suppose you could tell me more about it when we're standing out in the sunshine? I'm afraid Transylvania inspires my imagination differently than it does yours."

Kitt took in Garth's huge body, half in shadow beneath the floor of the old church. His head was slightly cocked because there was not enough room for him to straighten. A spiderweb draped off one shoulder. A yellowed femur lay near his shoes.

"Sorry." Suppressing a giggle, she headed for the first door on the right. Antiquities were her love. She didn't see the past and all its mysteries the way others might—as slightly spooky. She understood how Garth might be uncomfortable in the crypt. But she was glad he was with her. It had felt good to share her dreams as they poured out.

"This must be the door." Garth turned a big iron ring. At first he thought the door had rusted to the floor. Heaving his shoulder into it, he heard it squeal, and finally it began to open.

"A metal door in a damp crypt. That doesn't make sense—it was bound to get rusty." Kitt held the lantern high and walked into the small room.

Garth caught his breath. "Books—and they're not just records."

Sagging wooden shelves lined the four walls. Row upon row of books, some tattered and worn—others hardly used—filled each shelf. Two old locked trunks sat on the bare stone floor. Grabbing Kitt's shoulders, Garth directed her to a row of gold-lettered volumes. She lifted the lantern.

"These are religious books. Missals. Scriptures." He slid one out and gingerly pried open the yellowed pages. Illuminated, gold-leaf figures filled the borders. "This has got to be a medieval or early renaissance text."

"See what I mean? Treasures are everywhere, Garth. But we're looking for records of Black Dove." She moved away, leaving him staring at the old text in the darkness.

"Black Dove! Kitt, these are probably really valuable manuscripts. They're Latin, see? I bet they were brought over during the conquest."

"By the Spanish missionaries, I'd expect."

Garth closed the book and carried it across the room to where Kitt was scanning an old journal. He glanced at the door, wondering whether he should have wedged it with a stone. The place made him think of those old movies where the door suddenly slams shut, trapping everyone inside.

"This is it." The excitement in Kitt's voice pulled him away from his Lon Chaney imaginings. "The Guadalupe Y Calvo burial records for the late 1800s. Look at this strange, old-fashioned penmanship."

Garth took the lantern and held it over her shoulder as they read line after line in search of Black Dove. The 1850s, 1860s, 1870s, 1880s. A lot of people had passed away in the little town. But none of them were named Black Dove.

"Maybe he went by some other name while he was here," Garth said as Kitt set the book in its place.

"Everyone in this town who knows the legend calls him Black Dove. Or *Paloma Negra*. I looked for both."

"Well, I guess the padre was right. He wasn't buried here."

Flipping through page after page, she grew more frustrated. How could a town hire a man to help them and then refuse to acknowledge him? It was as if Black Dove had not even been considered a human being here. Had he been unable to marry because of his race? His religion? Or had he elected not to marry but instead to live with the schoolteacher's daughter? And what sort of woman had she been—to have chosen the Indian despite the disapproval of the whole town?

"I've got something." Garth's voice held a note of controlled excitement. He cradled a heavy brown volume.

"What is it?" Kitt closed the book of marriage records, marking her place with her thumb.

"A baptism. Right here." His brown finger pressed the page while Kitt read aloud.

"The baptism of Maria, girl child of Maria Cristina Gallegos and Black Dove, the Indian. April 23, 1858."

"So Black Dove *was* here. He did live with the schoolmaster's daughter. Her name was Maria Cristina Gallegos."

"And they had a baby girl whose name was also Maria. If Maria was born in 1858, she would have been twelve years old in 1870—the year she was taken from her father because her mother had died."

"There ought to be a burial record for Maria Cristina Gallegos in 1870." Garth spoke the words, but Kitt was already reaching for the volume of burial records.

It took only a moment. There was the name in faded ink. "Maria Cristina Gallegos, died May 17, 1870. Buried May 18, 1870. Guadalupe Y Calvo."

"We've got a man. We've got a wife. We've got a daughter. But what happened in 1870 after Maria Cristina Gallegos died and the twelve-year-old Maria was taken away from Black Dove?''

Kitt shut the book with a smile of satisfaction. ''Let's go see old Santiago. Maria's son. He'll know.''

# *Chapter 14*

The padre looked faintly surprised when Kitt and Garth emerged from the crypts. Perhaps he hadn't expected to see them again, Kitt thought. After all, it would have been tempting to explore the underground passageways. Who could tell what might be discovered beneath the old Sangre de Cristo church? Perhaps the site went back to the precolonial era. But Kitt and Garth had more pressing matters than a long trek through a maze.

They thanked the padre and climbed the gentle hill to Señor Martinez's store.

"It's true what the brochure said." Kitt studied the bustling village as they walked through it. "I don't see any wheeled vehicles at all."

"Sort of gives you the feeling you've stepped back in time."

"The clothing is so colorful—all handwoven reds and blues. Have you noticed how bright the children's eyes are? Everyone looks well-fed and content. It's not the way I imagined the Third World."

"They're self-sufficient, I expect. Agricultural, without much need for imported goods."

"Matches and soap and dye."

"And gasoline."

Garth took in a deep breath of fresh mountain air. He didn't mind chasing drug smugglers through Juarez, or tracing a murder case across the back alleys of downtown Albuquerque. But strolling around in a crypt was not his idea of a good time. Kitt continued to fascinate him with her enthusiasm and store of knowledge. He decided she'd probably go just about anywhere if it would solve some archaeological mystery.

"You know, Santiago has got to be pretty old," she was saying. "If his mother was born in 1858, he'd have to be upwards of ninety—even if she was in her forties when she gave birth to him."

"Like Hod...I wonder how he's doing, poor old guy. Probably still hanging around his bar. I keep thinking about that picture of James Kirker—Santiago Querque. And now we have another Santiago. Do you suppose Maria named her son for the renegade white hunter?"

"Who knows. There are some things we'll probably never know." Kitt waved at Señor Martinez as he ambled down the steps from his shop. "I hope we're not going to get involved in another discussion of his light bulb."

"Garth! Kitt!" He pronounced her name *Keet*. "I have been waiting for you. My wife is very concerned that you were lost in the caves beneath the church. After you left, we began to worry—perhaps the padre will send you down instead of going down himself. I am so glad he fetched the books for you."

"We went beneath the church by ourselves, Señor Martinez," Kitt informed him.

"*Caramba!*" He shook his head. Then he leaned over and whispered. "Sometimes when I am praying in the church, I think about the maze beneath the floor." Señor Martinez shivered. "Come, you will want to meet old Santiago? This is his house. On the left, with the blue posts. I will take you."

The door was opened by a dark-skinned, white-haired, wizened fellow who had no teeth. Dressed like the other villagers in a brightly knit sweater and dark wool trousers, he had a pair of worn leather boots on his feet. He smiled widely upon introduction and waved a wrinkled hand into his house.

"Santiago will serve your lunch. Return to my house for dinner," Señor Martinez said on parting. "You will not see the light on the porch, but I think you know my shop."

Kitt nodded, but Señor Martinez wasn't through. "The generator is too expensive to run until the sun has gone down," he said by way of explanation, "even though some days are very dark in Guadalupe Y Calvo. One evening the bulb burned out just as I lifted the switch . . . well, I will tell you about the light bulb while we eat our dinner."

Kitt glanced at Garth. He wore the faintest trace of a grin on his face as he stepped into the warm front room of Santiago's home. The old man gestured for his guests to be seated, then settled on a small stool beside the fire.

"I live here alone," he said softly. "My children and my grandchildren all have homes in the village of Guadalupe Y Calvo, but I wish to live here in the house of my mother."

Kitt nodded, trying to think how to begin a conversation about the past. She wasn't sure Santiago was totally alert. His thin fingers traced patterns on his trousers. His head was turned to the fire, and he seemed to have forgotten his guests.

"I am lonely," he murmured in Spanish. "In the old days many of us lived in the little house."

"How many children did your mother have, Santiago?" Kitt asked.

"Nine brothers and sisters. All dead now, but me. I was the youngest. Santiago, the baby." He chuckled, but kept his eyes on the fire.

"Your mother, Maria, was the daughter of Maria Cristina Gallegos and the Indian, Black Dove, wasn't she?" Kitt asked gently.

"I was born when my mother was forty-seven years old. A big surprise for everyone, even for my mother when she first learned a baby would be coming."

"Did you know your mother well, Santiago?"

The old man turned and laughed. His bare gums gave him a childlike expression of innocence. "Of course I knew my mother. She died when she was almost one hundred years old. We live a long time, we who have descended from the Indian war chief. My father was not so lucky. Kicked in the head by a horse when I was five."

"So Black Dove *was* your grandfather?"

Santiago nodded, then rubbed his hand across the air as if to erase the subject. "Let us eat now."

While Garth and Kitt sat in silence, the old man shuffled over to his stove and began preparing a meal of frijoles, fresh fruit and glasses of creamy milk. Glancing at Garth, Kitt realized he had slouched in his chair, one arm hooked over the back. His lazy-lidded blue-gray gaze traced over her face, pausing on her eyes, her lips, her neck before moving down. She tried to force his attention to her face, but his eyes followed a line to her breasts.

Shifting a little, she let her eyes dart downward. Her blue sweater clung to the outlines of her breasts. Their tips, tight from the cold walk through the village, poked against the thin cotton knit. Beneath Garth's comfortable scrutiny, Kitt felt her breasts swell and her nipples contract into hard, round beads.

Santiago was humming a tuneless melody as he stirred the frijoles. Kitt thought about where she was, and the necessity of concentration. She was a professional on a business trip, after all. Clearing her throat, she tried to capture Garth's attention.

His gaze had slid to her legs. Tracing the line of her jeans, he allowed his eyes to linger on her feet. Then he slowly moved his focus to her thighs and the gentle curve of her zipper. Remembering his promise of the morning, Kitt realized it wouldn't take much from him to rekindle her desire. Her knees felt limp, and she was grateful for the support of the stiff wooden chair. A tingle spread from her stomach to her bottom then curled deep between her thighs at the memory of his lips on her breasts, his tongue lapping at her nipples.

His eyes caught hers and held them for a full minute. She knew what he was thinking. It was the same look he had sent her across a classroom full of high school seniors. It was the look that meant, I'm thinking about us. I'm thinking about your lips and how wet they are. I'm thinking about stroking your wet lips with my fingertips, teasing you with my touch until you think you're about to die...

"Frijoles." Santiago thunked a chipped porcelain bowl on the table beside Kitt. She gave an involuntary little start. Garth chuckled in a low voice. Standing, he lifted his chair to the table and placed it in front of a second bowl of mud-brown beans.

"So, Santiago," he said, all charm and aplomb, "tell us about Black Dove, your grandfather."

Feeling like a kid caught with her hand in the cookie jar, Kitt awkwardly turned to the table. All Garth Culhane had to do was stare at her zipper for a minute and she began acting like some out-of-control teenager. This was *not* how she normally behaved. She dipped her spoon into the beans. Other men took her out, other men gave her longing looks. Why did it have to be this one certain man—and only him—who could transform her composure to chaos?

There he was across the table, chatting with Santiago, waving his spoon around as he spoke. Did he know how much she wanted to crawl across the table and touch that little curl of dark gold hair that was sitting on the collar of his sweater? She was practically shaking from wanting to run her palms over the hard plane of his chest and feel his crisp hair beneath her fingertips. Here she was, thinking about dipping her tongue in his navel, while he was glibly conversing over a bowl of refried beans.

"But Black Dove himself died when he was still quite young, we understand," Garth was saying. He glanced at Kitt.

She smiled with as little emotion as possible.

"My grandfather was killed on the side of the mountain," Santiago said. "You see, they took my mother away from him when she was twelve years old, after my grandmother died. From that time, Black Dove did not wish to live. He was careless, my mother told me. One day, he was trying to stop an Apache attack on the burro trains carrying gold to Chihuahua City. During the attack, my grandfather Black Dove was killed by Apaches. Much of the gold was taken away by the the Apaches that day."

"After his death, wasn't your grandfather buried in the church at Guadalupe Y Calvo?" Kitt asked, forcing herself to concentrate.

"Of course not. He was the Indian. My mother told me no one knew of the massacre for many months. Not until word came from Chihuahua City that the gold train had never arrived. Then searchers went looking. There they found the dead.''

''And your grandfather, Black Dove, was among those killed during the attack?''

''Many months after death, it is difficult to tell about such things. One man whose body was found at the place of the massacre was wearing the cross my grandmother had given to Black Dove. My mother believed that man was her father. Black Dove always wore the cross, and so Black Dove had been killed.''

Santiago held up a hand and began digging into the folds of his shirt. Kitt looked at Garth. He had set his spoon on the table and was watching as the old man fumbled with the buttons beneath his sweater.

''Here is the cross of Black Dove.'' Santiago slid a bright chain from his shirt and held it out. In his leathery palm lay a large but simple crucifix of yellow gold. It might have been any cross of gold. But Santiago took the end and carefully turned it over.

Kitt leaned forward. Tiny words had been engraved in the gold. *''BD—Ma C G,''* she read. *''Mi Esposo En Dios.''*

''My Husband In God,'' Garth said to Santiago. ''What did your grandmother mean when she had that inscribed to Black Dove?''

''The church would not marry them. So they were married by God. It is better, no?''

Garth focused on Kitt. ''Either way is good…isn't it, Kitt?''

Kitt had that fragile look again—the one she hadn't worn when he'd first met her after all those years. But now it kept appearing on her face, flitting across so fast he almost missed it sometimes. She was still herself—the new, tough Kitt who could look out for her own interests. But she was bending some, too. Allowing herself to feel things, and to want what she hadn't wanted for such a long time.

''Come and sit with me beside the fire again,'' Santiago said. Kitt picked up the empty bowls and glasses and set them in a pot of warm water by the stove. Garth wiped the table with a cloth. Then they joined the old man in a semicircle around his beehive fireplace.

"My mother told me about that day," Santiago said. His voice was barely audible. "It was the day she remembered most out of all the days of her whole life."

"Which day was that, Santiago?"

"The day her mother died. My mother told me she crept like a little mouse into the room of her mother. From the door she watched. Her father was sitting on the bed where her mother lay. He was weeping. Can you imagine—the warrior Black Dove weeping and holding the hand of his wife? No doctors would come to tend her. Black Dove did not know what was wrong with her. She had great pain. Black Dove climbed into the bed with his wife and held her very close to his chest. And then she died. He screamed and beat his chest and ran out of the house to his horse. He rode away into the mountains. My mother told me she was very afraid then—only twelve years old. She wanted to be with her father, but he had gone away in his grief."

"What happened after that, Santiago?" Kitt asked.

Santiago began tracing patterns in his trousers again. "Then the schoolteacher came to the home of Black Dove and Maria Cristina Gallegos—who had been his daughter. He took little twelve-year-old Maria—my mother—away from the house. They buried Maria Cristina Gallegos in the church the next day, but my mother was not allowed to see her."

"What about Black Dove? Did he ever come back for his daughter?"

Santiago smiled. "He came back, all painted for war—with red and black colors on his face. He rode up to the house of the schoolteacher and waved his tomahawk. He shouted that he wanted Maria and he would kill anyone who stood in his way. Then the schoolteacher, who was much afraid, forced my mother to go out onto the porch and tell Black Dove that she wanted to be safe and live in the village with the school-teacher."

"Was that the truth?"

"Oh, no." Santiago sighed. "My mother loved her father very much. Black Dove was a gentle man. He taught her many games, and words of his language. He was quiet and good to her always. But that day the schoolteacher told her that if she didn't make Black Dove leave the village, the whole town would go after him and kill him. Black Dove was a bad man, the schoolteacher told her—a murderer, a woman thief."

"So Black Dove left?"

"He went into the hills and soon he got killed by those Apaches."

"And what happened to Maria?"

"She lived with the schoolteacher for many years. But she never loved him. He had taken her away from her father. My mother always told me that the Indian was a good man—loving, kind, generous. No matter what the others said about him, she told me she would believe only what she knew. Black Dove was a good man."

"So Maria grew up and got married and had nine children."

"The last one was me!" Santiago chuckled. "Now, I have the cross of my grandfather Black Dove... I have something else, too."

Garth's eyebrows lifted a little. "What do you have, Santiago?"

The old man shook his head. "You would like to know—but I cannot tell you."

"Why can't you tell us?"

"Because it is the secret of Black Dove."

Kitt leaned forward. "The secret of Black Dove... Santiago—do you understand why we're here, asking about your grandfather?" She heard the note of pleading in her voice.

"Many people want to learn the story of Black Dove. I tell it often."

She briefly related the discovery of the grave in New Mexico and the importance of confirming or denying the theory that Black Dove might have left Guadalupe Y Calvo and gone to Muddy Flats.

"If you have anything at all that might lead us to the truth, Santiago, we need to know."

The old man closed his eyes and sat without speaking. Kitt waited, studying him, then decided he might have gone to sleep. She glanced at Garth. He shrugged. Remembering the way Garth had gone through her house and Hod's, she decided she'd better keep her eye on him. No doubt Garth would want to go exploring and see what he could find in Santiago's home while the old man slept. She was about to suggest they leave when Santiago opened his eyes.

"This, I think, will be proof that the man killed on the mountainside was Black Dove. But if I show it to you—you must not speak of it to anyone."

Kitt nodded. It would present some difficulties in compiling her book, but she decided to go along. Maybe Santiago had something worthwhile, maybe not. The cross was interesting, but it didn't really prove anything. She felt her heartbeat speed up as the old man rooted around in the bottom of a large metal chest beside the fire.

"Here." Santiago turned to them, smiling his gummy grin. "I have the treasure of Black Dove."

He carried a small leather pouch tied with a thong. Settling back in his chair, he placed the pouch on his knees and carefully untied it. As he loosened the thong, Kitt tried to see inside.

"What is it? What do you have, Santiago?"

"Gold!" Santiago held up to the firelight a rough nugget the size of a walnut. Laying it carefully on one knee, he lifted another to the light, this one roughly as large as a pecan. Then another and another.

"Where did Black Dove get this gold, Santiago?" Garth asked.

"From his mine. In the Sierra Madres, not far from Guadalupe Y Calvo." Santiago closed the pouch without offering Kitt or Garth a chance at close inspection. "There is no more gold at the mine now. Black Dove removed it all before he died."

"So how does this prove Black Dove was killed on the hillside?"

Santiago pulled at the drawstring. "This pouch was found on the body of the man who wore the cross. A sign is burned into the leather of the pouch—the sign of a black dove. See?" He showed them the tiny insignia. "So, the man killed by Apaches had both Black Dove's crucifix and his pouch of gold. It could only have been Black Dove."

Kitt thought for a moment. "What about the teeth?"

"Teeth?"

"Did the man killed on the hillside have two gold front teeth, Santiago?"

"My mother never mentioned gold teeth. Why do you speak of gold teeth?"

"Black Dove was said to have two gold front teeth."

"I know nothing about this. My mother said only that Black Dove was her father—good and kind, loving and gentle. Nothing about gold teeth."

Kitt's eyes followed the old man as he replaced the pouch in the chest. Maybe Maria hadn't even noticed her father's gold teeth. Children rarely saw their parents' flaws. To Maria, Black Dove clearly had been perfect in every way. Inside and out.

She let out her breath. As hard as it might be to accept in light of the Muddy Flats excavation, Black Dove apparently *had* been killed and later buried in the mountains just outside Guadalupe Y Calvo. The evidence was simply too convincing: the remains of a man wearing Black Dove's crucifix and carrying a pouch inscribed with his insignia and filled with nuggets from his gold mine. Maria certainly believed her father had been killed. All signs indicated the warrior had been distraught—his wife had died and his daughter was taken from him.

So, the mighty Black Dove *had* been murdered by the Apaches.

And the Muddy Flats man was another person entirely, even though he bore a striking resemblance to the description of Black Dove.

"Thank you, Santiago," Kitt said gently. She reached out to take his hand, but he sat gazing at the fire, his face slack.

"I am a very lonely man," he remarked. "Will you stay with me here, *señor* and *señora*?"

Garth stuck another log on the fire and prodded the flames. "Santiago, we already have a room at Señor Martinez's store. Would you like for us to find your family—one of your children would come and sit with you, I'm sure."

"So busy, they are. Plowing and harvesting. Not much time for an old man. But you have nothing to do. You like to sit and talk. You like the stories of old Santiago. Stay and I will tell you more stories."

Garth observed Kitt's face as she gazed at the old man. Making a quick decision, he reached into his pocket and pulled out his little tape recorder.

"Here, Kitt. It's what you said you always wanted to do. Listen to his stories and spend as much time as you want. I have something to do. I'll come back for you at dinnertime."

Kitt looked down at the little machine on her knee. "Thanks," she said. "I'm sure I can find my way to the store."

"I'll come get you."

Giving Santiago a firm handshake, Garth headed out the door into the afternoon. Through the window, Kitt watched him disappear down an alley. Where was he going? Or did he really just want her to have this time alone to collect an old man's tales?

"Santiago," she said, pressing the little red button on the tape recorder. "Tell me your stories."

"Did anything come of that?" Garth asked. "You were there three hours."

"I'd have stayed longer but I ran out of tape."

"Must have been some good stories. Anything about Black Dove?"

"Wouldn't you like to know." She felt his hand brush against hers as they descended the hill to the store. It had grown dark, and Señor Martinez's two light bulbs were burning.

"I couldn't stay with you, Kitt. I had other things to do."

"Like what?"

"Things."

"Things to do with what? Black Dove?"

"Wouldn't you like to know." Garth led Kitt through a side gate and deflected her course when she started for the Martinez house. "I made another plan for our dinner."

"I think Señora Martinez will be expecting us, Garth."

"No, she won't."

"What have you done?"

"Just close your eyes and walk into the room. Close your eyes, Kitt."

"You're treating me like a kid."

"Sixteen years old. Right where we left off... Close your eyes."

Making a face at him but obeying, Kitt stepped into the warmth of their tiny room. She could hear Garth moving around, striking matches, clinking dishes. The scent of smoke and candle wax drifted around her.

"Smells like you're lighting a pyre in here. What are you doing to do, set me on fire or something?" she asked.

"That's the plan."

"So when do I get to open my eyes?"

"You really have gotten a lot wordier in fifteen years, Kitt. You're impatient, too." His hand touched the side of her neck. "I like that about you. And I like *this* about you."

She took a deep breath as his fingers traced the curve of her jaw. Though her eyes were closed and he was barely touching her, she could sense the nearness of his body. He had moved behind her. His breath warmed her hair. The presence of his chest not an inch from her back was as palpable as a magnetic field. Then his hands began lifting her hair. His mouth covered the line of her neck. Instinctively, she lowered her head.

"Open your eyes, honey."

For a moment, she couldn't. His tongue was burning a ring of fire behind her ear. His teeth caught her lobe and pulled it gently downward. She could feel his chest now, hard against her shoulder blades. Waiting for his fingers to touch her somewhere—her neck, her hands, her breasts—she tensed and held her breath. But he didn't move.

She opened her eyes.

The bedroom sparkled with the lights of a hundred tiny candles that perched on windowsills, bedposts, chairs and floor. Shadows danced across the ceiling. A small table draped with a white cloth stood beside the bed. It held a platter of fresh fruit, a plate of steaming tortillas and two covered bowls. A bottle of wine lay between the pillows.

"It's magical," Kitt whispered, turning to him. His eyes reflected the golden light of the candles. "It's all been magical, you know? Seeing you outside my motel door that night...and finding out we still enjoyed each other... it's all been sort of unreal. I never expected this to happen. It's been... just magic."

"It's not magic, Kitt. It's destiny."

"You don't believe that."

"Yes, I do."

"You're supposed to be one of those cynical reporters I'm always butting heads with. Reporters don't believe in things like destiny. They only buy hard, cold facts."

"Archaeologists aren't supposed to believe in magic. Only in things you can touch." Putting action to words, he ran his fingers down her shoulders and took her hands. Lifting them, he pressed his thumbs deeply into her palms. His eyes held her, pinning her with a fierce intensity.

If this were a mating dance, she sensed it was her turn to whirl away and do something coy. But with Garth it had never been that way. It had always been bare, unpretentious desire between them. A wanting that couldn't wait for games.

"I suppose we could . . . eat," she whispered, making a stab at the dance.

"Kitt." He pulled her roughly against him. His fingers tangled in her hair, tugging her head back. His mouth covered hers, his tongue finding hers eager for his taste. With a groan of pleasure, he covered her with his hands—roughly, almost clumsily taking her hips, her waist, her breasts. Her arms wrapped tightly around his chest. Her fingertips explored the valley of his spine and the taut rise of his buttocks.

"Love me, Garth." Her voice dripped into his bones and made them liquid. "Love me the way you used to."

He cradled her head in his palms and met her eyes. "I can't do that. I'm not seventeen anymore. And you're a woman now."

"Then love me like a man."

Their eyes locked, they began undressing. Kitt slipped her sweater over her head. Her hair tumbled out of the sweater neck like a waterfall, spilling over her shoulders and down her bare breasts to lap at her waist. The rosy tips of her breasts peeked through the tangle.

Tearing off his sweater, Garth took her eagerly. His lips nuzzled through the thick hair and found her nipples. First one then the other. Suckling them, he felt them pucker under the stroke of his wet tongue. Her breath suddenly shallow, she slipped her hands over his chest and raked her nails lightly against his flat brown nipples.

Each worked the other's zipper, fumbling and laughing at their clumsiness. Their eagerness turned to moans of mutual pleasure as their hands slid down naked flesh to discard jeans, silky panties, shorts, wool socks and shoes.

"Look what you do to me, Kitt."

But her lips had already found him. He caught moundfuls of her hair as she knelt and tasted the essence of her lover. Then she kissed his thighs, the flat skin of his belly, the rough mat of hair as she rose up his body like a vine.

Catching her shoulders, he plunged his tongue into the warm, wet depths of her mouth. He didn't want to wait any longer. Driven as if he still were that uncontrolled teenager, he cupped her bottom in his hands and slipped his shaft between her thighs. But as he tensed there, aware of her lips moving down his neck and her fingers across the muscle of his shoulders, aware of her tiny mews of hunger, he remembered he did have control—he was a man. It was time to pleasure the woman Kitt had become. He could wait.

Lifting her in his powerful arms, he carried her to the bed. She stretched out on the cool sheets, grateful for some relief to the burning dampness of her skin. But Garth wasn't about to let her curl up in their bedding and relax. He knelt over her, one palm on either side of her head, pinning her to the bed by her hair. Then his tongue began to work its magic.

Down her neck, over the full rise of her breasts, his mouth moved. His lips and teeth taunted her nipples. A deep tickle of electricity plunged through her and set her hips dancing against his parted legs. The more he teased her breasts, the more she thought her body might involuntarily reach up and grab his, pulling him deep inside her.

But he wouldn't allow her weaving hips to work their magic. Instead, he moved his mouth slowly down, tasting the fine sheen on her belly, nuzzling in the warm fragrant triangle between her legs.

She writhed, wanting to take him in. But his body came down upon hers and he rolled her onto her side. While his mouth sapped her and sent white lightning currents down to her toes, his hand cupped her and slipped into the dewy recess between her legs.

"Garth—oh, I can't stand it. Please!" She had never felt such wanting, such an ache of unbearable desire. His fingers probed and stroked her, sliding in a rhythmic play until she knew she was at the point of abandonment.

"So beautiful," he murmured. "Every part of you is tight and wet and hungry for me."

"Don't keep me waiting, love," she pleaded.

He smiled at her, his eyes full of golden light. "Are you ready?"

She knew what he meant—about the precautions and the consequences. But she had made sure she was ready this time. Ready for his love.

"Come home," she whispered.

With a raspy moan, he felt her knees slip apart beneath him. Her legs curled over his back. She lifted toward him, seeking him. Unable to hold back, he plunged deeply inside her. Aware of hot lights and a constricting ache that sent him near the point of madness, he rose and fell within her. Her body welcomed his, her hips rotated, her legs curved around his thighs and her heels pressed into his buttocks.

"You're like new, Kitt," he whispered.

She felt new. She felt like the wildest, freest cloud floating high over the mountaintop. And she wanted more. She let her mouth follow the rest of her body—suckling and drawing him out.

His hips crushed against hers, his rhythm lifted her higher and higher until she lost track of time and space. Her head arched as wave after unbearable wave washed over her. His body tensed for a moment, suffused with the pleasure of her ecstasy. And then he, too, was lifted up and over the brink.

They lay tangled together, hair and arms and legs and breath all mixed up. Kitt's tongue reached out to taste his skin. His fingers squeezed her hair, released it and squeezed again as his body drifted slowly down.

"Kitt," he murmured against her ear.

His voice sent a shiver down her spine. "Yes?"

"Don't *you* believe in destiny?"

She closed her eyes, thinking about Garth Culhane and how many years she had loved him. Thinking about how his body fit with hers like a hand in a glove. Thinking about the way they could talk and laugh together. Yes, maybe it had been destined.

"I believe in destiny," she said softly. "And I believe in magic. But I'm not at all sure about tomorrow."

"Tomorrow?" he said, rolling up on one elbow and brushing a strand of hair from her cheek. "If we'll let it, tomorrow will bring us everything."

# *Chapter 15*

"Any idea what day this is?" Garth lay on the bed with one leg dangling over the edge and one hand running careless little circles around Kitt's bare breast.

"Thursday, I think."

"I bet it's Friday."

"Doesn't our plane come in on Friday?"

"Right after lunch. We might want to think about getting out of bed."

Kitt closed her eyes and laughed. The passage of night and day had evaporated in the little room. The hundred candles were nothing but white stubs. The fruit bowl held only a couple of brown apple cores and a banana peel.

"Haven't we been out of here since Monday?" she asked.

"Don't you remember—I got us that package of cookies from the store the other day. And you went out once for another bottle of wine."

Kitt thought for a moment. "We went for a walk, too, remember? We took a look at the old gold mine in town and then we had a picnic on the mountainside."

"I just remember the dessert."

Kitt curled into Garth and kissed the hard muscles of his shoulder. He smelled of love. She licked his neck with quick, flirty strokes. Groaning, he rolled against her. His hands slid up and down her nakedness, now so familiar. Knowing her again only made him want her more. It was like her body had melded into his and become a part of him.

"You know what I liked best about these past few days?" he asked, lightly rubbing her back.

"I think I can guess."

"Nope. What I liked best is the talking we've done."

"Come on, Garth!" Kitt tweaked his nose. But she knew what he meant. At some point everything inside him had come pouring out. He'd talked for hours in the silence of one night, telling her about the years he'd been without her.

While she cradled him, he told her of the lonely months in the Asian jungle. And she came to understand that Vietnam had been more to him than a time of coming to terms with the end of his marriage. It had been a horrifying, almost unbelievable time of growing up. Somewhere amid the death and destruction, he'd found himself. He'd risen above it, and come through with his head high.

College and his job as a journalist had expanded on that experience. He had learned what it meant to live with loss—and keep going.

She, too, had talked. Not about the past, but about the future. Garth had encouraged her to expand on her vision. She'd outlined the dream she mentioned in the crypt. It had been fun, mind-expanding, to talk about things outside the realm of probability.

But now, in the vague light of early morning, Kitt realized that she wasn't any clearer about the rest of her life than she had been the first night Garth walked in and turned all her plans into tossed salad.

"Kitt." The word held that quiet, ragged tone she had come to hunger for. His deep, adult male's voice—it was not cocky and defiant like the boy's had been. Low, assured, the sound seeped into her bones and turned them to liquid. "Where have you gone?"

"I'm right here."

"You're somewhere else. Thinking about something. Tell me."

She rolled over and stared at the white ceiling. "I'm having a hard time understanding myself right now, that's all. I don't usually do completely brainless things like this. I'm always thinking ahead, making plans, putting my life in order."

"Brainless?"

She grinned. "You have to admit—that part of me hasn't been terribly active these past few days."

"So what is it you want, Kitt?"

She met his steady blue-gray gaze. He was holding her a little apart, studying her with more solemnity than she wanted. She hedged. "Well, I think I probably ought to rent a car in El Paso and make a quick trip to Catclaw Draw. I have to take a last look at the new site—"

"Kitt—what do you want from me? From us?"

"Nothing! I mean...I don't know, Garth. I like being with you. It feels right to sleep with you and make love with you. But—"

"But you don't trust me. Damn it, Kitt—you *still* think I'm going to run off and leave you like I did before."

"I don't know! I don't know whether it even matters. I mean—people do this sort of thing, don't they? They go away together and spend a whole week in bed. And then they go back to their separate homes and their separate lives...and that's really all there is to it. You know what I'm saying?"

"Is that what you want this to be?"

"Well, what do *you* want?" Kitt's anguish boiled over.

"Hell if I know." Garth sat up and dropped his feet over the side of the bed. Kitt watched his muscles flex as he walked pantherlike across the room to the adjoining bathroom. He was a beautiful man—animal sleek, almost wickedly smooth. Dark blond curls tangled at the nape of his neck. His back formed a well-defined V that tapered into tight buttocks.

As he stood over the sink splashing his face with water, it occurred to Kitt that she really could not imagine ever being without Garth again. She wanted to look at his naked body every morning for years to come. She wanted the taste of him on her tongue and the damp trace of his loving on her thighs.

She wanted the chance to grow with him, fight with him, learn with him. She wanted to bear him children . . .

"Kitt—there's something I need to tell you." He stood outlined in the bathroom doorway, a towel dangling from one arm. "It's about the future. About us—"

"Please, Garth. I don't want to hear it right now." She slid out of bed and went to him. He would either want to make commitments—or bring about a painless but definite ending to their time together. She wasn't ready for either. And the fact that she didn't know which direction he would choose was enough proof that she really didn't know Garth as well as she imagined.

"I need to talk to you, Kitt." He covered her shoulders with his big hands. "I don't want to leave this place without working things out. There's a lot we still need to say. When I was back in Albuquerque—"

"Garth, could you just pretend you're seventeen again and you aren't really into talking?" She placed one hand on either of his thighs. "Could you let it go just this once?"

"Kitt—"

"No talking, Garth . . ."

"But—"

She shook her head. His hands teased the ends of her hair as it flitted across her bottom. "If we're leaving this afternoon, I have another idea of how we might want to spend the time."

"Oh, you do?"

Her tongue traced a wet circle around his flat nipple. Pressing her hips against him, she found him already hard and wanting. She cupped her hands around his buttocks and kneaded them lightly, aware of his fingers circling her breasts.

"Not that I don't enjoy talking, Garth," she whispered. "But there's this other thing—" her breath caught as his thumbs flicked over the tips of her nipples "—that you do awfully well. And I was just wondering if you might consider . . ."

He lifted her against him, his hands cradling her thighs, and settled her neatly over himself. She wiggled down, feeling the pleasure of his hardness filling her up. Her breasts trailed down his chest. The coarse hair stirred them to tightness.

He knew she wanted him exactly the same way he wanted her. He could feel her loving him with the very deepest part of her. But she was afraid. And what he had to tell her wasn't going to help. For now, he would pleasure her again. Take her places she had always wanted to go.

His mouth found hers and words were forgotten.

"Catclaw Draw hasn't changed."

Garth swung the rented compact into the motel parking lot. "The Thunderbird Motel hasn't changed, either. Same turquoise doors."

He caught Kitt's wrists as she leaned to open her door. Turning to face him, she read the message imprinted in his eyes. We *have* changed, Kitt. We're together now.

"I'm not running away, Garth," she said softly. "I'm still just searching."

"I love you, Kitt."

It was the second time he had said it. And it wasn't where or when she had expected to hear the words again. She still didn't know how to respond.

Garth saw that frightened-cat look in her eyes. Kitt was scared to death of him. But he couldn't take the pressure off. He'd lost her once—thanks to her long silences and her withdrawals. He'd be damned if he'd lose her again.

"Come on, honey. Let's go in," he said.

They settled their bags on the motel bed and Garth put in a call to the bureau in Albuquerque while Kitt showered. When she came out, she began sorting through their things looking for something to wear. Watching from the phone, it gave him a strange pleasure to see that their clothing was all mixed together.

Finally Kitt pulled one of his T-shirts over her head and began braiding her hair.

"I'm going out to the site," she mouthed.

He nodded. Then his face grew deadly serious. "When?" he demanded into the phone.

Kitt jammed her fists into her pockets. His boss had evidently told him something he didn't want to hear. Garth was shaking his head, trying to butt into the long harangue.

"No!" he said into the receiver. "I told you, Steve, I can't do it until next month. I'm not ready. I've got things—" He glanced up and caught Kitt watching him. "Go on, honey. It's all right."

She stood for a moment, wondering what had gone wrong.

"Absolutely not, Steve." His eyes had gone gray and hard. "Yes, I told you I'd accept. But I can't be ready that fast. There are more important things going on right now. I'm working through some—"

He glanced up and saw Kitt still standing there. Frowning, he jabbed a thumb at the door. She jangled the keys to indicate she was taking the car and headed out.

The new cemetery was an almost exact replica of the Muddy Flats site. Kitt trudged through the tall, dry grass with a sense of satisfaction. Restored headstones stood in a symmetric pattern facing west. New granite stones labeled Unknown marked the graves uncovered in the second phase of the project. The huge monument listing every name and every grave location was not yet in place. It had only to be filled with the tiny scraps of coffin wood that were being examined in Santa Fe, then it would be settled at the front of the site.

As she climbed into the car, Kitt debated whether to return to the motel. Garth's conversation had disturbed her. What was his boss asking him to do? In the weeks she had been with him again, she had never seen him that adamant. But, she decided, it *was* Garth's business. She pulled the car onto the highway and headed for Muddy Flats.

The familiar road lay bathed in a pink light. She watched the sun sink lower and lower over the horizon. As she drove down the dusty tracks to the project site, she could see how changed it was. The contractor's trailer had pulled out. All the stakes and string were gone. Even the ground was bare of stone and grass. It looked flat and empty.

As she pulled to a stop, a glint of reflected sunlight caught her eye and she swung around. Old Hod's battered pickup sat beneath the cottonwood tree. Squinting against the sunset, Kitt climbed down and walked over to the tree.

"Hod?" she called. "Hod, are you out here?"

There was no answer. Kitt walked around the pickup. Nothing. She checked the area around the site but found nothing. Standing on tiptoe, she looked into the cab. Old Hod lay crumpled on the seat like a wadded-up candy bar wrapper.

"Hod!" Kitt flung open the door and climbed in. "Hod— are you all right?"

The old man looked at her in silence, his eyes bright. Trying to remember her first aid, Kitt felt for a pulse rate and tried to hear him breathing. He smelled of beer.

"Hod—have you been drinking?" Then she noticed the florid blotches that covered his neck and cheeks. "Talk to me, Hod. How long have you had this rash?"

"Rash?" His voice was barely audible.

"You're covered in spots. Look at your arms! Your palms— oh, Lord, Hod!" Breathing heavily, Kitt combed her mind. "Can you move? No, that's obvious, Kitt. He can't move. Okay. I'll drive you to the hospital."

"Hospital! No—" Hod coughed out the words. "No, Dr. Tucker. Not the hospital!"

"Hod, you're a very sick man. You need to see a doctor."

"Not the hospital! Not the hospital!" He closed his eyes for a moment, then dragged them open. "Take me home."

"We'll go get Garth." She slid into the seat and propped Hod's burning head on her lap. How long had he been lying out here in the desert? And what was wrong with him? Oh, he couldn't die. Not yet. She had to get help.

Wind and dust blew into her face through the empty windshield as she sped down the highway. Hod's eyes were shut and his head lolled back and forth across her thighs as she worked the clutch. Don't die. Don't die. She chanted as she drove.

Slamming the truck to a halt in front of the motel, she leaned on the horn. Garth ran outside, his shirttail hanging out.

"It's Hod, Garth. Something's wrong with him!"

"Where's the car? We'll take him to the hospital."

"It's at the site. Garth—he won't go to the hospital. He wants to go home!"

Garth leaned through the window and looked at Hod. "God, what's this rash? It looks wicked. We've got to get him to the hospital."

"No!" Hod's head lifted off Kitt's lap. "Home!"

"Damn..." Garth could see the hazard of upsetting the old man. "Okay, you drive him to his house, Kitt. I'll call the paramedics and we'll get them out there. They can make the decision."

Without responding, Kitt threw the truck into reverse and barreled onto the highway. After minutes that seemed like hours, the pickup skidded to a halt in front of the rambling adobe. She sat gripping the wheel and breathing in deep gasps of honeysuckle-scented air.

"Hod?" She touched his cheek. "Hod, we're home."

"I want to go to bed, Mother."

Kitt closed her eyes. "Can you walk, Hod? I'll help you in."

She lifted the frail shoulders. Hod leaned against her as she slid him off the seat. For a moment she thought he would crumple onto the grass, but his knees somehow held. Hanging heavily on her shoulder, he stumbled up the path and into the house.

"There now. Your bed, Hod. Doesn't that feel good?" Kitt took off his old shoes and set them on the floor. Gingerly, she eased him out of his jacket. Red spots covered his face, neck and limbs. But his torso was clear and healthy looking.

"Hod, can you talk to me about this sickness you've got?"

The old man smiled and took her hand.

"Have you had a fever?"

"Pretty hot...I wanted to go and visit my mother. She wasn't there anymore."

"That's why you were out at Muddy Flats? Hod, the graves have all been moved to Catclaw Draw. Remember?"

Hod's laugh was dry. "I forgot all about that. You moved 'em, didn't you? Then you left and I thought you weren't coming back to see me. But here you are."

Kitt squeezed the paper-thin fingers. "Here I am, Hod."

"I want the picture."

"Which picture do you want?"

"My mother." He swung one red-spotted hand at the table where a group of daguerreotypes sat. "Getting married to my father."

Kitt leaned over and peered into the silvery photographs on the bedside table. The only one with two people in it was the one she had decided earlier must be a father and daughter. Blowing the dust from the top of the frame, she handed Hod the picture.

He stared at it in silence, a little smile playing at his lips.

"My mother," he whispered. "Elizabeth Hodding. She's in that box you put her in, Dr. Tucker. Number fifty-one."

Hod seemed to be slipping away, and Kitt grabbed for his hand.

"Hod!" She felt frantic for some reason, panicky. "Hod— tell me about your mother."

The thin eyelids fluttered open. "Elizabeth Hodding with the dress she sewed all them beads on that my Papa gave her. She was a seamstress, you know. She sewed him up when he first came to town that day. Such a pretty little thing she was, Papa said . . ."

"I'm sure she was, Hod."

"She took him in and nursed him back to health. Never mind that he was an Indian and mean as hell. She loved him. Married him."

"An Indian?"

"Sure enough. With a name like Black Dove, what else could he be? Me, I'm Hodding Black Dove—not just plain old Hod as everyone thinks."

"Black Dove..." The words hung at the end of her tongue.

"My papa was Indian, see. I remember him pretty good. Old fellow with a couple of bad teeth, a bunch of scars and the end of a knife stuck in his shoulder. But my mama loved him. No matter what all the town thought, she married him."

"You're Black Dove's son. Your mother married Black Dove in Muddy Flats."

"Ain't that what I said?"

Kitt studied the old man. She felt numb. "So Black Dove *is* buried in the Muddy Flats cemetery."

"I don't know where they buried him. They sent me off to Carlsbad to live with another family. I never did know where they put him."

"Hod, your father was buried in the Muddy Flats cemetery. I found his grave."

Hod nodded. His eyes were closed. "Him and my mama together. That's good. They belong together."

Kitt looked at the old daguerreotype on Hod's chest. Elizabeth Hodding—young, beautiful. Wearing a beaded dress. Standing beside her was the old man. Strong, his head held high and proud.

And now she saw what she had missed before. In the midst of the man's brilliant smile were two slightly darker front teeth. They shone.

"I don't feel so good, Dr. Tucker."

"Garth's gone to get help, Hod. Just hold on. Hold onto me."

The sparrow-bone hand gripped hers. "I'm hot."

"I'll get you a cool washcloth."

"Stay with me."

"I'm here, Hod."

He opened his eyes. "When I was born, my mama died. I never knew her. Not for one day."

"I understand, Hod."

"I loved her, but I never knew her. She was my mama. I was a part of her. I grew inside her. But she died."

Kitt nodded. "I know."

"I think I made her die."

"No, Hod. No, you didn't. It wasn't your fault she died."

They sat quietly. Kitt thought of the emptiness inside her. The part of her that had died too soon. The tiny boy buried in the cemetery.

She didn't hear the front door open. She didn't see Garth's shadow behind her as he stood in the hall.

"I loved my son," she whispered. "He died."

Hod patted his stomach and Kitt put her head down. He weakly stroked her hair.

"Babies and mothers," he said. "You lost your boy. I lost my mama."

Kitt turned her face into the coverlet. Everything she had hidden had risen to a hard knot in her throat.

"Tell me about your boy, Dr. Tucker."

"I . . . I can't."

"Tell me."

Her eyes stung. Hod kept stroking her hair.

"He was almost ready to be born. Three weeks away," she whispered into the quilt. "He stopped moving. The doctor . . . doctor couldn't hear his heart beating any more. I had to wait for the labor to start. I sat in a chair and rocked."

"You were waiting."

"I wanted my son so much. He was everything I'd hoped for. He was Garth and me."

Now the hand stroking her hair was Garth's. But the voice in the little bedroom was Hod's.

"You loved your baby, even though you never knew him."

"He was part of me. And then he was born. He was . . . he was so stiff and hard. Like a little . . . like a little mummy. His cord was tied in a knot. That's what made him die. The delivery room was so quiet."

"It's always quiet when the good go."

The quilt was soaking up her tears. Garth ran his fingers through her hair as he knelt by her side. Some part of her knew he was there. He was crying silently, but she could feel him.

"I just went home," she whispered. "I just kept rocking thinking about nothing."

"You felt empty inside," Garth said.

"I felt dead."

Hod made little clucking sounds. Kitt cried. She cried for the life that had been inside her. The hope of birth. The love she had shared with Garth. All the dead, lost years. Her shoulders shook and Garth leaned against her, holding her.


"Mr. Culhane—we're ready now . . ."

Two paramedics moved into the room with tubes and a stretcher. They hovered over Hod, examining. "What's wrong with him, Dr. Tucker? What can you tell us?"

Kitt brushed her cheek and put on her professional face. Hod was submissive as they worked over him. In five minutes the ambulance drove off with Hod, leaving a cloud of dust to settle on the honeysuckle vine.

Kitt stood on the porch hugging herself.

"Talk to me, Kitt."

She turned to find Garth just behind her. "You look different."

"What do you mean?"

"Everything feels . . . okay."

"About our baby."

"About everything."

His face was solemn for a moment. Then his mouth tipped up. "You cried. I'm glad, honey."

She gave a little laugh as she nodded. "Me, too."

He walked to her and caught her in his arms. She clutched his shirttail as his mouth came down on hers. Relief flowed through the kiss. She felt alive, glowing in his arms. The relief turned to elation.

"Kitt, honey," he said, holding her at arm's length. "Kitt, are we over this hump?"

"I'll never completely get over what happened, Garth. You know that."

"I do know it. But I also know it's possible to heal."

She looked into the gray-blue eyes she loved. "I think it's time for me to heal."


Minutes later they stood in the waiting room at Catclaw Draw General Hospital. Charles Grant from the Catclaw Draw Museum hurried down the hall just as a doctor swung open the emergency room door.

"I need to talk with you folks," the doctor said calmly. "Come this way please."

"Thanks for calling, Garth," Charles whispered, following them into an unoccupied patient's room.

"We're having trouble getting a grip on Hod's illness," the doctor explained. "You seem to know him better than anyone else. What can you tell me about his activities? Anything he may have been exposed to?"

"We've been away from him for a couple of weeks now," Kitt said. "We just got back to Catclaw Draw."

Charles shook his head. "I hadn't seen him for days, either. He hangs out at a bar in town. Maybe some of the people there know what he's been up to—"

"Get them on the phone please, Charles. I need to know anything they can tell me."

As Charles vanished, Garth laced his fingers through Kitt's. "What's going on here, Doc?" he asked.

"I've never seen anything like this. Hod apparently had a high fever for ten to twelve days. He's indicated signs of prostration and toxicity. As you can see, he's now developed a macular rash on his face and extremities."

"Macular?"

"Spots. His palms and the soles of his feet are covered with them. His trunk area is minimally affected. The rash apparently started out as papular—small, conical lesions. It's moved into a vesicular stage, now. He's weathering it all pretty well. But I suspect it may develop into something worse."

"Worse, like what?"

The doctor fiddled with his stethoscope. "If it moves into a pustular stage, there could be secondary infection. If the lungs, heart or brain become involved, he'll be in serious trouble."

"What do you think he's got?"

He shook his head. "To tell you the truth, it reminds me of some sort of primitive virus. Something rare."

"Smallpox." Kitt said it without hesitation.

"Smallpox has been eradicated from the earth, Dr. Tucker."

"It's smallpox."

"I hate to contradict you, but there is no smallpox in existence. It's a completely eradicated disease."

"Not in skeletal remains. Smallpox can live in bones for years."

"How many years?"

"I've been told up to three hundred years. Check with the Centers for Disease Control in Atlanta. I know that all the archaeologists working on cemetery sites have to keep their immunizations up for that reason."

The doctor's face took on an uh-oh look. "Has Hod been at the Muddy Flats site where you were working, Dr. Tucker?"

Kitt had to nod. "His parents were buried there."

"So Hod may have been exposed to a living smallpox virus."

"Yes."

"Oh, boy." The doctor heaved a sigh. "Well, looks like we may have a little problem here. I want you two to go back to your motel for a while and stay near the phone. Smallpox is highly contagious—don't make contact with anyone else at this point. I need to check with CDC on the ramifications of this thing."

Garth nodded, wrapping one arm around Kitt. "What about Hod? Can we see him?"

"I'm afraid not. He's in isolation."

The doctor hurried down the hall, his white coattails swinging behind him.

Kitt opened her mouth, but Garth kissed it closed.

"I know what you're thinking, Kitt. Don't even start to say it."

"But it *is* my fault."

"You tried to keep him off the site. Dr. Dean is a witness to that. All your summer workers saw you trying to keep Hod away. You even told your boss you were having trouble. *Hod* insisted on being there."

"But if he dies—"

"He's not going to die."

"He's a hundred and five years old, Garth."

"And tough as an old turkey. Besides, he can't die yet."

"Why not? He's got *smallpox*. People died of smallpox."

"He hasn't found his gold mine."

"Oh, Garth!" Kitt felt like screaming.

Instead, she rode out to Muddy Flats with Garth to pick up the rented car, then drove it to the motel. Charles Grant called from the hospital to say that Hod had been responding to medication. He also reported that half the tavern regulars had gathered in the waiting room. Some of them had decided to hold an impromptu prayer meeting for the old man. It was a bit of a circus, but kind of an upbeat way to deal with everyone's concern.

"You never did get Hod registered, Kitt," Charles said on the phone. "Any idea of his age?"

"He says he's around a hundred and five."

Garth was on the bed taking off his boots. "Tell Charles to talk to that barmaid who knows Hod."

Kitt started to relate the information, but Charles interrupted her. "Any idea of Hod's full name? I know he won't have insurance or anything, but they need his full name to register him. None of the bar patrons has any idea."

"Black Dove," Kitt said evenly. "His name is Hodding Black Dove."

"What?" Garth and Charles said it at the same time.

"Hodding Black Dove. His mother was Elizabeth Hodding. His father was Black Dove—"

"We'll call you back, Charles." Garth slammed down the phone, which he had jerked from Kitt's hand.

"Garth!"

"What are you talking about, Kitt?"

"That was rude! Charles was just trying to help—"

"What were you telling him?"

"Black Dove is Hod's father. While you were getting the ambulance, he told me all about it. There's even a picture. You can see the gold teeth."

"You mean I was right? Black Dove really was buried in Muddy Flats?"

"Yes."

"I'll be damned."

The phone was ringing. Kitt reached for it, but Garth grabbed her hand with his fist. "This is a story, Kitt. My story. I don't want it to get out."

"I don't see what the big deal is."

"Don't you get it? If Black Dove really did come to New Mexico—and if Hod really is Black Dove's son—and if Black Dove really did take Hod to a mine when he was a boy—then that gold is probably what he dug out of the mine near Guadalupe Y Calvo. Hod really did see gold, Kitt."

"So?"

"So, that gold is somewhere near here."

"So?"

"I'm going to find it."

# Chapter 16

"**H**od has been hunting for that gold mine for almost a hundred years, Garth. What makes you so sure you can find it?"

"I can do it."

"I'm calling Charles Grant right this minute and I want you to apologize for cutting him off."

Kitt hauled herself onto the bureau where the phone sat. She dumped the phone book into her lap and began flipping through it.

"Kitt, listen to me. I want us to look for that gold. It would be a great ending to the story."

"If Hod couldn't find it, how could we?"

"Maybe there's something Hod overlooked. Something he didn't know about."

"Garth, the story is just fine the way it is. Hod turned out to be Black Dove's son. That's just amazing. It'll blow everyone out of the water."

"I need to write—"

"But not the gold part of it."

"Why not?"

"Because everyone and their dog will start combing the area looking for Black Dove's gold. You don't know how treasure hunters are. They'll tear up everything in sight. It's something in their blood."

"How can I do the story and leave out the gold?"

"They'll destroy valuable historical sites. I'll never forgive you for printing that, Garth. You won't believe the mess it'll cause."

"Kitt, for heaven's sake—" He stopped when he saw Kitt's face go still. All the breath went out of her.

She was holding a slip of paper that had slid out of the phone book. Garth recognized it. He grabbed for it, but she jerked it away.

"Nairobi."

She said the word like it was something alien. Then she looked at him, her brown eyes almost black. "This is an airline flight schedule from Albuquerque to Nairobi, Garth. One way."

"Give me that."

"What is this?"

"I wanted to tell you in Guadalupe Y Calvo, Kitt. I need to explain this."

"This is what you were talking to your boss about, isn't it?"

"I got the overseas bureau job."

"Nairobi."

"It's in Kenya. Africa."

"I know where it is," she snapped.

"I found out when I was in Albuquerque. That's part of the reason I came to see you. Why I wanted to go to Mexico with you."

"One last fling?"

"Kitt—"

"When are you leaving?"

"Next week."

Kitt carefully placed the slip of paper in the phone book. She could feel herself overreacting. Garth was going away. Leaving. Just like he'd left before. Only this time he'd be in Africa.

She gave a little laugh. "Well, I guess that settles that."

"What settles what?"

"I need to check on Hod. Excuse me."

She slid off the dresser and made for the door. Garth's hand clamped on her arm. She tried to pull free but he swung her around.

"What do you think I am, anyway, Kitt?"

"You're separate from me, that's all I know. A completely separate person."

"After what happened between us in Mexico?"

"I'm not going to go through this all over again with you. I have to leave."

"You'll stay right here."

"Damn it, Garth. Let me go! Don't drag this out."

"Kitt, will you just listen to me?"

"No, I will not listen to you!" She saw him standing over her, a giant barely contained by ropes of restraint. But she wasn't afraid of him. She was more afraid of herself.

"I've been through this before with you, Garth. You told me you loved me. You told me if I ever needed you, you'd be there. But then you just walked right out. Well, this time *I'm* the one who's walking out. Go to Africa. Print your gold story. Just leave me alone."

She didn't wait for him to say anything. She didn't pick up her bag. She just headed out the door, got into Hod's old truck and drove away.

Kitt didn't know it was possible to cry for five hours straight. It was. She sat in Hod's adobe house, playing the Victrola, drinking wine and crying.

Hod was going to be all right. He had a mild form of smallpox—variola minor, the doctor called it. His friends had set up a vigil. Around-the-clock praying and waiting, with a little card-playing thrown in. She had stayed a while. But Garth hadn't come.

Hod needed clothes, so she volunteered to go out to his place. She swung past the motel, but the compact rental was gone.

So that was it.

She forgot about getting Hod any pajamas. Instead, she sat in the Victorian chair playing old records and getting drunk. It was easier than facing everything.

Of course, everything didn't go away. She had to remember that Garth had danced her around this very room. She had to remember that she probably had gone overboard when she found the itinerary. Way overboard.

But *Africa*?

He'd be at least ten thousand miles away. And he *was* going. He'd accepted the bureau job. He had a plane ticket. That was that.

Why had she thought it would be any different this time?

"Dr. Tucker, am I glad to see you." Hod stretched out his hand.

He looked out of place in the crisp, clean hospital bed. His face had been newly shaved. The pale green gown revealed his long, sinewy arms. He patted her hand as she sat on a high stool.

"They tell me I been in here almost a week now."

"How's it been?"

"Hell. I want out. You gonna get me out, Dr. Tucker?"

"When you're well enough."

"Aw, I'm tough as an old turkey buzzard. I want to go home."

Kitt smoothed the thin wisps of white hair on his forehead. His spots had dried and were clearing up. He gave her a little grin.

"You look worse'n me, Doc. What you been up to?"

"I've been staying out at your house, Hod. I hope you don't mind. I did a little straightening and cleaning."

"Them newspapers. Kinda got the better of me, didn't they?" He looked sheepish.

"You have some valuable material there, Hod. You ought to think about letting Charles Grant put it in the museum."

"Hell, he can have whatever he wants. I don't need the stuff. Just the pictures—he can't have my pictures."

"I brought the one of your mother and father the other day. You were sleeping."

"I got it there on my table. Thanks."

"Hod . . . you told me your father was named Black Dove. Is that right?"

Hod closed his eyes. "You ain't gonna turn against me 'cause I'm part Indian, are you, Doc?"

"Of course not, Hod. But there's something you should know."

"What's that?"

"Your father was quite a famous man. No one knew what became of him after his days with James Kirker."

"The scalper? Oh, Papa went to Mexico after he quit with Kirker. Lived there a few years. Had a damn rough time, he told me."

"Most people thought Black Dove died in Mexico."

"Died there!" Hod cackled. "Why didn't they ask me? I'da told 'em he come on up here to Muddy Flats and married my mama. 'Course he had a little trouble along the way. Got ambushed. He was near dead when he rode into town. My Mama sewed him up, see. She was a seamstress."

"Yes."

"So they fell in love and got married. Papa didn't die till I was around ten. He was old as the hills by that time. He told me folk with his Indian blood live a long, long time."

Kitt pondered what she had been turning over in her mind. "Hod, there's something else you should know."

"What's that, Doc?"

"Your father had a daughter in Mexico. Her son and his children still live there."

"I'll be damned." Hod gripped Kitt's hand. "You mean to tell me I got a sister? I got *family*?"

"Your half-sister passed away some time ago. But her son is still living. He's in his nineties. He has several children and grandchildren."

"Hot damn! I got a family! A family!"

"Take it easy, Hod."

He had raised up on the bed and was gazing at her with bright, shining eyes. "Tell me about my nephew, Doc. Tell me everything."

Kitt settled him onto his pillow and related her long chat with old Santiago in Guadalupe Y Calvo. Hod's expression went from one of elation to pure ecstasy. Every few sentences, he would interrupt.

"I got me a *family*!"

"You'd love them, Hod. I'm sure of that."

"I'm going to see them. You get me out of this damn bed and I'm going to see my nephew."

Kitt considered pressing the nurse contact button. Hod was almost beside himself with happiness. "You can't go see them, Hod," she explained, trying to smooth him onto the bed. "They live far away in Mexico. You're a sick man. Besides, they all speak Spanish—"

"You don't think I've lived a hundred and five years in New Mexico and ain't learned to talk Spanish, do ya? Now, you just get me a plane ticket and I'm going down there. I'll just move right in there with my nephew—"

"Hod, please. You have to settle down."

"You said he was lonely. You told me that, didn't you? Well, I'm lonely too. Let me tell you something, Dr. Tucker—"

Hod jerked her close with surprising strength.

"I always told myself if I ever got a chance to be part of a family, I'd grab it." He squinted at her appraisingly. "And so should you."

Kitt's eyes clouded with tears for the hundredth time. "Hod—"

"I ain't finished, young 'un. Now my papa and my mama had a lot of things goin' against 'em. But they stuck it out, 'cause they loved each other. Me—I spent my whole life lookin' for some stupid gold mine. I kept on puttin' other things ahead of love. Don't you do that, young 'un. You go find love and hang on for dear life *no matter what.*"

Kitt reached for a tissue and blew her nose. "I've just had a lot of difficult things—"

"Difficult things be damned! Life is hard, gal. Believe me, I ain't lived no hundred and five years 'cause it was *easy.*"

"Hod, the way things are today—"

"Ain't no different than the way they used to be! Don't think I ain't read them newspapers I been stackin' up in my kitchen. Folks want marriage handed to 'em like they get everything else—all wrapped up in pretty packages. If it ain't workin' just right, they toss it out like some old fast food hamburger in a plastic carton. Uh-uh, young 'un. It just ain't thataway with family. You listen to old Hod."

Kit nodded, blotting at her cheeks.

"What about your young fella, now? That newspaper reporter. I seen the way you two been lookin' at each other."

"He's gone. He's . . . well, we just couldn't make it work. I lost my baby, you know. And my marriage—"

"Aw, hell, there you go again. Ain't you strong enough to get over them humps, Dr. Tucker?"

"I don't think I'm—"

"Hell, you're tough as an old turkey buzzard, just like me. Wipe your eyes, young 'un. Go find your own happiness."

"I love you, Hod."

"I love you, too, sweetheart." He brushed a tear from his cheek. "Now when you gonna go get me my ticket? I'm headin' for Mexico!"

# Chapter 17

The old adobe house held a healing power. Maybe it was the power of the love that had lived there so long ago, Kitt thought.

She stayed all week, cleaning and arranging rooms. It felt like she was putting herself back in order. Garth had gone to Africa in the middle of the week. She'd thought about his plane flying overhead, taking him away for good. She'd gone back to her cleaning.

She had made one trip to the post office with a letter for her boss. Dave and Sue would be wondering what had happened to her. She was supposed to start the ditch project. She'd written Dave she was taking an extra week of vacation.

Hod had gotten feistier by the day. The nurses could barely hold him down for his medication. And every day it was the same— "You got my plane tickets for Mexico, yet, Dr. Tucker? You written my nephew to tell him I'm comin' to see him? Tell him to get the grandkids ready. Old Uncle Hod is movin' in!"

Kitt was up early, dusting the glass-fronted rosewood sideboard in the parlor, when she heard a car pull up to the front of the house. For a moment, she was afraid it might be bad news about Hod. Then she remembered Charles Grant had promised to come that morning and haul away the last stack of old newspapers.

Still in her robe, Kitt padded across the warm tile floor. The smell of honeysuckle enveloped her as she opened the door.

"Morning, ma'am." A thin young man stood framed in sunlight. "I've come to put up your sign."

Kitt glanced at the dusty brown car behind him. "Are you from the museum?"

"I'm with the Miriam Morgan Realty Company." He held a big green metal sign. "Didn't Mr. Black Dove tell you we were coming?"

"Come in. Please." She stepped back from the door, but he didn't move.

"Mr. Black Dove is selling his house. I thought he would have mentioned it."

"Selling his house? Why?"

"He called up my boss and said he wanted to list the house. She told him he probably wouldn't get much for it, way out here like it is—and with no plumbing or electricity. But he's insistent, you know. I need to look around and make an appraisal so we can set a sale price, and then I'll just put the sign in over there . . ."

He turned as a sleek gray compact car pulled up to the front of the house. Kitt's heart did a double flip-flop and nearly stopped.

"You can put your sign away," Garth said, getting out of the car. He slipped his sunglasses into the front pocket of his blue oxford shirt.

"But I was sent out here—"

"I just bought the house. You can head on back to town."

The young man gaped as Garth strode onto the porch. Kitt couldn't move.

"I'm with Miriam Morgan Real Estate—"

"I know who you're with. I've already talked to Mrs. Morgan. Hod and I have worked out a deal on the house. Your boss knows all about it."

"You mean I don't need to do the appraisal? Or put up a sign?"

"Neither."

Turning to Kitt, the young man gave a little shrug and carried his sign off the porch.

As the brown car pulled away, Garth stuck his hands in his pockets and leaned against a wooden post.

"You're supposed to be in Africa," Kitt said.

"You're supposed to be filling in ditches with colored cement."

He'd never looked so good. His blue shirt made his eyes lose their gray and take on an almost clear-sky quality. His face, tanned and smooth even this early in the morning, held a faint trace of a grin.

Kitt glanced at the shaggy brown robe and worn slippers she had found in Hod's wardrobe. Her braid, sprigs of loose hair hanging out, had slipped over her shoulder.

"You bought Hod's house?" she asked.

"He wants to go to Mexico to live with his nephew."

"I know."

"He needed money, so I bought the house. Furniture and all. How do you like it?"

"I . . . well, I love it. But—"

"Aren't you going to invite me into my own home for a cup of coffee?" He strolled past her into the cool depths of the hall.

"What are you doing here, Garth?" She hurried after him, trying to smooth out the sprigs.

"I came to find you."

"I thought you were going to Africa."

"I am." He swung around as he passed the parlor. "What have you done with the place? It looks great in here."

"I've been cleaning house."

"You didn't throw out all the newspapers, did you?"

"Charles Grant has them down at the museum."

"Good. I intend to do some reading. Where do you keep the coffee? I've been up almost all night. That Hod is a cantankerous old devil. He tried to give me the house for the cost of his plane ticket. It was all I could do to—"

"It's up here."

"What?"

"The coffee. I keep it up here."

She took a can from one of the shelves she had painted in white enamel. Mechanically, she filled the old speckled tin coffeepot. What was Garth doing here? He was supposed to be in Africa.

"Your boss gave me a call two days ago, Kitt." Garth had settled into one of the big oak press-backed chairs at the kitchen table.

"Why did he do that?"

"He thought I might know where you were."

She fiddled with the cups on the shelf, then took one down and stared at it. "If you thought I was going to come apart again, Garth, you were wrong. If you thought you'd find me sitting here in a rocking chair—"

"That's not why I came."

"I just needed some time to readjust."

"Readjust to what?"

"To everything. To getting my old life back."

"Your old life. You didn't think I was going to go off and leave you again, did you, Kitt?"

She looked at him. He had propped the heel of one boot on the toe of the other. His eyes held a curious light.

"You're going to Africa, Garth. You just told me that."

"That's true."

"Then what are you doing here?"

"We've already been over this. I came to find you."

"What for?"

"Several things."

"Like what?"

"The gold, for one."

"Oh, Garth. You're not still on that, are you?"

He stood and took the cup of steaming coffee. "I like this."

She looked at him, confused.

"This—taking a cup of hot coffee from you in the morning. Being together in our kitchen."

She tried to fathom what he'd said. *Our* kitchen.

"So, how do you think you can find Hod's gold?" she asked.

He grinned. "Evasive, Kitt."

"It's *your* house. You bought it."

"Hod told me it would be a good house for a family. For the sort of love that lasts a lifetime."

Kitt began unbraiding her hair. She couldn't look at him. "He's been talking about family nonstop. He's just excited about his nephew."

"I've got a bunch of stuff out in the car, Kitt. All your files on the Muddy Flats cemetery. Dr. Oldham's notes. Want to see if we can find that mine?"

She considered for a moment. Whatever he was doing here, she was glad to see him. In fact, the more she looked at him standing in the big bright kitchen, the more she wanted him to take her in his arms and kiss her.

"I thought you were leaving for Nairobi last week."

"Affiliated Press owed me a couple of weeks of vacation. I changed my departure date."

"I think I know where the mine is."

He took a step closer. "I thought you might."

"Is that why you're here?"

"No."

"Why are you here?"

"I came to find you, Kitt."

She fumbled the lid onto the coffee can. "I need to change clothes."

"You look beautiful this morning."

She laughed. "This is Hod's old—"

"I love you, Kitt."

"I was trying to give you up again."

"Don't give me up."

She looked out at the honeysuckle. A ruby-throated hummingbird darted from blossom to blossom. Its emerald-green feathers shimmered in the early sunlight.

"There's a photograph in my files," she said softly. "It's of a scrap of newspaper I found in Black Dove's grave. Do you have it?"

"Marry me, Kitt."

The hummingbird dipped its long beak into a yellow flower. She couldn't see its wings, they were moving so fast. Behind her, Garth walked down the long hallway and out the front door. His front door. She could see him rooting around in the back seat of his car. His lean legs, his leather loafers. The back of his head with its sunlightened gold curls. His blue shirt molding to his muscles.

She'd love him even if he got old and skinny and stubborn, like Hod. She seemed to see them dancing around and around on the porch of the old adobe. The honeysuckle vine scented the air. She was wearing glasses, and one of those old-lady checkered dresses. Her hair was white and cottony. His knees creaked as he shuffled her around. She could hear his heartbeat beneath his old red wool cardigan.

She knew she could dance all night.

"Well, here's your stuff, Kitt. Think you can find that photograph?"

It hadn't really taken all that much figuring. As she'd cleaned out the house, her mind had put together all the pieces of the past. Black Dove and Kirker. Guadalupe Y Calvo. The gold mine and the Apache massacre.

"Black Dove took that gold, you know," she told Garth. "He set up the whole massacre so he could get away with the gold train."

He followed her into the bedroom. She changed clothes in the bathroom while he studied the clusters of daguerreotypes on the tables.

"I figure he planted that cross and the pouch of nuggets on someone else's body."

"Of course. He was no fool. If the citizens of Guadalupe Y Calvo were heartless enough to refuse to let him marry in the church—"

"And they took his daughter away when her mother died."

"That's right. Black Dove had no compunctions about stealing their gold."

"No wonder Hod remembers seeing both nuggets and bars in Black Dove's hideout. The bars were Chihuahua government gold. The nuggets were from Black Dove's little mine in the mountains."

Kitt shoved her foot into her boot and smoothed her jeans over her thighs. Garth watched appreciatively as she brushed out her hair and flipped it behind her.

"So, where's the gold?" he asked as they walked down the hall.

She began digging through her files on the kitchen table. "Are you going to make a big production out of this if we find it?"

"I'm going to put it in my story."

"You haven't done the story yet?"

"I need to put in the gold part. I figured if we could find the gold ourselves, then nobody would be tempted to tear up historical sites looking for it."

"Here." She sat and leafed through the pile of photographs. One showed a picture of a glass bottle they had found in the crook of one woman's elbow. Another was of the head of a ceramic doll.

"These are Elizabeth Hodding's beads," she said, handing him a picture. "She's Hod's mother, you know."

"The seamstress."

They both smiled. Kitt finally located the photograph she had been seeking. "I found this scrap of paper in Black Dove's grave."

"Looks like cattle market prices to me."

"Dr. Dean and I thought that's why it had been saved. Here's what was on the other side."

"An advertisement for maps."

Kitt held the photograph under a beam of thick yellow sunlight. "This is the part I had forgotten. See this writing scribbled on the side of the newspaper scrap? I thought it was an address—you know, the place to write for the maps."

Garth studied the photo. "It's not an address, Kitt. It's—"

"It's the coordinates for the location of the gold mine."

"I'll be damned. Hod *told* us his father had promised to write it down for him so he'd always have it."

"But the directions were buried with him. Poor old Hod didn't have a chance of finding it."

"Any idea where this is?"

Kitt carried the photograph into the parlor. "No. But I bet if we can find the map listed in this ad, we'll find the location."

The thought of all those rolled-up maps he had stumbled over gave Garth a moment's hesitation. But Kitt calmly went to an oversize desk and lowered the lid. All the maps were neatly arranged.

He thought about grabbing her and giving her a great big kiss. But the hurt was still too near the surface. He knew she had thought he was running off and leaving her again. He'd forced himself to stay away just long enough to give her time to think over her feelings. Just long enough to prove to her that he wasn't leaving her again. Ever.

"Here it is." She was unrolling an old yellowed map on the floor. He stared at the way her hair draped over her arms and spilled onto the document. Her long finger traced the directions as she looked from the photographs to the map. Her boots were curled up beneath her little round bottom, and it was all he could do to keep from touching her right then.

He knew that she'd abandon the map and curl right into his arms. She'd lift her lips to his and stroke his mouth with her tongue. She'd take off that T-shirt and her full breasts would come tumbling out into his hands, eager for the brush of his fingers—

"Here it is!" She swung around on the map, her face alight. "Look at these coordinates. Black Dove hid the gold in the Guadalupe Mountains—right here on a spot called Baldy Peak. Can you imagine that? The gold is from Guadalupe Y Calvo and he put in the Guadalupes. And Calvo means bald in Spanish!"

He watched her leap to her feet—a young girl again. All the sadness had gone out of her face. She was rolling up the map, grabbing her jacket from the coatrack.

"Wasn't that clever of him?" she asked, shrugging on her jacket. With the movement, her breasts lifted then fell beneath her T-shirt. She caught up the length of her hair and pulled it out of her collar. "Guadalupe Y Calvo. Baldy Peak in the Guadalupe Mountains. You'd think Hod might have figured that out. Of course, without the scrap of newspaper, he really didn't have any idea. I mean that's what first tipped me off—"

In two strides Garth had caught her in his arms. Her lips covered his, warm and just as hungry as he'd imagined. She didn't resist for one instant. The map fell to the floor. Her hand covered his back, moving down the ridges of his muscles, sliding beneath his belt. He tasted the early morning sweetness of her skin. Her breath, as she groaned against him, was warm and damp.

"Oh, Garth. I thought you'd gone."

"I told you I wasn't leaving you again, Kitt. When are you going to start believing me?"

"I believe you. I believe everything you tell me. Just...just don't stop kissing me. Right there—kiss me right there. Oh, Garth. I'm aching. I want you. I want you right now—"

His lips closed over her breast. She felt her body melt into a liquid pool that seeped between her legs making her ready...so ready for him.

"You'll want me more later," he murmured.

"No—Garth!"

"Come on, Kitt. Let's go find that gold."

Before she could protest, he grabbed her around the waist and hauled her out to the car.

It was a wonder they ever found the gold. The Guadalupes were more than an hour southwest of Catclaw Draw. By the time they had driven into the shadow of the chain of giant, flat-topped mountains, Kitt thought she was going to come apart.

Garth hadn't allowed her hands to touch him once, but as he drove, he'd let his fingers dangle carelessly all over her body. It had started as just a teasing, sensual tickle. But as the minutes ticked by, his hands seemed to find every single private place she had. The car was silent, Kitt writhing on the seat, as his fingers pulled her tight nipples, then rolled them and pressed them until she thought she couldn't stand it. His hands found the soft skin of her belly, slipped apart her jeans' zipper, tested the warm, damp source of her hunger. She begged for release. He would take her just about as far as she could go, then slip his hand away and find some other place to touch.

"Baldy Peak," he murmured. "Here we are."

She couldn't have cared less. The car swung up to a vista parking lot and Garth tried to get out. Kitt grabbed his shirt and dragged him back.

"You're not getting away with this," she said.

"I'm not?" He feigned innocence.

"Absolutely not."

"You mean you don't want to look for Black Dove's gold right this minute?"

"Never have."

"Well, what do you have in mind?"

"Follow me." They wandered up a shaggy trail that meandered between a couple of boulders. The realization that a fortune in gold was somewhere nearby held little pull. The old compelling force between Kitt and Garth proved much stronger.

In a sheltered field, Garth pulled off Kitt's shirt and dropped it onto the ground. The sun kissed her breasts, then Garth did, too. She caught his head and held his mouth to her nipples until her skin sang. It took two seconds for her to get his shirt unbuttoned and his pants unzipped. The pile of clothing on the ground grew until a pair of silky panties topped it off.

As they tumbled onto a dense patch of yellow grass, Kitt felt Garth part her thighs. She was so ready for him, she could hardly believe the force that drove her onward. His fingers slipped around and around, intensifying every sensation.

"I've never wanted you so badly, Kitt. Never."

"Don't ever stop wanting me."

He entered her slowly, but it was all he could do to hold back. He'd never felt her so hungry. Like a wild thing, she clutched him, satisfying herself and carrying him upward to a peak he'd never imagined reaching.

"Marry me, Kitt. Just say you will."

"I never stopped being your wife."

With her words, his moment came. She felt him fill her, the pulse of his life-giving seed. She was ready for him. Ready for life and everything it had to bring. She paused, feeling his body wrack with shuddering release. Then she let herself slide over the brink—her body and soul one with his.

They hiked up a shaggy trail, Garth looking at his compass and trying to remember his Boy Scout training. Kitt found herself paying more attention to the terrain than the map. She had never cared much for the idea of piles of gold—and the lust for it that drove men mad. Garth was all business again, but she felt reborn. A warm glow spread through her body and settled on her face in a soft smile.

It was nearly sunset when Garth finally found the old pine tree bent in the shape of an upside down L. The tree was right where it ought to be, just as the coordinates had been written. Somewhere near them lay Black Dove's fortune. They scouted around, searching for anything that might look like the entrance to a cave.

"Didn't Hod refer to the cave entrance as a sort of chasm?" Garth called from the top of a boulder.

Kitt nodded. "I don't see any chasms around here. Do you suppose it could be under a pile of these rocks?"

"If it is, it's going to take a bulldozer to find the opening."

Kitt flicked a pebble and watched it roll down the mountain. She thought of Hod rolling stones there almost a hundred years earlier. The old pine tree bent in the shape of an L certainly was the right landmark. But nothing seemed to suggest a cave of any sort.

Garth scrambled behind the boulder. She could tell he was getting frustrated after the half hour's fruitless search. She scanned the old pine tree, guessing the wind had twisted it into such an odd shape. At the crook of the tree, the branches forked. There, a strange-looking branch stuck out like some sort of odd appendage...

Wandering closer, Kitt set one foot on a small rock and lifted herself up to the crook.

"Garth! Garth—get over here!"

He ran around the boulder and joined her at the base of the pine tree. "What have you ... what *is* that thing?"

"It's some kind of metal tube. Definitely man-made." She stood on tiptoe and grabbed the end of it. It wouldn't budge.

"The tree's grown up around it. It must have been there a long time. Here—let me take a look."

They traded places.

"It's the barrel of a gun," Garth said. "A muzzle loader barrel."

"A muzzle loader. What's it doing stuck way up there?"

"I don't know. It's just the barrel. There's no stock, and the breech-plug has been taken out."

"So it's just a hollow tube?"

"I'll get closer and see if anything's been written on the barrel—or if there's anything with it in the crook of the trunk."

Kitt shaded her eyes while Garth heaved himself into the branches. He tried to wiggle the barrel but the tree's growth had wedged it firmly in place. "Nothing here."

"Look inside. Maybe Black Dove stuck some more directions inside the tube."

Garth gave her a quick grin. "You're sure Black Dove put this up here?"

"Who else?"

"You're the expert."

He fitted his eyes to the barrel and squinted. The setting sun had nearly obliterated the light, but it was clear nothing had been inserted in the old gun. The sides were a little rusty and corroded, but through the center there was nothing but the view of a limestone face.

"What do you see? Any gold?"

He looked down at her and laughed. "If you think of this barrel as a sort of scope, it focuses right on a blank wall. I guess somebody just stuck the gun up there and the pine tree grew around it over the years."

As Garth climbed down, Kitt again imagined the young Hod. That long ago, the pine tree would have been just a sapling. If someone had placed the barrel of a gun in the crook of a tree, in time the tree would have wedged it tight and lifted it high.

"I think I know where the gold is," Kitt whispered. For all her certainty that the treasure meant nothing to her, the realization that she might have found some had made her mouth go dry. Garth leaped down from the tree and dusted off his hands.

"Kitt, I don't think—"

"Boost me up."

Her tone left no room for argument. Kitt crouched on the branch and gazed down the barrel of the muzzle loader. A blank face of limestone. She memorized the spot and moved her head to one side of the metal tube. Then she let her focus drift slowly downward.

"Black Dove wrote down the coordinates for the muzzle loader barrel," she said softly. "He positioned the muzzle loader in the pine tree so that if you look down it, you see the entrance to the cave."

Garth frowned. "I just saw a blank wall."

"A hundred years ago the tree was shorter. If you look down the limestone face about fifty feet, you'll see the crevice."


The gold was just like Hod had described it. Bars on one side, nuggets in saddlebags on the other. The slender scar at the base of the stone mountain face had been so covered with dirt and pebbles it was no wonder the place had been hidden for over a hundred years. Another fifteen-minute hike had taken them to the site, and a serious shoveling effort had revealed the narrow opening to the cave.

"Looks like we're set for life," Garth remarked as he shone a flashlight over the stacked bars. "We can buy a penthouse in New York and a cabin in Aspen."

Kitt straightened. "This isn't *our* gold, Garth. Ownership will be worked out between Hod and the Mexican and United States governments—"

He was grinning at her. "So how does an old adobe house in New Mexico sound instead?"

"It sounds like heaven." She tossed a bar onto its stack. He stood only inches away. "What about Africa?" she asked.

"What about it?"

"Are you going?"

"I thought you might want to see Kenya. Wasn't that where Louis Leakey found those old skeletons—"

"*Proconsul*—a primitive creature who lived twenty million years ago."

"And there'll be lots of tribal legends you could record—"

"I'll have to tell Dave Logan."

"I already told him. Sue's planning the wedding. There's this old chapel in Santa Fe . . ."

Kitt stared at the shaft of light filtering into the narrow cave. Life with Garth was worth more than all the gold of Guadalupe Y Calvo. Hod had been right. This time they wouldn't give up—no matter what.

What had passed before was only the twilight of the dawn. The day of their love had come at last.

# SILHOUETTE·INTIMATE·MOMENTS®

# FEBRUARY FROLICS!

This February, we've got a special treat in store for you: four terrific books written by four brand-new authors! From sunny California to North Dakota's frozen plains, they'll whisk you away to a world of romance and adventure.

**Look for**

L.A. HEAT (IM #369) by Rebecca Daniels
AN OFFICER AND A GENTLEMAN (IM #370) by Rachel Lee
HUNTER'S WAY (IM #371) by Justine Davis
DANGEROUS BARGAIN (IM #372) by Kathryn Stewart

They're all part of February Frolics, coming to you from Silhouette Intimate Moments—where life is exciting and dreams do come true.

FF-1

*Silhouette Books®*

# SILHOUETTE·INTIMATE·MOMENTS®

## NORA ROBERTS
## Night Shadow

People all over the city of Urbana were asking, Who was that masked man?

Assistant district attorney Deborah O'Roarke was the first to learn his secret identity . . . and her life would never be the same.

The stories of the lives and loves of the O'Roarke sisters began in January 1991 with NIGHT SHIFT, Silhouette Intimate Moments #365. And if you want to know more about Deborah and the man behind the mask, look for NIGHT SHADOW, Silhouette Intimate Moments #373, available in March at your favorite retail outlet.

NITE-1

*Silhouette Books*®

## Silhouette Special Edition

proudly presents
the long-awaited "prequel" volume of

### ★ LOVE AND GLORY ★

## by
## LINDSAY McKENNA

### *Dawn of Valor*

In the summer of '89, Silhouette Special Edition premiered three novels celebrating America's men and women in uniform: LOVE AND GLORY, by bestselling author Lindsay McKenna. Featured were the proud Trayherns, a military family as bold and patriotic as the American flag—three siblings valiantly battling the threat of dishonor, determined to triumph... in love and glory.

Now, discover the roots of the Trayhern brand of courage, as parents Chase and Rachel relive their earliest heart stopping experiences of survival and indomitable love, in

*Dawn of Valor,* Silhouette Special Edition #649.

This February, experience the thrill of LOVE AND GLORY—from the very beginning!

DV-1

Silhouette Books®